Death on ZigZag Trail

A spooky legend twists grave matters

Sheila Mackey's dislike for cemeteries can't fend off her friend Clara's determination. Amid eerie legends, including a tailgating hearse, the accidental investigator is lured into sorting through deadly questions a century old, revolving around an unidentified victim known as ZigZag Jane.

Nothing follows a straight line in this historic inquiry, including conflict over their sleuthing with Teague O'Donnell, newly hired as a part-time detective in North Bend County, Kentucky. Especially when the past doesn't stay in the past and the victims multiply.

Secret Sleuth series

Death on the Diversion
Death on Torrid Avenue
Death on Beguiling Way
Death on Covert Circle
Death on Shady Bridge
Death on Carrion Lane
Death on ZigZag Trail
Death on Puzzle Place

Other mystery by Patricia McLinn

Caught Dead in Wyoming series

Sign Off

Left Hanging

Shoot First

Last Ditch

Look Live

Back Story

Cold Open

Hot Roll

Reaction Shot

Body Brace

Cross Talk

Air Ready

Holiday Bullets

Cue Up

The Innocence Trilogy

Proof of Innocence

Price of Innocence

Premise of Innocence

DEATH ON ZIGZAG TRAIL

Secret Sleuth, Book 7

Patricia McLinn

SUNDAY

CHAPTER ONE

"DO YOU KNOW about the Legend of Sleepy Hollow?" my friend Clara Woodrow asked casually as we watched our dogs cavort.

I felt as if a bowling ball lodged in my stomach.

Not for any external reasons. The externals were fine.

It was early afternoon of a sunny and not too chilly day for late October in North Bend County, Kentucky.

We were watching the dogs at the Torrid Avenue Dog Park, where the main topic of conversation broadened—temporarily—beyond dogs to whether the warm and dry spell would last for Halloween Trick or Treaters the day after tomorrow.

Cavorting is something our dogs do every day. If we don't take them to the dog park to cavort, they do it in our houses, which is something experience has taught us to avoid, if at all possible.

Clara's Lulu was the white Great Pyrenees mix cantering joyfully along a path that would nauseate a snake. My Gracie was the sable and white collie clacking her teeth at Lulu's shoulder, telling her to straighten that line. Collies are a bossy breed.

The third member of their triumvirate, lab mix Murphy, departed not long ago with his owner, Teague O'Donnell.

Teague and I were … dating? … seeing each other? … sort of a couple?

We'd spent a laid-back, dog-centric weekend together. Teague's early departure from the dog park was to prep to substitute teach a new class tomorrow at an area high school.

We didn't kiss goodbye—too public. But his look promised to make up for that the next time we said hello.

I enjoyed looking forward to that.

Until Clara asked her question.

The Legend of Sleepy Hollow haunted me.

Not for the reasons you might think, even with Halloween coming.

In elementary school, as punishment for talking in class, I read the story aloud. The memory of my fellow students' faces—divided between boredom and avid anticipation of my making a mistake— swam into my mind's eye before every one of innumerable readings I did as an adult.

Especially since attendees at those latter readings thought I was reading *my* work.

I wasn't.

That was all Kit's doing.

I call her Aunt Kit. She's actually another generation removed from me, though she maintains the appellation *great* is one she's earned by deeds, not by family tree. She does not like to be contradicted on that subject. Or others.

She supported herself her entire working life by (mostly) happily writing genre fiction. That, alone, is a feat.

Then she wrote another book.

An amazing book. A once-in-a-generation book. A book called this century's *To Kill a Mockingbird*.

Aunt Kit had been around publishing enough to know *Abandon All* would not get the star treatment if presented as the work of a career-long midlist writer. She asked me—fresh out of college at the time and passably attractive in a wholesome Midwestern way—to be the book's public face. In other words, pretend I wrote it.

It worked. Beyond Kit's dreams, I think. Certainly astronomically beyond mine. Bestsellerdom. Sequels. Movies. Big money. Fame.

Thankfully, the readings I gave as the purported author of *Abandon All* did not morph into *Sleepy Hollow*-like nightmares. The faces in those audiences were eager and interested, unlike my childhood classmates. More important, Aunt Kit wrote in a style infinitely more conducive to being read aloud in our times than Washington Irving did.

The opening of *The Legend of Sleepy Hollow* takes six chunky phrases to get through the first sentence.

I still shiver at the commas and semicolons littering every sentence. In an agony of phrases, I stumbled along to reach the fat fourth paragraph, which introduces the apparition, though it is not until the end of the fifth paragraph that the sobriquet the Headless Horseman of Sleepy Hollow is introduced.

That got the attention of my ghoulish classmates.

Their ghoulishness was not news to me.

I wasn't a chicken.

I wasn't.

I just wasn't destined to like horror movies or other methods of being scared.

As a kid, I could dash through Old Town cemetery in my hometown on a dare with the best of them. Possibly faster than most and always sticking to the paths, because it's rude to run on people's graves. But I didn't care how much harassment Bryan Ferris poured on my head, I was not going to stretch out for a "nap" atop a grave. Not going to do it.

Actually, I'm not going to run through a cemetery again, either. Not after Bryan Ferris jumped out from behind a headstone at me.

Yes, I screamed like a girl.

However, Bryan Ferris couldn't gloat about it, because I also swung and kicked at whatever grabbed at me. The swings knocked him down. The kicks got his nose and jaw. He wasn't laughing—or talking—for a while.

Pushing down memories of childhood punishment, Bryan Ferris, and trepidations before readings of Aunt Kit's works—none of which Clara knew about—I answered her question.

"Yes, I know *The Legend of Sleepy Hollow.*"

"Why do you say it that way, Sheila? Oh—do you mean the one by the writer? Made into movies and stuff."

"Washington Irving. Exactly."

"No, no, I mean *our* Legend of Sleepy Hollow. North Bend County's. The one where a hearse tailgates you."

"A hearse. Tailgates you."

Clara nodded, clearly glad I had it now, even though I didn't. "Although when the old lady who lived behind us when I was a kid first told me, she said a horse-drawn hearse and I said it couldn't keep up with a car, so you'd drive away. Then *she* said it modernized over time and now it's a vehicle with a really strong engine and it comes up behind you and tries to run you off the road. And I said how can a ghost change? It's stuck being partially what it was before, that's what makes it a ghost. Otherwise it would go to the other side and be done with it. She said—"

"Wait. Clara, just wait." I felt dizzy, what with whiplashing from a childhood trauma to a tailgating ghost hearse transforming its mode of horsepower. "What is this all about?"

She cast an experienced eye toward our dogs, checking they remained within an acceptable level of mayhem, then considered for a moment. "I asked if you knew about our Legend of Sleepy Hollow, because if you knew the stretch of ZigZag Trail in Sleepy Hollow where the hearse tailgates it would be easier to explain where the cemetery is."

"Cemetery." I did not like the turn in this conversation.

"Right. Because we're going there to meet somebody. I'll drive. But don't worry, I don't have to be anywhere until later, so there's no reason to hurry away if the conversation's going well."

"There's no reason for me to go at all."

"Sure there is. ZigZag Cemetery is one of the oldest cemeteries in the county. Lots and lots of history there from even before it was called ZigZag Cemetery. And you like history. You're energized after you visit Urban Parhem at the historical society, telling me stories I never heard before, even though I've lived here my whole life. At least it's among the oldest formal ones."

In a move worthy of someone trying to avoid a tailgating hearse, she'd made an abrupt topical U-turn to return to the cemetery.

I hung on—barely—as she continued, "Because, you know, the early settlers and later, on larger estates, people established family graveyards. Not to mention people being buried kind of where they died. There's a legend about a headless pioneer woman who haunts a particular area. So we have a Legend of Sleepy Hollow and we have a headless person, but ours are not in the same place." She seemed to find that superior to Washington Irving's version. "The woman and her daughter were killed while her husband was away. They cut her head off and took it. Some people say she's still looking for it. I think trying to find her daughter is why she hasn't passed over. I mean, if it were the horrible way of dying, the little girl should be haunting, too, and I've never heard of—"

"Clara—"

"You're right, you're right. I'm getting off track. The headless pioneer woman ghost is not at ZigZag Cemetery—or any cemetery, because that's her problem—so no need to worry. Now."

Her bright smile did not reassure me the way, I'm sure, she intended.

"With or without headless pioneer women, I'm *not* a fan of cemeteries."

Cemeteries reached by way of a road known for a ghostly hearse being particularly low on my list.

"Did you know there's a word for that? Not for *not* being a fan of cemeteries, but for being a fan of cemeteries. Taphophiles are people fascinated by cemeteries. It's so interesting you're an anti-taphophile, because you're so practical and death is just part of life. But it's okay you're not a taphophile, it's just the meeting spot Doug Vonner and I picked for us to get acquainted."

"Not going to happen. You got me to go to your high school reunion and look how that turned out."

"Yes," she said happily, "we figured it all out, the not guilty are free and the guilty get punished."

"I was thinking about what happened when someone was murdered."

"Oh, that."

CHAPTER TWO

DO NOT ASK me how she talked me into it. I still don't know.

Clara was mild-mannered, unless stirred to action by a perceived inequity or danger to anyone she cared about, human or canine. She'd single-handedly—more accurately, single-mouthedly—rousted two tough guys in motorcycle gear with four even tougher acting mixed-breeds last spring from the dog park while I prepared to pack up Gracie, LuLu, and Murphy and get the hell out of Dodge.

Getting me to a cemetery was only slightly harder.

Clara insisted we drop our dogs off at her house—which was not on a direct path from the dog park to ZigZag Cemetery in the northeastern corner of the county, but closer than my house.

Her reasons for dropping off the dogs seemed muddled to me. Was she sparing the cemetery potential degradations from the duo? Or sparing their delicate spirits' exposure to … well, spirits?

If the latter, why didn't her thoughtfulness extend to me?

I really didn't want to go to a cemetery.

Still, a cloudless blue-sky day helped.

Clara answered a phone call hands-free, while I concentrated on the cheerful sky.

"Sorry to cut you short, Molly, but I'm on the way to an appointment," Clara said. "I'll call you back later."

As soon as the call ended, Clara said to me, "Did you hear what she was saying?"

"No." I'd been trying to not eavesdrop … and to ignore we were getting closer and closer to Clara's objective.

"You remember Molly, Ned's cousin's ex-wife who lives in Blue Grass Estates? We talked to her about Bob after the murder at the dog park. She has a lab named Bart."

Ned was Clara's husband. Blue Grass Estates was not far away. Bob's death was the first we investigated together. But the dog was the clue that did it for me. "Right. Nice neighborhood."

"She's having a terrible time with doing short-term rentals in the neighborhood. The county and the owner keep blabbing about the rental company having rules against parties or dirty conditions, while doing nothing to prevent them. Molly is forever cleaning up their trash after sleepless nights because of noise."

"Renters break the rules?"

"All the time. Molly said these rental parties routinely include people screaming and physically fighting in the street, and swearing at neighbors who're in their own yard. When the neighbors complained, the owner said it was the *neighbors'* responsibility to call the police. Plus, he takes so long to clean, there were—" She lowered her voice. "—rodents."

"What did the county say?"

"Hah! After passing a regulation allowing short-term rentals, they washed their hands of it and told neighbors to deal with the owner. The neighbors *tried* to. But, first, he didn't answer for hours and hours while all the noise and trashing and fighting went on. When he finally did answer, he complained they called him so late—while they were being kept awake by the noise at *his* property." Clara's outrage grew with each phrase. "And *then* he said the party would be over before he could get there, anyway, and hung up, saying he was trying to sleep. Like they weren't! And he must have turned his phone off, because they couldn't get him again."

"What a mess."

"It is. You might not be affected because you're in the town of Haines Tavern, Sheila, but otherwise, it's all over the county."

"Why'd they let these rentals happen in the first place?"

Clara pulled a cynical expression unsuited to her face. "Why do you think? Money. Taxes, license fees, all to make their jobs more important.

"I've heard from good sources—*very* good, only I can't tell you who because I swore not to tell—that a few bigwigs, including some of those who voted for it, wanted to rent out houses themselves. I swear, they think they're going to make a fortune renting houses for a night or two in North Bend County, Kentucky. I mean, I love my home, but this is not exactly Palm Beach, you know?"

"I do know."

"And it seems like most of the people renting these places are locals or semi-locals who want to have a blowout party and won't mess up their own house or neighborhood, so go elsewhere, which is incredibly rude."

"That's one word for it."

"Well, I might have other words for it, too, but I generally try not to use them. Also for the people making money by renting out the houses, because it's not where they live, either. Oh, no, not them. Stinkers," she said emphatically.

With Clara apparently prepared to sink into steaming silence, I sought another way to distract myself from our destination. "So, this road's called ZigZag Trail?" I asked.

"Uh-huh." That was uncharacteristically uncommunicative for Clara.

"Is there a story behind the name?"

"Story? It just makes sense. The road zigs and zags."

It truly did. As Clara drove, I'd been leaning left, then right, then left so often I could have matched all the politicians who zigged and zagged for the sole purpose of their personal ambition.

To Clara, I said, "There's no secret, macabre history?" Like the rest of North Bend County.

"Why would it have a secret, macabre history?"

She wasn't kidding.

"Let's start with building a high school on Carrion Lane," I said.

"I explained that."

Not to my satisfaction, but no sense rehashing. Instead, I asked, "Was the cemetery named after the road or the road after the cemetery?"

"Dunno. Besides—" She interrupted herself with an exhalation of satisfaction. "We're here."

Cemeteries are bad enough. But at least well-tended cemeteries convey a sense of dignity, of well-deserved rest. Not this one.

Remember the help from the cloudless sky?

It didn't stand a chance against the other side of the ledger, starting with an ironwork arch listing over the entrance with letters in a dour font the Addams family could love. The unreadable swirls definitely didn't spell ZigZag. I thought it started with an R, followed by several letters I couldn't read, and ended in *em* or *en* or *on* or *om*. Maybe *ow*— how appropriate.

Overgrown ivy and weeds in varied stages of death and decay festooned the uneven iron fencing extending from either side of the entrance.

Just beyond the cemetery stood a single, ghost-white tree stripped of bark. It retained main branches but lacked a network of leaf-supporting branches. Smaller, darker vegetation formed a backdrop to this apparition tree, but with a gap, as if the living drew back, not wanting to be too close.

Clara pulled in behind a neat, mid-level sedan parked alongside the fence.

She hopped out and jogged around to the passenger side, calling in through my unopened door. "That's Doug's car. He's here already. C'mon."

She was on her way before I could protest that meeting this guy outside the cemetery was weird, but meeting him *inside* was ... what I was about to do.

I exited the SUV and followed while she skipped along one of four paths dividing the space into quadrants of graves.

Well, not actually skipped, but walked really cheerfully.

Where the four paths met, a stilled and dusty stone fountain stood. In the first ring, the tallest and most impressive memorials rose. Farther away from the fountain, the markers became less and less distinguished.

"Doug!" Clara called.

A man on one side or the other of fifty, stepped back from a monument in the first ring, and raised a hand to her in greeting.

He wore a pale blue shirt tucked into neat jeans, revealing a slight paunch. Casual shoes, not brand new, not too worn. A canvas jacket with subtle pocket bulges, ruling him out as a neat freak.

He was gray from the temples through short sideburns with more sprinkled into weekend bristles on his chin, but otherwise had medium brown hair. A little intense around intelligent gray eyes, but with smile lines at his mouth.

In other words, he looked reassuringly normal for someone who set meetings for graveyards.

"I'm glad you could come. Both of you. Thank you."

We shook hands as Clara performed the formal introductions. Doug Vonner's manner was polite, with a trace of edginess underneath. Like a basically honest guy who really, really wanted you to buy his used car.

In other circumstances, I'd probably have enjoyed meeting him. But the nearby monument engraved with the name Vonner, along with its many neighbors, put a damper on my conviviality.

"I'm glad you found me. I told Clara I'd be by Jane's grave—"

Bad enough meeting at a cemetery, but at a specific grave … I sent Clara a laser look.

It bounced off.

"—but I stopped here. Meant to only be a moment, but started remembering…" He looked at the monument's inscription of names and dates. "My grandparents. I barely knew my grandmother, but my grandfather…" Rough math said he'd been an adult when his grandfather, also named Douglas Vonner, died. "He was an impressive man. Knowing him formed me."

"Are you…?" What did I want to ask? Obsessed with dead people? A ghoul who liked hanging out at cemeteries? "In a profession involving history?"

"No. I'm a construction analyst for a hospital in Cincinnati."

"That must keep you busy," Clara said.

"Yeah." He twitched his shoulders. "My grandfather would be the first to say you weren't here to see him. I'll lead you to where Jane is."

He said it like we'd know who he meant.

Clara started to follow him, then turned back to me. "Are you okay?"

Tempted to claim a twisted ankle, I said, "I told you, I've never liked cemeteries."

"Really? Why? It's not even Halloween yet." As if only on that day might it make sense to not find cemeteries—especially ones like this— welcomed surroundings. She whipped her head around to me. "Oh. You don't dislike Halloween, do you?"

She made me sound like the Grinch and Scrooge rolled into one, wrapped in black and orange.

"I'm not anti-Halloween. Pumpkins and mums and handing out candy to kids in costumes are all good—as long as I don't have to do it in a cemetery."

She looked around with genuine curiosity.

"But why?"

She certainly didn't appear put off by the lone, skeletal tree, other vegetation scraggling into unhealthy thickets on both sides of the fence. Unlike the monument where we'd met Doug Vonner, most of the graves we passed now were grown over by browned grass, topped by broken or tipped headstones.

If I told Clara about Bryan Ferris, she'd sympathize. But my antipathy pre-dated him.

I said, "The headstones look like books, only in a really sad library, with gaps of missing books and others half tipped over."

"Huh." She looked around. "We'll have to talk about that more. But right now Doug's waiting."

I trudged on, trying not to look too closely at anything around me until we reached Doug Vonner, standing beside a grave off the main path and near the back fence. This grave was marked by a rectangle about waist high.

He faced the front of the headstone, while we remained on the path, looking at its back. It appeared to have had carving at one time, but it was worn to shallow smudges.

At the grave next door, so to speak, the headstone leaned back sharply as if horrified to find itself in such company.

While I tried to read the tipped headstone, Clara clasped my arm— I didn't jump much—and tugged me toward Doug Vonner.

Above a pile of dead leaves the front of the headstone read:

Our Girl

"Jane's body was found a few feet from here, by the back fence." Doug Vonner tipped his head toward it and the tree beyond it. "There'd been a storm the night before. The sky was bright and clear. It was warm for early November. She was lying on her face, covered with leaves brought down by the storm, so her brown hair almost blended in. She looked like a child playing hide and seek in the pile. Except for the two ends of a scarf crossed at the back of her neck and of course she wasn't moving."

Confused, I stopped him. "You know the scene very well. When was this?"

"November 8. The anniversary is nearly here."

Clara ordered Doug Vonner, "Tell her the rest of it."

Before answering, he bent and gently scooped away enough leaves for me to read the entire inscription.

Our Girl
d. Nov. 3, 1921
Rest in peace

Then he said, "It's more than a hundred years since she was

found—and since she was murdered."

"A hundred years?" That sure explained the wear on the back of the stone. Yet the front was still readable.

"No name," I murmured.

"We've called her Jane for Jane Doe," Doug said.

"Most often known as ZigZag Jane because of being found here," Clara said.

"Grandfather didn't want to put that on her headstone—not Jane Doe, and definitely not ZigZag Jane. He said it made the lack of her real name too permanent. Guess a century's pretty permanent, huh."

CHAPTER THREE

DOUG **V**ONNER **HARKED** back to my earlier comment. "The reason I know the scene so well is my grandfather was the one who found her. He was seventeen years old."

I couldn't imagine coming upon the body of a dead stranger ... and in these surroundings.

"Grandfather used to run through this cemetery—"

Ah. I had something in common with Grandfather.

"—to and from school. He was on the track team, but with chores on the family farm, he couldn't stay after school, so he ran to and from as training. Including hurdles." Some sections of fence wouldn't pose much of an obstacle these days. "He always said his favorite part was through the cemetery. He found it peaceful, but also like everyone here cheered him on."

I had *nothing* in common with Grandfather.

"For practice, he'd hurdle the fence around the outside and some of the gravestones."

"He must have been quite the athlete," Clara said.

"Held a bunch of the high school track records. And he was spry and athletic until he died at 97."

Admiration and love for his grandfather came through clearly.

"From the moment he found Jane, he was determined to give her justice. A decent burial, too. He got an article in the paper about how this poor young woman died in our community, so we owed her. Quite the turnout, from the ancient clips.

"He raised funds to get her a headstone. Went door-to-door collecting. Also asking questions about if anyone knew her, if she looked familiar, if they'd seen anything the night before he found her … anything. He raised enough for this headstone, but never got much in the way of clues.

"The mystery of who she was and what happened to her consumed him the rest of his life. Eighty years. My father helped awhile, but Grandfather saw me as the torchbearer." The words carried both pride and burden. "At the end of his life, he was certain science and all the advances could finally…"

He shook his head. "But to even have a chance of taking advantage of DNA, we'd need to have her exhumed and that costs money, much less the tests, as county officials keep reminding me. An unknown woman, dead for a hundred years, doesn't have clout." From bitterness, his tone changed to something infinitely sadder. "What it amounts to is I've failed. Failed Jane and failed Grandfather."

I spotted something on the back of what appeared to be an even older headstone than Jane's, near where Doug said Jane was found.

"What's that? A Z?" It was at an angle on the headstone, to the side of the rest of the carving.

He glanced toward it without interest. "Looks like it. Maybe he found carving too hard, so he stopped."

"Who? What carvings?"

"Later," Clara said to me, then—bracingly—to Doug, she added. "You haven't failed. You've worked so hard and you're still working. No more talk about failing."

He gave a flat-lipped grimace, combining thanks with dismissal of her reassurance. "I've had no luck raising funds for private testing. But I thought if … Well, everyone says how good you two are at untangling mysteries that baffle the local authorities."

I fought off a reflex to flinch.

Not only did I not want *everyone* noticing me, but Teague O'Donnell was now among those local authorities. Newly hired by the local sheriff's department and on a part-time basis, true, but I didn't think he'd enjoy being called baffled.

What he enjoyed and didn't enjoy was becoming increasingly important to me, despite … complications.

"There are all sorts of things they can do with DNA these days," Doug continued. "But I can't get anyone official to consider it. There's even one guy trying to get the cemetery closed. I guess when there's no guarantee there will be usable DNA, much less with no one but me urging them to do it, it's easy to say no," he acknowledged.

"Do you have a possible relative you want to match her DNA with?" I asked.

He shook his head. "No. We could check it against what's in public databanks, but that's the Catch-22. Without DNA, we can't advance on who she might have been. Without knowing who she might have been, we can't get support for financing DNA."

"That is hard," I started, aiming to let him down easy.

Clara talked over me. "But if there's any way we can help, Doug…"

"There is," he said promptly, recognizing her invitation. "If you would look over what we know about Jane, maybe see something we've missed. If you can open a crack, take even one step toward identifying her, that might stir interest. Raise funds for private DNA…" His voice ran down.

After a pause, he said, "You see, I promised my grandfather as he was dying to find out who Jane is. I promised him."

"I'm sorry—"

My words had no chance against Clara's, "Of course we'll help."

CLARA HUSTLED ME out before I could contradict her.

I did not resist.

I figured leave the cemetery first, contradict later.

But now, in her SUV, zigzagging away from the cemetery, other matters surfaced.

"All the stuff about Kentucky's Legend of Sleepy Hollow and the headless frontier woman was to distract me from what you were up to."

Clara looked at me with the same utter innocence Gracie employs when she rushes up like the idea just occurred to her that what would most please her in the world was being at my side, and aren't I really, really happy the idea occurred to her? When—in fact—I'd been calling her to come all along.

"I was explaining where the cemetery's located," she said.

"Another sleight of hand. Look over here, a spooky cemetery. Pay attention to the spooky cemetery. Don't look at the other hand where you're being sucked into a quicksand pit."

"You're mixing your metaphors, Sheila. You need to watch that in your writing. It can confuse your readers—"

"You followed it perfectly." Besides, I had no readers. I never finished anything, much less published. "A hundred-year-old victim with no name? Really, Clara?"

"Actually, she was probably in her early twenties, so if you're going from when she died, she'd be a twenty-something victim. If you're going from now, she'd be a hundred and twenty-something victim."

I rolled my eyes. "The point being it's hard enough to figure out things that just happened, much less a century ago."

"He's only asked us to *try* to find out who she is—was."

"You know he *really* wants us to figure out who killed Jane."

"That's natural," she said serenely.

"It might be natural, but it's also darned near impossible. A century old death? We don't even know for sure she *was* killed."

"Doug's grandfather's account from when he saw the body said she'd been strangled."

"Yeah, Douglas Vonner's account. How reliable is that? We don't know. We don't know how reliable Doug's account of his grandfather's account is."

"I don't think he'd forget. After all, it's not like something he heard once and never again. They talked about it a lot."

"It's not his memory I'm wondering about."

"You mean... But why would Doug lie about it?"

Confronted with her Pollyanna face, I backed down. "Maybe not lie. Maybe misremember and not be aware of it. We could spend all sorts of time looking into this and find out everything we based it on, was full of holes."

"Hmm."

"Hmm, what?"

"Isn't that what happens a lot? We start with one direction in mind, then adjust as we get new information and sort through what stands up and what gets discarded."

After a reluctant moment, I said, "I suppose."

"We'll look over the material Doug has tomorrow, like we told him."

"What we should do is check material not provided by Doug Vonner—or his grandfather. I mean, we should if we were going to—"

Too late.

"Great idea. Historical society?"

"Clara, I don't think—"

"Oh, c'mon. You know you're interested. Besides, this should be interesting. Fun, even. Look at it this way, we don't have to worry about a killer striking again or someone being in danger, because everybody's already dead. There's no deadline, so to speak."

I twisted to get a better look at her face. Yep. She was as cheerful as she sounded.

"You like talking to Urban Parhem at the historical society," she continued. "I'll drop you off, take LuLu to the vet for her checkup and swing back to get you. You and Urban will have a fine time discussing this."

"He might not be there."

There was the Old Old Courthouse, which housed North Bend County's historical society.

This county's motto should be *Never Abandons a Courthouse*. The Old appellation is necessary because there is also the Old Courthouse, the Old New Courthouse, and the New New Courthouse. Only the last currently operates as a courthouse, but they forever carry the name.

Clara snorted at my suggestion that Urban might not be at the tiny white-painted Greek Revival building.

She was right.

CHAPTER FOUR

URBAN PARHEM APPEARED mild with his mostly gray hair, all gray mustache, and solid citizen dark glasses.

But he shocked me by responding to my introduction of the topic of ZigZag Jane with, "I'm not interested."

Urban not interested in an aspect of North Bend County history? Unheard of.

"Why?"

"It's like Jack the Ripper."

"How is ZigZag Jane like Jack the Ripper?"

A glint behind his glasses was as good as a smirk. I'd given him the response he wanted. "It's been hashed over a thousand times, the evidence doesn't get any better, and the theories get weirder and weirder."

"DNA could provide new evidence."

He snorted "Is Doug Vonner trying another fund-raising drive? I'll say this, the man doesn't give up. Though at some point, you'd think he'd give his head a rest from bashing it against multiple brick walls."

"*Multiple* brick walls? He indicated it's county officials blocking his request for support to pursue DNA on ZigZag Jane."

"Why do you think that's happening?"

"No push from the community?" And then I heard myself making Clara's argument. "But if something renews interest—"

I let it drop because he shook his head. "It's not just that nobody other than Doug urges authorities to gamble money on a chance of finding her identity. Most of North Bend County—the old guard that knows about her, anyway, because there are plenty now who've never heard of her—is actively against the idea."

From his expression, he knew I fell into the never-heard-of-her category before today.

"Does the old guard object to exhumation on religious grounds or—"

"No. They want to keep ZigZag Jane belonging to the county. She gets identified and then she belongs to her family, not North Bend anymore."

And no longer part of North Bend County lore? Was that why Urban was against it? Not because he *wasn't* interested in ZigZag Jane.

"But shouldn't we want her to find her true home, her family?"

"It's like this building," Urban said. "When a new courthouse was built, it became a post office. Then it was sold to a bank. It's been moved twice and was painted blue at one point. Now it's here, where it belongs. Like ZigZag Jane. She's home with us."

"Urban, I was at that cemetery. If anyone visits her grave or pays attention to it other than Doug Vonner, there's no sign of it."

"Oh, some pay attention, including wanting to close it, no doubt to benefit a very few." He peered at me, then clicked his tongue. "Why you'd want to know about her, when it leads nowhere and the tale of the ZigZag Hermit is far more interesting, I don't know. But if you insist, I can try to answer your questions."

If you think that was a straightforward invitation, you haven't met Urban Parhem.

We were like a couple of old hagglers coming to an agreement without ever being so crass as to mention price or product. Listening to the history of the ZigZag Hermit—whoever that might be—was the toll I'd pay to get him to talk about what I wanted to know.

Accepting his terms, I nodded and said, "Let's start with what you've heard over the years. Give me the general outline."

"Well, I wasn't around when she was found a century ago, if that's what you're thinking," he said tartly.

I chuckled, as he'd intended.

"An attractive, white female in her early twenties was found at the cemetery. They determined cause of death was strangulation by her own scarf. She was either killed there or dumped in the forty-eight hours before she was found, because Douglas Vonner took the same route to school two days earlier. She wasn't from around here."

"How did they know that?"

"They would have recognized someone from around here. If not Douglas Vonner when he found her, the authorities for sure. There weren't many people living here a hundred years ago."

As I knew from house-hunting almost a year ago, the building boom hit this county in the early 1990s.

"From contemporaneous articles and oral histories of people alive at the time, the dead woman at the cemetery on ZigZag Trail was all anyone could talk about for quite a while. The collection to erect a headstone reached its goal faster than anybody expected.

"At the beginning, they put ads in papers, contacted neighboring police and sheriff's departments, watched for notices of missing women ... But the longer it was from when she was found, the less and less chance of turning up anything new. No Internet databases, no DNA, not even much connection among law enforcement departments in those days.

"Douglas Vonner kept trying to rally interest in ZigZag Jane, but it got harder and harder. His last big push wasn't long before he died, mounting another round of remembrances, tied to raising money to have the headstone redone. You said you saw it?"

"Yes." I didn't feel any need to expand on my time in the cemetery.

"Then you know how successful he was—spruced up the front, but not enough money to do the back, too. Here I pulled some things for you." Automatically, I took the folder he held out. "A lot of this material isn't digitized yet, so I made copies you can take home. What is digitized, I emailed to you."

"You pulled...? How did you know...?" I took a leap. "*You* told

Vonner to talk to us—no, wait. You told him to try Clara first, go for the soft touch."

"I believed—hoped—Clara would identify with his connection to his grandfather and his desire to carry on his efforts."

Clara would empathize. She had a close relationship with her grandmother, even though the woman was in Belize now with her septuagenarian *boyfriend*.

But Urban said he wasn't interested in ZigZag Jane, so why…

"You didn't want to take this on yourself," I said.

"No, I didn't. I have enough here to keep me more than busy."

True. However, subtext oozed out around his words and tone that I didn't understand. I probed more. "You weren't willing to turn Doug Vonner away and forget it."

"Like I said, he's trying to carry on for his grandfather."

Yet Urban didn't want him to succeed in that quest, because that would—or could—take ZigZag Jane away from a county that was at least half unaware of her existence. Something was missing.

"Did you know Douglas Vonner, Doug's grandfather?"

"Yes, I did."

"What did you think of him?"

"In what way?"

Kit calls responses like that a confession question. By asking it, the person thinks he delays answering, but the question itself serves as an answer.

With Kit's voice whispering in my ear, I said, "In the way of what was your opinion of him in all facets of your interactions?"

He scrunched his face, but then relaxed the muscles.

"Didn't have that many interactions. He was considerably older than me."

"But you interacted enough to have an opinion of him."

Still, he didn't answer directly. "We didn't see eye to eye on matters of local history."

"Beyond differing priorities on local history—"

"He didn't care about local history. He had a monomania. He

married a fine woman, whom he neglected. Not sure how they married in the first place, since he barely paid any attention to anything or anybody other than ZigZag Jane. You know the expression of not being able to see the forest for the trees?"

"Of course."

"He couldn't see the forest for a single tree. If he'd had his way, every resource that came the historical society's way—time, money, hands to help—would have been devoted to Jane. He pushed around some of the previous chairs. But too many other aspects demand our resources."

"Do you oppose exhumation and checking for DNA?"

"Not under all circumstances. But with the information and technology available then, yes."

"What about now? Technology's improved vastly."

He said nothing, yet his silence opened the curtains on my understanding.

"Ah. But the information hasn't advanced and without that, you don't think it's worth the investment of resources. Then why send Doug Vonner to us?"

He shook his head once. "That should be obvious. If there's information that would make a DNA test more than a shot in the dark, you and Clara are most likely to find it."

I wasn't sure I bought that, considering his views on identifying ZigZag Jane.

Maybe, though, he saw it as an opportunity to shut up the Vonners—past and present—for good? And to have Jane secured forever in North Bend County?

"You know why it's called ZigZag Trail?" His question stopped my speculation and told me we'd reached the payback portion of the program.

In other words, Urban's turn.

Clara's commonsense explanation came readily. "Because it zigs and zags and has no similarity to a straight line."

"A coincidence. It acquired its name from other circumstances.

That trail cut through woods along the Ohio River, where a ferry operated. A man took refuge in those woods and became something of a legend in a short time, known as the ZigZag Hermit or ZigZag John. He carved zigzags in trees along the road to the ferry. The proliferation of his zigzags quickly gave the road, the cemetery, and himself their names.

"But after some time, he began to carve zigzags on wood markers in the cemetery—used until replaced by a monument or permanently for poor people. Perhaps it was easier to carve them than trees."

And far easier than the one Z in the headstone. This must be the story Clara had promised for *later.*

"Why do I have the feeling the people of North Bend County at that time didn't care for him applying his skill in the cemetery?"

"They didn't. A group of men went to the hermit's house, a shack, and burned it down. He, in turn, became enraged and carved zigzags on the arms of a couple people he caught at the burn site and then on the leg of a woman who was the wife of the leader of those who burned down the shack. Looking for revenge, the husband went into the woods alone. It's not known what happened exactly, but the upshot was the hermit cut zigzag lines on the man's throat, cut deep enough that the man died. They captured the hermit, tried him for murder, and hanged him in 1922. He was only 27."

"So the ZigZag Hermit must have been around and the name applied to the road and the cemetery before Jane's death." I wondered if Doug's grandfather didn't want to put ZigZag Jane on her headstone because of that association. "She wouldn't have been called ZigZag Jane otherwise."

"Sound reasoning," he said.

Idly, I asked, "What was it called before ZigZag?"

"Kielwegen." He wrote it in his nicely legible hand on a piece of scratch paper from a pile at his work area.

"*That's* what the ironwork over the entrance at the cemetery says? Not sure I ever would have guessed that."

"The Trail, the cemetery, the ferry were all initially called Kielwegen. The family was all over that section. The ZigZag Hermit was a Kielwegen, too. Before he became ZigZag John."

"What have you got against the Kielwegens?"

He did not take the question amiss, which I'd based on his sucking-something-sour expression.

"My father—and his father—never cared for the family, while feeling sorry for John. He'd been in some of the worst fighting in Europe in World War I, though his breakdown, if that's what it was, did not follow immediately. Some said the cause was a broken romance, some said from things he'd done working for a gangster after the war, but most likely from what he'd seen in the war. Went out in the woods by himself and pretty much left everybody alone. Well, until the end."

CHAPTER FIVE

THROUGH THE PHONE connection, I heard Clara *tsk* after I recounted the tale of the hermit called ZigZag John.

"That poor soul. Why those men burned down his home … Have you ever noticed how often trouble escalates when a group of men get together and get riled about something? Except Madame Defarge."

"Madame Defarge?"

"You know, the woman in Dickens' *A Tale of Two Cities*, who sits and knits as heads fall from the guillotine. Oh, of course you know about that, because you're an author."

"Trying to write. And, yes, I do know who Madam Defarge is. Anyway, you can't say any longer that you don't understand why I say there's a definite ghoulish cast to this county."

"Every place has history like that."

"I walked around New York—New York state, the area where I lived before I came here—" I amended quickly to align with my cover story. "—without ever once thinking about some hermit carving zigzag lines into someone's throat. I never heard about ghoulish things in my hometown, either."

"Really?" She seemed to be both surprised and inclined to feel sorry for my deprived childhood.

"Really. But here, I feel like every step I take it's on somebody's grave."

She gave my comment serious consideration. "I've never lived anywhere else—well, except for college at UK and you don't focus on things like that at college, what with dating and basketball games and parties and football games and—"

"Studying?"

"That, too. Anyway they could have had stories in Lexington and I never heard them. But I do know that in North Bend County there's a good chance you *are* walking on someone's grave. Native tribes had burial grounds dotted around, then people not buried in cemeteries like I told you before, plus the Civil War, and—"

"This not reassuring."

"On the other hand—" She sailed on, unperturbed by giving me the heebie-jeebies. "—you and I have encountered more current murders than I'd ever known about. The things I've told you have been spread out over years and years—even centuries."

A fair point. "You really do think we've encountered a higher concentration of murders lately?"

"Oh, yes," she said cheerfully. "It's so interesting and challenging."

"I don't think Ned and Teague would agree."

"Probably not." Still cheerful. "And like I said before, anyone who committed murder a century ago is not around anymore. Unless-."

"Do *not* say vampires. Or ghosts."

"Okay, okay. Still, if we find out who Jane was and who killed her, that would be a kind of justice."

"I think we concentrate on who she was. That's what Doug Vonner asked us to do and it alone is a shot at the moon. Trying to find out who killed her is aiming for an unknown galaxy far, far away that hasn't been heard of yet."

"If we had the backing of the community, we could pay to have her DNA traced and that might get us to her identity."

"I was thinking about that. I see two avenues. One, for you to contact the reporters who interviewed you in the past."

"Great idea. I'll pitch them the story—I've been studying how to pitch for my author assistant clients." She'd started her business earlier this year and was growing it carefully. "An innocent woman whose identity has been lost to murder all these years, the devotion of Doug and his grandfather. They'll love it. We can stir support—moral and financial. Start a DNA fund."

"We might even get someone who knows something to come forward." My feeding off her enthusiasm abruptly died. "Although, with it being a century ago…"

"Around here a hundred years ago is barely yesterday. What's the other avenue?"

"I talk to my great-aunt Kit."

BUT NOT YET on calling Kit.

First, the Internet can be a bonanza of information.

…but not so much on ZigZag Jane.

What I found were sporadic updates that quoted older stories and quoted Douglas Vonner, then later Doug, for "freshness."

None added new information.

Worse, they were the journalistic version of the game Telephone, with less of the original being reported with each rendition.

I took the folder of material from Urban to bed with me. I sure would have preferred Teague.

I made it through the first article—far wordier than today's news accounts, with laments at the tragedy and exclamations of a fair, young beauty sent from this earth far too early. Underneath the flowery language, it had a lot of questions about who she was, what happened to her, where she came from, had she been killed there or when she'd been left. It did add that Douglas had not run to school the previous day because a passing neighbor gave him a lift.

With the choice of reading another article or going to sleep, I opted for sleep.

What had Clara said about no deadline? Maybe I needed the threat of murderers roaming free to keep me working past yawns.

MONDAY

CHAPTER SIX

AT MY INVITATION, Gracie hopped in the back seat willingly, but with a hint of reserve.

She looked a lot like Lassie, but had a tough start in life and came to me through collie rescue. She's relaxed a lot over these past months, but maintains a veneer of skepticism to protect her wounded heart.

That skepticism noted that this was significantly earlier than our usual departure for the dog park. This was more like vet appointment time. She wasn't counting her dog parks until they hatched.

When this one did hatch with the turn into the Torrid Avenue Dog Park entrance, there was joy, oh, joy in the back seat.

True, she looked puzzled and disappointed when a circuit of the big dog enclosure informed her neither LuLu nor Murphy was on hand. But she discovered a Chesapeake retriever acquaintance happily fielding balls from an owner equipped with a tennis ball thrower.

The owner threw, the retriever retrieved, Gracie herded the retriever back to his owner with much fanfare. Worked out for all concerned, while we waited for Clara and the other two dogs.

Clara has the spare key to Teague's apartment for exactly such missions of mercy as picking up Murphy while Teague taught. Also, her having the key rather than me eased any potential pressure on my gradually developing relationship with Teague.

There are important facts about Teague.

First, he was a former police detective who topped the list whenever I wondered how people might view my charade as *Abandon All's* author.

Second, he is a detective again, now working for the North Bend County Sheriff's Department on an as-needed basis for big cases. So it wouldn't matter only how *he* viewed that charade, but how other people might, because it would reflect on him.

My dog remained blissfully unaware of such issues, not to mention an unidentified dead woman from a century ago.

I kept my eye on the reason for our earlier-than-usual trip to the dog park, but didn't approach until Clara arrived with LuLu and Murphy, who galloped over to join Gracie and the retriever.

Clara and I met where a bright-eyed woman named Donna stood with Hattie, her golden retriever with a grayed muzzle. We both stopped to pet and love on Hattie, as required by dog park protocol. It was required because it's what most dog park regulars enjoyed doing.

Donna watched with approval … which didn't reach her voice as she said, "My, my, to what do we owe this early arrival when no one's been murdered lately." Her attention sharpened. "Or has there been a murder?"

"Not lately," Clara said cheerfully.

"Unless you count at Clara's recent high school reunion," I muttered.

"Donna knows that's been resolved, so we wouldn't be here about that."

"She could think that's barely in our rear-view mirror and—"

Donna cut across my retort. "Why *are* you two here at this hour?"

"ZigZag Jane," Clara said.

Both Donna's eyebrows rose. "ZigZag Jane? My, I haven't heard much about her in … I suppose it's years. What got you two interested?"

"Doug Vonner."

"Ah." Understanding crystalized as Donna breathed the syllable. "Another generation of Don Quixotes tilting at the same windmill. Poor man."

"Doug or his grandfather?" I asked.

She tipped her head. "Both, I suppose. His grandfather because the accident of finding that dead young woman remained with him his entire life. Doug because the accident of birth meant he inherited that quest. Although, if he'd wanted to, he could have put it aside as his father did. What does he think you two can do now?"

I shrugged. Clara said, "Find out who she was."

Donna snorted. "And then who killed her, too?"

"That would be great, wouldn't it?" Clara said.

"It would be a miracle. Douglas Vonner spent his life trying to find out who she was."

"Did he really?" I asked. "Or did he come to share the feeling of others in the community that she belonged here and finding her identity could take her away?"

She partially turned her head away, side-eyeing me with a clear what-makes-you-say-that?

"*Our girl* on the headstone," I said.

"Now that's interesting." Donna considered it, her gaze sweeping the dog park, making sure all was running—or lying in the sun, depending on the dog—as it should. "There certainly is—or has been—a good deal of that feeling about ZigZag Jane, though it's faded. People alive when she was found are gone. The connection's not as close these days.

"But I would say the Vonners—Douglas and Doug—did and do want to find out who she is. Was. They could have held onto her by keeping quiet. Heck of a lot easier than all they've done over the years."

I nodded acknowledgment of her logic.

Taking another tack, I asked, "What do you remember about her history?"

One eyebrow quirked. "Comparing my story to Doug's?"

"Getting additional viewpoints," I said firmly.

"Can't imagine my story is any different from Doug's because it's settled lore around here. Douglas Vonner running to school, with his usual path through the cemetery to practice hurdles. Comes across a woman's body, face down with leaves partially on top of her. She'd been strangled—there was a scarf around her neck that matched her dress.

"She was not known locally. Efforts to find out who she was failed. Douglas raised money to have her buried and erect a head-stone."

She raised one shoulder. "There'd be stories about her now and then, but spread more and more."

I knew that firsthand from last night's scrolling.

"The person you should talk to is Ruby."

That surprised me. Ruby Zweydorf, who ran the post office, was no kid, but didn't come close to first-hand knowledge of the 1920s.

"Okay," Clara said cheerfully. "Anyone else?"

"Imagine you've already connected with Urban Parhem." Clara and I nodded in unison. "There are a couple more people, but that will develop naturally. No need for you two to do a thing."

I regarded the amused glint in her eyes warily. "A hint—"

"Nope. That would ruin the fun."

"Our fun? Or yours?" I asked.

"Oh, mine. Definitely mine. C'mon, Hattie. Time to get on with our day. Good luck on this one." She grinned at each of us in turn, then she and her dog headed for the gate.

"You think we could persuade the dogs to leave now?" I asked Clara.

"No way. They just got here. Anyway, we have plenty of time before we have to change for yoga, since we don't have to shower."

In the summer, a shower and change of clothes between those activities was required. This time of year we could get by with a change of clothes to avoid dirty looks for smelling like fido while doing downward dog. Dirty looks take the edge off zen-like feelings.

Also taking the edge off zen-like feelings—at least mine—was the Beguiling Way Yoga Studio switching its schedule. Instead of going Monday nights and Tuesday lunches, it switched to Monday lunches and Tuesday nights.

Not only do I suspect they do that just to confuse me, but this week it meant no yoga on Tuesday. It was Halloween and I wasn't going to skip handing out candy during Trick or Treating.

But we'd signed up for a special class Saturday … after complaining to Clara that billing it as a way to relax at the start of the holiday was stretching it, barely a few days after Halloween.

"C'mon," Clara invited, "let's sit and you can tell me everything Urban told you yesterday."

We sat. I told.

After I finished with last night's unrewarding Internet searches and reading the first article, I said, "I'll copy everything so you can read them, too."

"There's not much chance I'd find anything you missed, but I do want to read them." She flashed a grin. "If nothing else, so you're not suffering alone." Serious again, she added, "I was thinking it over last night and didn't come to any great conclusions, but I did sort of wonder about one thing. Did they call people Jane and John Doe back then? Or is that more modern? Not that I think Doug would lie, but…"

"You wondered," I concluded for her. "Aunt Kit would say that was an excellent example of critical thinking."

Clara perked up. "She would?"

"Absolutely." She'd also think Clara needed to crank her skepticism to full volume because she thought everyone's skepticism should be full volume. "As a matter of fact, using John Doe—along with Richard Roe—as placeholders in English law started in the 1300s and using Jane started in the 1700s. It took longer to extend the names for use with unidentified bodies." All learned from Kit. "Jane or John Doe is far more humanizing than Dead Body One and Dead Body Two."

"True … Doug and his grandfather certainly don't think of ZigZag Jane as Dead Body One."

"No."

Was that a point worth considering?

The grandfather might not have thought of her that way because she was roughly a contemporary—a young woman in her twenties, the first article said, while he was in his late teens.

Yet not someone he recognized, or she wouldn't be Jane Doe.

Unless...

The possibility that Douglas Vonner *had* known who she was would not be one Kit would let pass. Have I mentioned she's more of a skeptic than I am? She'd say it was because she was older and wiser, especially wiser. It certainly made her adept at writing murder mysteries.

On the other hand, I'd been involved in real-world murders, so in that arena, I could claim being the expert.

And if you think I would say that to Kit, you don't know my great-aunt. Or my instinct for self-preservation.

As for Doug, could he have inherited more than a sense of obligation from his grandfather?

If his grandfather knew her identity, but kept the secret—for whatever reason and a couple occurred to me—what were the chances he'd told his grandson?

Not a hundred percent, but enough to make me wonder and keep that possibility in mind.

And then there was Urban Parhem's view of Douglas Vonner.

On the flip side, would Doug have reached out to Urban and Clara if he knew who Jane was?

"Are you done?" Clara asked me.

"Done?"

"Thinking. I didn't want to interrupt, but I thought you'd reached the end..."

I bumped my shoulder against hers. "You are amazing to know I was thinking *and* when I reached the end. It's not much, really. Just some questions."

As I told her my thoughts, she gaped at me.

To give her a chance to recover, I concluded with, "In other words, what did Grandfather know and when did he know it?"

"That sounds like a quote."

"It is. Watergate. Howard Baker, senator from Tennessee at the time."

"How do you know that?"

"Aunt Kit."

"I should have known. I just have to meet her, Sheila."

"You will. Someday." I wouldn't mind putting that off longer. My great-aunt freely sharing her opinion that I should Tell All to Teague was why I hadn't called her yet. And she was more forceful in person. "Anyway, that's a famous quote. And it applies here."

"The *question* might apply, but the *answer* is they don't know who she is," Clara said flatly. "They said so. Well, Doug said, but he was speaking for his grandfather, too, so it's nearly the same as *they* said."

"I know what they said. But what if they're lying? Or maybe only the grandfather was lying. Doug repeats what he was told."

"But why?"

"Guilt."

"Guilt over what?"

"Douglas Vonner killed her. Or he didn't save her. Or he knew who killed her and never told."

"Wow. I never would have thought of those things. That's why you're the writer," Clara said.

"Would-be writer," I muttered.

She pretended not to hear. "But I can't believe Douglas Vonner would do that."

"You know, Clara, there's actually a better argument you can use for Doug Vonner."

She grinned. "And you're going to tell me what that argument is so I can use it on you, because you're my friend."

"Exactly." My grin back faded, "If his grandfather knew ZigZag Jane's real identity and if he told his grandson, why would Doug go to Urban? Why involve us? Why not keep the whole thing to himself? Let it die, so to speak."

She hmm'd softly, then said, "To get it resolved?"

"Now who's arguing the opposite side? But you're right. That's a possibility. The human instinct to close what Kit calls open loops. Though, she most often means stories and characters rattling around in her head. With Doug Vonner, it might be more complicated—say, to get it resolved, yet not have the resolution on his plate?"

Clara raised one finger as she pulled her thoughts together. "Because his grandfather was involved and Doug doesn't want to be the instrument of that revelation, yet feels it's time to resolve this at last. Oh, Sheila, that really is complicated." She exhaled slowly. "I have to admit, it could make sense. But I still think it's more likely the Vonners truly don't know more than they've said."

"I guess we'll find out—if we're lucky. In the meantime, let's see if we can pry the pups out of here, get changed, and maybe have time to talk to Ruby before yoga."

CHAPTER SEVEN

We parked midway between the post office and the yoga studio, which happened to be near a café we liked. But the café wouldn't come until after yoga. And the post office came before either of the other two.

Ruby Zweydorf, who was proportioned perfectly for the historic brick post office, which was only slightly wider than its front door plus the two narrow windows that flanked it, greeted us with a big smile that faded as she said, "What? No Lulu and Gracie?"

"We left them at home. We're on our way to yoga. Sorry, Ike," Clara apologized to Ruby's husband, who sat in a chair not far from the door. A horrible car accident years ago left him with brain trauma, but he retained his love for animals. "I'll bring LuLu next time."

He nodded and kept nodding, until Clara put a gentle hand on his shoulder, slowly bringing the motion to a stop.

"Molly was here earlier," Ruby said. It took me half a beat to connect the reference to Ned's cousin's ex. "There was another big mess at that short-term rental over the weekend. Loud music, fights, broken glass, trash. They called the deputies fast this time. And *then* wasn't there some shouting and swearing, with these people saying they'd paid and they could do whatever they wanted."

"Oh, no," Clara said. "I hadn't heard that."

"Yup. Big Halloween party, apparently. The renters were from Stringer." That was the biggest town in the county. "The nerve of them, coming here to trash the place. And Molly said when they called the owner—like the county said they had to—he said he'd sold the place and to stop bothering him.

"Sure enough, she was at the courthouse first thing today and records show it sold to some company she'd never heard of. Has an address in Nevada, of all places."

"Some people incorporate their business in Nevada or a few other states because it's cheaper," I said.

"You know that from Kit?" Clara asked.

"Of course. It's not going to make it easy for Molly and her neighbors to find the owners."

"Poor Molly. I'll have to call her this afternoon."

"I'm sure she'd like to hear from you, Clara," Ruby said. But if that's not why you came and since I don't see Sheila bringing a package of cookies to send to North Carolina…?"

"Sure, pile on the guilt." I hadn't sent Kit any of her favorites lately. "You're as bad as my aunt."

She chuckled. "Guess you're baking for someone else these days."

Clara rescued me from the not-so-subtle reference to Teague. "Actually, we're hoping to hear what you could tell us about ZigZag Jane, Ruby."

"Oh, my, I haven't heard that name in a month of Sundays. Seems like she's forgotten more and more, poor soul. But what do you want to know?"

"Anything you can tell us."

Ruby relayed the basics already covered by Doug, Urban, and Donna.

"If not for Douglas Vonner the whole matter would have slid into obscurity. But he made other people ashamed of ignoring her death. Got obsessed, people said, and some whispered about it, but not above a whisper. He got a good number of people to chip in for that headstone and the burial.

"They raised enough to get her buried in ZigZag cemetery, but it took a considerable longer time to get the headstone." She pressed her lips together. "My mother always said her mama said the donators scrimped on that headstone because they thought the family would come along and take her away and people of the county would've paid for a headstone and not have anybody in the grave anymore."

"Why did they think that?" I asked.

Ike grunted.

We all looked toward him. Ruby, clearly, saw more than I did, because she said, "Ike's right. His people said the same as mine. The sheriff and all at the time didn't worry themselves much about her once they decided she wasn't from the county. That sheriff ... well, as our folks said, he thought the sun came up just to hear him crow."

Clara nodded wisely while I needed an extra beat to decipher that the sheriff thought more highly of himself than Ruby's and Ike's families had.

"So, at the start, regular folks thought it made sense Douglas Vonner agitatin' about finding out who she was. Thought it would happen fast. But then there was all that about ZigZag John, which had the sheriff crowing like mad for sure."

Ike made another sound. Ruby immediately said, "That's right, Ike. It was more a cryin' shame than something to puff his chest out over. You know about ZigZag John?"

"Urban mentioned him, when I was asking about ZigZag Jane."

It occurred to me that ZigZag John and ZigZag Jane was the local twist on John and Jane Doe.

The hint of my preferred ZigZag topic rolled right off Ruby.

"It's not me so much as Ike who knows about ZigZag John. Not that he was around back then, even if you are as old as dirt, isn't that right, old man?"

They looked at each other and whatever cognitive and language issues dogged the man, these two communicated their feelings just fine.

"But his people lived in that part of the county for as long as forever, them and the Kielwegens, and a few others. They always said it was the sheriff and his cronies from Stringer way—you know they were trying their darnedest to take the county seat from us here in

Haines Tavern and put it in Stringer—that started all that with ZigZag John. The folks that lived around where he roamed weren't bothered the least little bit by him or his carving. It was wrong what they did to him. Pushed until he snapped, and then rushed him through a trial and hanged him."

"But after that ended, did interest return to Jane?"

"No. As time went on, most felt the moment had passed. She was staying ZigZag Jane forevermore and might as well get on with other things, you know?"

CLARA AND I went straight to our Monday lunchtime yoga class at the Beguiling Way Yoga studio, taking our favorite spots in the far corner.

We favored those spots because they were out of view of the mirrored front wall. Also mostly out of view of the instructors. Clara said this eased her insecurities about *doing it right* enough to get the full benefits from the classes.

As for me, I'd been known to think about murder in that back corner, and I didn't want the instructor or the mirror to recognize that. Though I suspected one of our fellow students did.

After class, Fern, well past eighty, and far more limber than I'd ever been, zeroed in on us, her eyes bright and curious … or downright nosy.

Another student gave us a sharp look, before turning her shoulder to us and joining the slow flow—that's a yoga joke—out the door.

"No need to worry about Berrie Vittlow," Fern said of our acquaintance and sometimes nemesis from the dog park, taking a hold of each of our arms. "She doesn't know what you're into this time, not yet, anyway."

"Fern, we're not—"

She cut short my fib. "Of course you are. You were at the historical society yesterday, Urban Parhem filled your ears and sent you off with homework, though an unbiased source he has never been. Was stubborn as a boy. Even more stubborn as a middle-aged man."

Middle aged? Well, I suppose to Fern he might appear to be that. Of course, that was if she didn't consider herself middle-aged.

"He won't lie to you, but he won't volunteer anything he thinks might take you in a direction he doesn't like."

"What was there between him and Douglas Vonner?"

"Ah. Urban's mother was second cousin with Douglas Vonner's wife, but close as sisters. She always felt Douglas neglected the living woman in his life because of his obsession with a dead one. Mostly a silly notion. The woman had some disease they could probably deal with these days, but not back then. Anyway, she blamed Douglas and passed that on to her son.

"And then there was the matter of history and their views of it. Urban's not one to romanticize the past, but he wants to preserve knowledge of it for future generations. Let them know what came before, help them appreciate that they've built their edifices atop the work of others. Douglas didn't care for any of that—not the broad past, not the future. He had this one incident in his life, finding that young woman's body, and it became the center of all for him."

Monomania, Urban said.

Fern leaned in. "Urban didn't like being told what to do, either. I *told* Douglas that trying to browbeat Urban wouldn't work. Tried the same thing with his own son—pounding into him that nothing was more important than ZigZag Jane—and that backfired, too. But Douglas wouldn't listen to me—I was a kid to him. He was a stubborn cuss as long as I knew him and wouldn't change his ways with his son or Urban. Don't know if he finally listened or if age softened him, because he took a different tack later. Only reason the boy's still trying to get the answers his grandfather wanted."

It took half a beat to realize she meant fifty-ish Doug Vonner when she said *the boy*.

"Cost that boy a marriage. Though it wasn't any great loss. Still, would like to see him settled. I'll tell you one thing about ZigZag Jane not in any files Urban could show you. She'd had a baby. At least one. They kept that real quiet. Only reason I know is I heard the woman who used to wash the bodies before funerals tell our cook that the doctor who examined her said so."

"They didn't put that in the report? Why—Oh. They viewed her as a fallen woman?"

"Probably. Thought they were doing her a favor by not further sullying her name." Her mouth twisted reminding me of the rumor that her family once ran a house of ill-repute. "You'd think she was past the point of anyone worrying about sullying her name—or lack of name."

Clara turned her phone back on at that moment. It beeped at her like a motorbike trying to get through traffic.

Fern and I watched as she checked her messages. "That TV reporter Evelyn Dermotte wants to do an interview with me about ZigZag Jane." She sucked in a breath. "In twenty minutes. At the cemetery. I have to go home, get changed, do something with my hair—"

"I'll drive. You primp."

"But first, tell her yes," Fern called after us as we went out the door.

✧ ✧ ✧ ✧

ONLY AS WE neared the cemetery with almost a full minute to spare did I ask Clara the obvious question.

"This is fast. Did you call her about an interview on ZigZag Jane?"

"I messaged her and Bianca Abernathy that we were looking into the mystery and the anniversary is coming up."

She paused in putting away her comb and mirror, and looked at me. "Do you *really* not mind the reporters talking to me and you don't get your share of the limelight?"

"Don't mind at all. I'm happy with the way it is." And relieved. Fame faded for the author of *Abandon All* before I came to Kentucky, but no sense increasing the odds of someone recognizing me on TV, even local TV.

As I watched Clara's interview from a safe distance, I thought about the secret I carried.

A secret from Clara, the only one who did know I was trying to write.

A secret from Teague.

Less than a month ago, I'd been prepared to tell him I never was a teacher, hadn't lived in upstate New York, no inheritance gave me financial freedom. Instead, I'd spent fifteen years with another identity—that of the author of *Abandon All.*

Yes, I know you could swear the author's name wasn't Sheila Mackey. You're right. I used a different combination of family names as *Abandon All*'s author.

For a long time it felt like a lark. Living with Kit in a Manhattan brownstone while she wrote away, traveling, hanging out with big name authors, spending time in Hollywood. And making money.

Kit handled that, but insisted I know the gist, which included enough zeroes at the end to set us both up forevermore.

Gradually, though, downsides became apparent. Hard to start friendships or romantic relationships while what you told the other person about your identity and occupation were not true. (*Not true* sounds so much better than *a lie.*)

Not to mention calculating if someone could be trusted with the secret that wasn't mine alone. It felt so much safer to not trust, to not tell. To not have relationships.

I felt a chasm open under my breastbone.

I did *not* want to assign Teague to the limbo where half-forgotten faces of non-relationships drifted.

Telling him about *Abandon All,* about Kit really writing it, about my former life as a different person who happened to be a public figure I wasn't… The worms in that required a very large can.

But I'd prepared to open that can with substitute teacher/carpenter Teague O'Donnell. Problem was, he'd also moved from once-a-cop to once-again-a-cop.

He was careful the way he'd told me about the part-time position with the county sheriff's department. Cautious. Because that job specializing in major cases overlapped with murder investigations Clara and I had pursued? Or not wanting to get his hopes up?

He'd been a full-time detective in a busy department in the Chicago area when something happened that he didn't talk about left him legally blind in one eye. He didn't talk much about that, either. Or why he didn't try to stay with his old department.

If my secret came out and his association with me ruined that for him…

Kit assures me she's covered all the legal bases, so the kind of fraud that could get you—could get *me*—arrested was not an issue. But what about notoriety, public outcry, lots of nosy questions?

It hurt my head to think of what that might do to his position with the sheriff's department.

My head and my heart.

Which also took a blow when I thought about telling him nothing and looped back to the non-relationship limbo of half-forgotten faces.

I suppose it could be worse. I could be a fugitive—not only from the public eye and publishing world, but from justice. *That* would put a cap on our relationship. Instead of just stunting it.

CHAPTER EIGHT

THERE WAS NOTHING stunted about the kiss we shared when he arrived at my house that early evening, bearing takeout from our favorite Chinese place, and accompanied by Murphy.

I suppose the dogs greeted each other with enthusiasm, but I wasn't paying attention. I had my own enthusiasm to enjoy.

"Let's eat in front of the TV," I said when the scent of food reminded us of that bodily function. "I want to catch the news."

His eyebrow rose, but he didn't question me.

After a few national stories, which came in second to cashew shrimp in my interest, he asked casually, "Something in particular you want to see?"

He also leaned back casually, resting the back of his neck on the top of the cushion. But I suspected it was to get a better look at my expression as I faced the TV, without blatantly studying me.

Instead of answering directly, I asked, "What do you think of Jack the Ripper?"

He rolled his head on the back of the sofa cushion to look at me directly. I'd surprised him. "I have to confess, I don't think of him much at all. What brought that up?"

"Was talking to Urban Parhem recently and he doesn't think it will ever be solved. What do you think?"

"Probably depends on if they kept evidence in a state that developing science can access it without destroying it. Though I'm not sure the desire to solve is universal. After all, that would be the end of a cottage industry. Jack the Ripper books, Jack the Ripper movies, Jack the Ripper tours, Jack the Ripper articles, Jack the Ripper—"

I added to his litany. "Jack the Ripper interviews on TV."

He raised his eyebrows. "Those, too. What's up, Sheila?"

"Clara's doing an interview on TV tonight."

"On Jack the Ripper?"

"No. On ZigZag Jane."

"Not one I've heard of. If that's a cottage industry it must be—"

"A very tiny cottage. Ha. Ha. Ha."

He grinned.

I grinned back. He had that effect on me.

"Who's ZigZag Jane?" he asked.

"*That* is exactly the question." I checked the time. "Let's listen to Clara's interview. That should answer your questions." Some of them.

He raised one eyebrow—the more skeptical of his two—but didn't argue.

✧ ✧ ✧ ✧

"…**CLARA WOODROW, WHO** has helped the authorities with solving a number of murders and other mysteries in the past months, will be with us to share a new—and fascinating—story after this break."

Teague turned to me before the anchor finished.

"*Clara* has helped the authorities? Alone? How do you feel about that?"

Grateful. Relieved.

As long as she stayed in the limelight no one noticed me in the shadows. And that made it less likely anyone would notice an inconvenient resemblance between me and the author of *Abandon All.*

"I'm good with it. She's so much better with the media than I am."

"Is she?"

Something in his tone had me giving him a sharp look. "Yes, she is."

He nodded slowly. "As long as that's the way you want it."

My shoulders relaxed. He was looking out for me. I put my hand on his thigh.

A nice place to rest it. "I wouldn't like being interviewed and all that. The makeup alone—Uh. It would probably make my face break out. At least from what Clara tells me about the experience. Not that she's complaining, because she does enjoy it. Besides—Shh, here comes her segment."

I needn't have shushed myself, because it took banter between the anchors, then with the reporter, Evelyn Dermotte, before we saw Clara.

"It's such a tragic story, with this young woman found murdered. Not only so young—in her early twenties the experts of that day said—but also without anyone knowing her identity."

"Tell us about how she was found, Clara."

"A local boy on his way to the high school on that November day a hundred years ago took a shortcut through the old cemetery and came across her body—"

"Tactful of her not to call it ZigZag Cemetery," Teague murmured.

And likely unnecessary. The locals knew where she meant.

"—and lying in a bed of leaves, with more leaves almost covering her. She had been strangled with her own scarf, the ends crossed and trailing down her back.

"She was not known by the local inhabitants. The authorities said there were no clues to her identity. And no one claimed her body. It was only through the generosity of the community at that time—led by Douglas Vonner, the teenager who found her—that she had a decent burial. Though, by necessity, it was under the name they gave to her of ZigZag Jane.

"We can't give her back the life she should have had. We can't even punish her killer, who is surely dead by now, but with the scientific advances of our day, we might finally be able to resolve her identity—to give ZigZag Jane her real name. That's an effort spearheaded by the grandson of that long ago student who found her body, but it requires all of us to help, to finally discover Jane's true identity."

Back to the reporter. "The cemetery in North Bend County, Kentucky, does have a long, sad history, with a number of suicides and other mysterious deaths occurring there. But as Clara Woodrow points out, we can all help resolve one of those mysteries. A donation site has been established—"

Over the wrap-up and segue to a commercial, Teague said, "You two are looking into another murder."

His neutrality didn't fool me.

"You can't object to this one. The sheriff's department isn't actively pursuing the investigation—according to our sources, it never did. On top of which, if there was a murder a hundred years ago when this woman was found, the murderer has to be long dead, as Clara said."

"Valid point. Don't suppose you and Clara would promise to only look at hundred-year-old murders."

"You suppose right."

He let that drop. "Wish she hadn't emphasized the suicides at the cemetery."

"Clara never said a word to me about that," I said a bit grimly.

"Not Clara—she did fine—the reporter. This time of year, talking about a cemetery with that kind of history is catnip to the curious and worse." He expelled a breath. "Which reminds me, I can't come over to hand out candy to Trick or Treaters tomorrow. It's all-hands-on-deck for the sheriff's department."

Through my disappointment, I teased, "Trick or treating has major cases?"

Deadpan, he said, "Somebody's got to prevent bad guys from stealing candy from babies."

"YOU REALLY THINK I was okay?" Clara asked when I finally got through to her.

"More than okay. You were fantastic."

"I'm so relieved it's over."

"You always say that, but you do a terrific job."

"Doug Vonner was pleased. He said he's already seeing an uptick in donations online."

"Wonder if they'd be even higher if you'd played up the cemetery's history more instead of the reporter only mentioning it at the end."

"You think so?"

"So you *did* know that history and you kept it from me."

"I knew a little, I guess." She overdid the innocence. "I mean, I think saying mysterious deaths—other than Jane, of course—is awfully strong. And, yeah, there've been a couple suicides … But the one I know about was someone who was sick and in a lot of pain. Besides, that happened way after Douglas Vonner found ZigZag Jane, so it doesn't have anything to do with her."

That was her way of explaining why she hadn't mentioned the history to me. Uh-huh. Had nothing to do with not wanting to give me the full spooky picture.

"Don't be so sure it's not related to Jane. Some places attract acts like that. The person committing suicide feels … understood. Connected to another tragic figure."

"That's profound, Sheila."

"Thanks, but if we're going to try to figure out who ZigZag Jane was, I need to know that you've told me everything that—"

"Oh, I gotta go. Gran's calling from Belize. She streams the news from around here and must have seen me. Talk to you tomorrow."

TUESDAY

CHAPTER NINE

THREE DAYS IN a row at ZigZag Cemetery. How did I get so lucky?

Once again, I drove while Clara applied makeup, with a far better sense of balance than I'd have. My mascara would look like a stretch of this road drawn down my face.

"You do know why they messaged you, don't you?" I asked, wanting her to be on her guard. "They're hoping for fireworks."

Two reporters, including Evelyn Dermotte from yesterday, messaged saying a local politician named Henderson Nickell was holding a news conference at ZigZag Cemetery this morning, advocating that it be closed permanently. They asked if she had a comment.

"They might get their fireworks," she said grimly.

I stifled a smile. Unless this politician—I wonder if he fit Urban's reference to efforts to close the cemetery benefiting *the few*—threatened harm to a dog, her version of fireworks included please and thank you.

A jumble of vehicles stretched along the road. "I'll drop you off and park past the cemetery."

I saw crew setting up to shoot the news conference as I let Clara out, then went around a curve and found plenty of roadside space much closer than if we'd parked at the back of the line.

As I neared the cemetery, the scent of autumn leaves, stirred and trodden by many feet, rose strong and familiar.

I've read passages saying fallen leaves, especially wet ones, smell like decay, reminding us of the cycle of life, heading for its nadir. In other words, death. But to me they smell like earth. The same smell as those tiny biodegradable pots of plants you dig into the ground in the spring.

At least they did when I wasn't visiting a cemetery.

At ZigZag Cemetery the smell did make me think of death.

I spotted the two rival reporters, each with her own small supporting tech cast busy placing microphones, cameras.

Another knot consisted of people I didn't recognize. I figured the tall man in his forties was Henderson Nickell. I based that largely on the fact that a younger man and younger woman fussed around him and he accepted their attention as his due.

Nickell had blond hair that in a few years would either leave him with a very high forehead or a gravity-defying combover.

The younger man, thin and darkly attractive in a slightly over-groomed way, spared time now and then to hit the younger woman with dagger looks.

She never noticed. All her attention was for Henderson Nickell. She was also blonde, with no sign of thinning in her flowing mane. She, too, counted as attractive with a heavy leaning toward cuteness.

She touched Henderson Nickell a lot. Too much? Borderline, I'd say.

The fourth member of their group recognized the touches, but showed no reaction.

She was the most arresting. Standing still, saying nothing, moving only her eyes, she gave me the impression of intelligence and … energy? That wasn't quite right, but—

"Ready," one of the tech people from Bianca Abernathy's group said. Immediately echoed by one of Evelyn Dermotte's. "Ready."

After a brief, heated exchange between Nickell's two younger at-tendees, the young woman started forward.

As she stepped in front of the microphones and smiled widely, I received a message from Urban Parhem. Wonder of wonders, having a connection to receive it. Or maybe not so wondrous, since the TV people were generating hotspots.

The young woman's soundtrack became background as I read Urban's message.

"I'd like to introduce Drain Commissioner Henderson Nickell. That's N-i-c-k-e-l-l." She also spelled the first name and provided contact information.

Someone asked if she was his press secretary. A faint titter came from somewhere, as she said no, but added winningly that she was sure she could help if they had any questions.

Puzzled, I acted on Urban's message, by clicking a link.

At the young woman's invitation—punctuated with an adoring look he did not return—Henderson Nickell took her place in front of the microphones.

I glanced from the screen to see him apply a veneer of concern to his expression as he started talking.

"We are here today to call attention to a grave matter—"

He didn't even get the pun, but several of the news people did.

"—for all of North Bend County. Although this problem is located in one small section of our fair county, this is a matter for all…"

I tuned out as I found what Urban's message pointed me to.

I tried not to grin too broadly.

"It's an eyesore and menace in our community," Nickell said in full politician mode.

Clara defended ZigZag Cemetery. "It is locked most of the time, and only opened when—"

"Locked?" Henderson Nickell scoffed. "Anyone could get in with the state of disrepair of the fences. That north section is practically flat. And the rest of the place is no better. Should have been closed up and moved a long time ago."

"In order to build more cheap houses on this spot, like you did on the site of the historic schoolhouse?" Clara demanded.

"I don't think this place's history would be a selling point. ZigZag Estates?" He smirked.

The two younger members of his entourage chuckled sycophantly. The remaining one did not.

I stepped forward and extended my phone to Clara, with my back to the cameras that were focused elsewhere anyway.

Nickell riffed for a minute on the dangers of the cemetery, clearly happier with himself with each word.

That was a mistake, because it gave Clara a chance to read what I'd pulled up on the screen.

Her eyes widened, then she looked at me.

The older woman was the only one of Henderson Nickell's group to catch that. She twisted around to spear me with a look, then back to Clara. She took a step forward, as if to reach Nickell or get his attention. She couldn't do either. Too many people between them. And his attention was deeply focused down the front of Bianca Abernathy's neckline.

Clara slid into his next breath-taking pause without hesitation.

"But surely, Mr. Nickell, you know North Bend County was among the first to enact regulations to protect historic cemeteries, with requirements for documentation and strong preference for preservation."

"The laws—" he started, but not with his previous confidence.

Clara gave no quarter.

"The laws of Kentucky do allow relocation of cemeteries—as a last resort—and I'm sure, since you've been advocating for the closure of Kielwegen Cemetery, popularly known as ZigZag Cemetery, that you're aware of the required steps, including contacting local authorities, publishing public notice of your intent, obtaining affidavits from descendants of those whose remains you would be moving, including necessary genealogical research to identify and contact those related individuals, and that's barely the first third of the requirements. Not only for ZigZag Cemetery, of course. Our county has any number of family cemeteries from those early days. Did you know that at least one previously unknown historic cemetery is reported in North Bend County every year? And the historical society asks anyone who knows of such historic family cemeteries to let them know so they can be documented and preserved."

"I don't—"

"You didn't know about our heritage of historic family cemeteries? That's a shame. Or did you mean you don't know about the requirements? You *must* familiarize yourself with them and be aware of all the obligations that would fall on you or anyone who favors closing ZigZag Cemetery and relocating the remains of those interred here. I say we preserve our history, leave these souls in peace who came before us, who are our North Bend County ancestors, whether related or not, because they made our home what it is now."

She delivered the rousing end directly into the cameras.

"Great!" Evelyn cried out.

Not to be outdone, Bianca said, "That was terrific. Both of you."

That was gracious of her, since Evelyn invited Clara. On the other hand, Clara had turned a politician blah-blah-blah-ing into energy-infused video.

"I had more—" Henderson Nickell's complaint sank under the clamor of techs disassembling gear.

I took Clara's arm and steered her out of there.

THE FIRST SHOWING of *Clara Woodrow Annihilates the Politician* aired on the early news. We would each record the dinnertime news, because Trick or Treating was six to eight. We also had the eleven o'clock news to look forward to.

We'd left the cemetery floating on a cloud of victory. We called Urban first to thank him for that juicy information. Then Clara called her husband Ned, before phoning Doug Vonner.

She interrupted his renewed thanks about her interview with Evelyn Dermotte by letting him know that was yesterday's news—literally—and he should not miss tonight's.

By the time she brought him up to date, I was dropping her off at her house to be sure we both caught the early news, then prepared for the evening's Trick or Treaters and—no doubt—accolade phone calls to Clara.

✧ ✧ ✧ ✧

THE GHOSTS, GOBLINS, princesses, football players, super heroes, firemen, and other pint-sized personas arriving at our front door initially startled, then delighted Gracie.

The kids might have been coming for candy, but to Gracie they were coming to see her. They oohed and ahhed when they saw her, distracted from the bowl of individually wrapped chocolate delights.

I had a ball.

I barely even missed Teague.

I didn't catch up with Clara until she called after the late news, when she'd triumphed again on both stations and, as expected, received many complimentary phone calls, including from Doug Vonner, who was taking the next day off work to explore the topic of protection for small and family cemeteries in North Bend County.

She also received three truly nasty comments on social media. Ned took care of them—report, block, delete—but they shook Clara. I reminded her to look at the percentage of negative compared to the percentage of positive.

In the end, logic and math soothed her.

Along with tomorrow's promise of a morning dog-park meetup and discussion of what to do next about ZigZag Jane.

WEDNESDAY

CHAPTER TEN

CLARA PICKED UP Murphy, then Gracie and me, for today's dog park trip, starting slightly earlier than our customary late morning. Though Donna and the other early dog park regulars were long gone.

Entering, our three dogs threaded around and through groups, leaving a wake of frothy excitement behind them.

Clara and I, making our way to our favorite picnic table, received a quick wave here and there from our fellow humans, along with one call of congratulations to Clara for last night's "starring role."

"Starring role," she scoffed, but she was pleased. "A few more calls today. No more of those social media nasties, thank heavens."

Probably thanks to Ned's ability to block them. Lift a rock and you rarely find just three slimy bugs.

"I called Doug a few times this morning, finally got him when I called on the way to your house. He said we should come over after lunch to look at the files his grandfather kept."

"Good. I copied all the articles Urban gave me for you. I left the file in your SUV. I read a couple more articles last night, but I have to admit I fell asleep before I got far."

"That's the way to make me enthusiastic about reading them." Clara laughed. "Anything else?"

"Like what?"

"Wondered if you'd talked to anybody. You know, maybe on the phone, somebody who might have ideas or suggestions or something?"

She couldn't mean Teague. She knew as well as I did that neither he nor Ned had much enthusiasm for us chasing murderers. The age of this one helped, but I didn't see that changing their views completely.

"Kit?" I asked.

"Of course. Did she? Have ideas or suggestions?"

"No ideas, no suggestions, because I haven't called her."

"Why?"

"We're not going to discover ZigZag Jane's real identity before the anniversary of her death, and there's no other specific date pushing us, right?"

I also didn't want to hear Kit pushing me on opening the door to my past to Teague.

"I suppose not," Clara said. "Though I'd be interested what she thought of all this. Well, will you look at that?"

She jerked her chin toward the unheard-of sight of all three dogs lying at the lip of a drop-off to an area called Las Vegas, because once out of sight the dogs treated it like Sin City.

"Quick, load them up before they get a second wind."

WE ACCOMPLISHED THAT goal.

As we got in the SUV's front seat from opposite sides, Clara said, "Oh, I almost forgot. I need to swing by the bank and grocery store. It won't take long. I could drop you and Gracie off…"

"No need. Which grocery?"

"Jolly Roger on Covert Circle. I placed a pickup order because I have to go to the bank, too."

A little delay in getting back to reading Urban's file on ZigZag Jane wouldn't hurt anything.

While I was thinking, she drove past the bank's drive-through.

"The bank…?" I asked.

"I have to go inside. Need to get my signature notarized for something in Ned's mom's estate. Still working on that, poor guy." She raised a wait-a-second finger. "I'll be right back."

She wasn't kidding. She'd barely left when the dogs' happy yips had me checking the side mirror … and here came Clara.

She slid into the driver's seat. Not with a happy yip.

"I'm beginning to think this woman doesn't exist. This is the third time I've gone to that bank to try to get this thing notarized. Early lunch, late lunch, filling in for people at another branch—she's never there."

"What are you going to do?"

"They suggested the library. Or come back tomorrow." She grimaced. "Though they couldn't say *when* tomorrow. The library is on the way home, if you don't mind another stop."

"Of course not. In fact, I was going to ask if we could swing by the dry cleaners. I've had a jacket there for weeks."

"Sure, we'll do that right after I call the library."

The library said they had a notary public on staff, she was at lunch, but expected back in twenty minutes and to call again when we were nearby.

The dry cleaners had a drive-through to drop off and pick up. My least favorite clerk came out. I leaned over to say, "I'm picking up" and gave my phone number.

"We don't have anything under that." It was an accusation of misbehavior on my part. "Can you spell your name?"

I did.

"I'll have to check inside," she complained.

As soon as she left, Clara said, "I hate when people ask if I can spell my name. I want to say I've been able to since before kindergarten. It brings out the nasty in me."

"Yeah, you're so nasty."

She proved my point by cooing at the dogs.

The woman returned—with my jacket.

Clara said, "Don't you have the loyalty card, Sheila?"

"Oh, I do. And it's one payment from getting the reward. It's right—"

"You can't use it." The woman recoiled as if the card were a snake.

"This order doesn't count. You pre-paid. Besides, we're dropping it soon."

"Well, here, put this in." Clara pulled a jacket of Ned's from behind her seat.

"That's *your* dry cleaning. You can't use *her* loyalty card." The woman's tone identified us as moral delinquents.

"I'll pay for it," I said.

In triumph, the woman said, "But then you'll be pre-paying and that doesn't qualify."

"We'll pay when we pick up," Clara replied.

"That will be too late. The card won't be good anymore."

"You're cancelling it that fast?"

"Yes," the woman lied.

I threw up my hands. "Forget it."

"No." Clara leaned toward the woman. "Her paid order counts as the last item on this loyalty card. She gets $5 off on her next dry cleaning. That's this item. Take five dollars off the bill and we'll pre-pay."

"I don't think…"

Clara stared her down. We exchanged jacket, money, and receipt.

"So much for loyalty. *Or* service," Clara muttered as we left.

Heading for the grocery store, she cheered up. "Did you hear what happened Halloween night?"

"Beyond an epidemic of sugar highs? And I don't just mean from the candy. There were some seriously cute kids Trick or Treating. Gracie wanted them all to stay with us forever. If I'd let her out, I swear she'd have herded every kid to our house."

"That's so adorable. LuLu kept going back to her bed, then dashing to the door when the doorbell rang. She never did figure out it would keep ringing. But that's not what happened. Maybe it was too far away from you to hear the sirens, but we sure did. And saw flashing lights from behind us through the trees now that half the leaves are down."

From a previous adventure chasing our errant dogs, I knew the

Woodrows' property ended at a creek that divided back yards on their side from those facing onto another street.

"Another dog escape?"

"No." Her eyes went big and solemn. "A police raid. They were having a party—"

"The North Bend County Sheriff's Department raided a Halloween party? Was Deputy Eckles in charge?"

The young and by-the-book deputy was the opposite of a dog person, which put him below slime in Clara's eyes.

She grinned at my gibe. "No. But we saw Teague there."

"What? At the party or—?"

"No, no. Let me start at the start. Well after Trick or Treating ended, we heard sirens. We'd been hearing noise from that direction for a while. First noticed it about ten, I think. Even with the windows closed. Loud voices and laughing—the kind of laughing when people aren't sober."

I confirmed I knew what she meant with a nod.

"Sirens started around midnight. At first it seemed like they were coming right to our house, then they turned off, but Ned could see the lights. We decided to walk LuLu over there."

That statement totally sidetracked me. "Aren't sirens one of the things she's afraid of?"

"Yeah. And flashing lights. That's why I thought it would be a good time to work on desensitizing her."

Uh-huh, satisfying Clara's curiosity had nothing to do with it.

Not hearing my internal skepticism, she went on. "Giving her lots of treats and praise, she came along eventually. Especially since the sirens were mostly done at that point. And then she saw Teague and it was like party on. *Oh.* I almost forgot. Hold on everybody."

She made a sharp U-turn that got us into the lane for the drive-through pharmacy window. "I have a prescription to pick up for my neighbor."

The window was covered from inside, with a small sign saying the pickup window was closed for lunch—neither the closed window nor the sign was visible from any distance.

Clara sighed. "This is taking a lot longer than I expected."

"No problem."

"We'll go to the pickup area." She matched her driving to her words. "The sign said the *window's* closed, so I'll run in and get the prescription inside. You stay here and accept the pickup order."

She was back much faster than I expected, frowning.

I told her, "The pickup order hasn't arrived."

"Despite what the sign said, the whole pharmacy's closed for lunch, for another ten minutes."

"So you have time to finish telling me about LuLu seeing Teague at a party."

"Right, right. We got LuLu around the block with treat bribes. Seriously, it was like she didn't trust me or Ned or the two of us combined, but when she saw *Teague*, it was like, oh, *now* it's safe. It was kind of disgusting she dissed Ned and me, actually, and also really, really cute she made such a fuss over Teague. He acted all nonchalant, but you could tell he was touched."

Which brought us back to the main thread I wanted to pursue.

"Teague was at this scene with the sheriff's department?" I asked.

"Uh-huh. Maybe not officially, because he did come over and greet LuLu. He said hi to Ned and me, too."

That coming as an afterthought—in Clara's recounting of the incident and probably in Teague's actions—was perfectly understandable, even expected in our circles.

But at this moment a non-dog thought had my attention.

"Teague never said a word about being at a scene to me." And we had talked last night—briefly, true. Still.

"Well, maybe he was on duty after all and couldn't talk about it. Or—" Her enthusiasm said she liked this excuse for Teague better than her first try. "—it turned out to be nothing, so it wasn't worth mentioning."

"*You* think it's worth mentioning."

"Uh. Yeah ... but, you and I talk about those sorts of things."

And Teague and I didn't talk about … a number of things.

Clara was about to say more when a store employee pulling a wagon of groceries arrived outside her window.

She exited to show the young woman where to put the groceries, keeping them safe from the dogs, who were mostly fascinated by the young woman, but would take eating groceries as a fallback position.

As they put in the last bag, Clara reached into one and pulled out an item. "I didn't order hamburger buns."

"Are you sure?"

"I'm sure," Clara said firmly.

"But they're in your order."

"I see that, but I didn't order them."

"I suppose you can take them to the front desk and see if maybe they'll give you a refund."

"Let me get this straight. The store messed up my order by adding hamburger buns I didn't order, but to make it right, I have to go inside, stand in line and see if—*maybe*—they'll give me a refund so I'm not charged for something I didn't order?"

"Um, yeah." The young woman departed without a backward glance.

"I did *not* order hamburger buns."

My extraordinarily slow-to-anger—unless you hurt an animal—friend had built a head of steam.

"You go to the pharmacy, Clara. I'll stand in line for the refund."

I'd advanced to being the next person to be helped when Clara returned—again, sooner than expected.

"It's still not open?" I asked.

"It's open. With fourteen people in line and as I stood at the end, a woman came right up behind me with two kids in a basket—the part closest to me—who clearly had whooping cough and have never been taught to cover their cough."

I *did* cover my grin as we became the front of the line and Clara explained the situation to the man behind the counter.

"You ordered hot dog buns," the man I hadn't seen here before said, contrary to everything Clara just told him.

"I did not. Nor did I order hamburger buns, which is what was in the bag."

"You want to return the buns as defective?"

"No. I want a refund for them because I did not order them."

"You don't want them?"

Clara released a breath slowly. "I do not want them."

"Well, we'll have to fill out the form and submit it to the front office and see if it qualifies."

This time when Clara released a breath, fast words came along. "Forget it. Forget the form, forget the refund, forget making me pay for something I didn't order. Just give them to somebody who needs them."

"We're not in the business of giving food away. And you did get the product."

"*Which. I. Did. Not. Order.*"

"It says here you ordered hot dog buns," the Jolly Roger employee said.

"Then why did you give her hamburger buns?" the man behind us asked.

The man behind the counter frowned. "You want to exchange the hamburger buns for hot dog buns?"

Clara turned to me. "Get me out of here. Now."

"Gladly." I took the package of hamburger buns from the clerk's hand. At the end of the line was a woman with a toddler beside her and a baby in a carrier in the cart. "Would you like these hamburger buns?"

She blinked. "Sure."

"They're yours." Clara, who was closer, handed them to her as we walked past.

The man behind the counter called after us, "You can't exchange them now."

We didn't look back.

But as we exited, a cart pushed by a mother with two hacking kids in it started to follow us.

We walked faster to Clara's SUV, closing the doors quickly.

CHAPTER ELEVEN

"**I STILL HAVE** to go to the pharmacy for Eloise, but the drive-through seems safer than inside," Clara said.

She drove back to the side of the store and got in line behind three other cars. The good news was the window appeared to be open.

"So what did Teague say about the party?" I asked.

"Nothing, really. But I learned more from my neighbor. That's Eloise Gareer, who lives catty-corner behind us. She heard the racket outside, called the sheriff's department, then went outside and told them so. She's almost ninety, but nothing scares her.

"She yelled at people for being on her lawn. One guy, uh, urinated on her rose bushes. She told him that with other men she'd warn them about the thorns, but since he had so little at risk, she didn't need to. He pushed her—can you believe that?—and then the coward ran off, still trying to get his pants closed.

"Neighbors helped her and the so-called partygoers scattered, especially with deputies arriving. Though they found plenty of people still there. Including the woman who rented the house. One neighbor said she overheard deputies talking and it wasn't the first time the party woman did this. She rents a house in a nice neighborhood, puts out the word there'll be a wild party, charges people to come, disrupts the neighborhood, then walks away with a profit. It's disgusting. I wish the deputies would charge her with *something*."

Our turn at the pharmacy window.

We were silent during the transaction, except yips from the four-footed passengers in back, who expected a treat at every drive-through.

As we eased forward to let the next car advance while Clara put away her wallet, I said, "They didn't ask for your ID to check if it's your prescription."

"Why do you think I get it here?"

As she spoke the last word, a pickup bounced over the wide curb dividing our lane from an ATM lane to our right, wildly cutting in front of us.

Clara jammed on the brakes.

"The dogs?" she said, fighting to keep the wheel under control.

I twisted around. "Fine." If a bit alarmed (LuLu), surprised (Murphy), and indignant (Gracie.)

I continued the twist to see where the truck came from, if law enforcement was chasing him, or possibly the hounds of hell.

Nobody was behind him.

Twisting back, the only explanation I could see was the little car in front of him hadn't moved fast enough, so he went … sideways.

His left tires came off the wide curb at an angle that tipped his vehicle dangerously.

A plastic bottle of something flew high and wide out of the unsecured pickup bed, hit the top of Clara's SUV with a bam that made all of us flinch, then dripped light yellow fluid thickly down her windshield.

The pickup's front left tire hit the far side of our lane and jerked back, possibly on its own, because it sure didn't seem as if the person behind the wheel was steering.

Once straight enough to avoid more ping-ponging from curb to curb, the pickup kept going, having missed a collision with us by a good two inches, thanks to Clara practically standing on the brake pedal.

We both breathed hard, while the dogs circled in a mixture of nerves, excitement, and searching for something that needed to be barked at.

That came in the form of a knock on Clara's side window.

After we both jumped—and possibly swore, though that would have been covered by the barking—Clara lowered her window.

I saw a face appear in the driver's window as he leaned down. It was the man from behind us in line at the counter mislabeled as customer service.

"That stuff that hit your vehicle? It's brake fluid."

"Okay. Thank you." Clara sounded genuinely grateful for that factoid.

"That matters, Missy. A lot. Brake fluid'll ruin the paint job if you don't get it washed off right quick. Get yourself over to that car wash over there and get it done right now."

"*Oh.* Oh, dear. Thank you." The words were heartfelt.

"Fast as you can, girl," he concluded, stepping back from the vehicle so Clara could obey.

The SUV was a long way from the showroom, but I knew she and Ned hoped to stretch its life several more years.

When Clara told the car wash attendant about the brake fluid on the roof, he solemnly informed her, "You should never put brake fluid on the roof. It's real bad for the paint."

"I know. That's why…" A deep breath from Clara. "Thank you. Can we get in right away?"

"Yeah, you better get in right away," he said as if it were his idea.

As she steered into the mechanism that grabbed the tire, I said, "Some days—"

She cut me off. "Let's not talk about it now. Let's talk about a hundred-year-old murder."

It seemed the best thing for my friend, so I gladly complied, even though I had to dredge up something to say.

"So, it's good we're going to see the files Doug Vonner has."

Surprisingly, she frowned.

"What?" I asked.

"Nothing really. Just a little strange Doug didn't answer my calls this morning. I'd hoped we could see him before the dog park, but it was too late by the time he called back. And it was almost like he'd forgotten he'd said he was going to spend today on ZigZag Jane. Never mind, never mind. You're right. It *is* good. What are you going to look for in the files?"

Anything more interesting than what I'd found in the articles from Urban.

But I didn't think Clara was in the mood to hear that.

I riffed on the usual—means, opportunity, and motive, with motive getting short shrift since it usually tied into who the victim was.

The flashing lights of the car wash dimmed as we neared the end.

Uber-cheery signage instructed Clara to put the car in drive and "Go." In case she didn't know what came next.

She seemed revived by our few moments of ... Calm wasn't right, considering we talked about murder. And it sure wasn't quiet with the machinery around us. But at least we didn't encounter anyone else for those few minutes.

Clara called the library again.

Her call went to hold. And stayed there.

Clara focused on driving as we left Covert Circle, took the highway briefly before leaving exiting onto what I'd swear was a cow path, connecting to an alley eventually, and somehow spurting out at the corner where the library stood.

A voice came through the phone. "I'm so sorry. I can't find her. She must have gone to lunch."

"But they said she was at lunch when I called before and would be back by now."

"I don't know what to tell you. Call back between eight and eight-fifteen Monday to try again."

"Monday—? No. I'm here. I'm coming in."

"I can't guarantee—"

"I understand. But we're here now."

The person on the phone might have warned the rest of the staff about our arrival, because as we approached the main desk, a woman intercepted us.

Clara said, "I'm looking for the staff member who's a notary public.”

“That’s me. I was leaving for lunch.”

“Oh, no. They said you were at lunch before.”

“That was a meeting. Now I’m going to lunch.”

Clara sighed. “I tried other places already and—”

“Let me guess. Banks? Don’t worry. I can delay lunch. I’ll get my stuff.”

“Oh. *Thank you.* It is one quick signature.”

The woman reached over and patted Clara’s hand. “We’ll get this done.”

Back in her SUV, Clara fended off LuLu’s kisses halfheartedly, then flopped back against her seat. “Thank heavens for that nice woman. Sometimes murder truly is easier than real life.”

I turned and saw through the rear window an all-too-familiar figure plowing toward us.

“Real life is going to get a lot harder if you don’t get the SUV started and get us out of here.”

“Why?”

“Berrie spotted us and appears to be headed this way.”

Berrie Vittlow’s habit of critiquing other dog owners and their dogs, while she and her cadre of Boston Terriers behaved obnoxiously—she far worse than the dogs—was annoying. Plus, ever since Clara and I helped figure out a murder for the first time, Berrie simultaneously derided our activities while pumping us for every last bit of information.

We regularly encountered her at the dog park and yoga. That was more than enough.

Clara executed a bit of driving that might not have been entirely legal, but did get us away from Berrie and aimed toward our favorite café to pick up lunch.

Back in the car with our goodies—while I tried to persuade the dogs the good scents emanating from the bags weren’t for them— Clara headed for her house, where we planned to eat before going to Doug Vonner’s house. “Maybe we should have talked to Berrie,” she said.

"Not a sentiment I expected from you, Clara."

"Her family is from the part of the county around the cemetery. She might have something useful to share."

Expressing surprise won out over the thought that Berrie rarely had something useful. "The Vittlows are? I thought that was Kielwegen territory."

"Them, too. Plenty of them buried there. She married a Vittlow—didn't last long but she kept the name—but she was born a Kielwegen."

I laughed. "I bet she loves that the road named after her family became ghoulish ZigZag Trail."

"Well, she probably *would* prefer if it stayed Kielwegen, but it's still named after her family, since it was her great-great-uncle or something who cut those zigzags and killed the man."

"*What?*"

She turned to me, surprised at my vehemence. "What, what?"

"Berrie is descended from the ZigZag murderer?"

"Not directly. As I said, an uncle. Must have several greats in there, too."

"That's close enough. Her ancestor's the reason it's called ZigZag Trail."

"Why are you grinning?"

"I can't wait to tell her."

"Oh, she knows. Everybody around here knows."

That dimmed my pleasure only momentarily. "But she doesn't know I know. I'm going to enjoy the reveal."

CHAPTER TWELVE

DOUG VONNER LIVED in a substantial two-story brick house. I liked that about it, along with its symmetrical windows with black shutters. Although a pair of small windows above the front door, each with a single shutter placed on its inside edge, made the house look as if it were cross-eyed.

Doug stepped back when he opened the front door to us, so we didn't get a good view of his face until we reached the family room at the back of the house.

He had scratches on his face and neck, with puffiness around them.

"Oh, dear, Doug. Are you okay?" Clara asked.

He grimaced and looked uncomfortable. "Took a header into the bushes. I was chasing kids who stole the pumpkin off the front step and went down. Of course they triumphantly smashed the pumpkin all over the sidewalk."

"That's terrible," Clara said.

He shrugged. "Petty stuff. Did as bad myself as a kid. But you aren't here to see evidence of my clumsiness. Do you want anything to eat or drink first? No? We'll go downstairs then. That's where the collection is."

The basement was nicely finished. The amount of dark wood might have been daunting coming from outside on a nice day, but with clouds piling up on each other today, this seemed cozy, especially the corner he led us to, with a wood counter atop two double sets of filing cabinets, beside a desk with a computer. Shelves above the counter held books focused on local history, cemeteries, identifying people.

He gestured us to two chairs and took the one at the computer, turning it to face an open filing cabinet.

"I was looking through the files, trying to think what you'd be most interested in. There's so much. It's hard to know where to start. The coverage at the time or—"

"We have copies of that from Urban," Clara said. "So maybe things directly from your grandfather?"

I added, "You said your grandfather didn't get much by asking questions while he was collecting for Jane's headstone, but did he ever tell you the exact answers he got."

"Ever tell me? It was what passed as a bedtime story with Grandfather. He recited what he'd heard time after time after time. When he got old, he'd have to consult his notes, but—"

"You still have those notes?"

"Yeah. Do you think—?"

I interrupted. "We don't think anything. Especially not at the beginning. We gather as much information as we can. And then we see."

"Well, to start, here's my grandfather's account of what happened that day and the next couple days, after he talked to the authorities." He handed us each a printout, already stapled together.

We read in silence.

There wasn't anything new after what we'd heard from Doug, Urban, Donna, and Fern. At the end, there was a declaration by Douglas Vonner that he didn't believe the sheriff was going to pursue this, since no one had identified the dead young woman as a local. Followed by his declaration that in that case, he'd do it himself.

"Don't know why this is in here," Doug said to himself as he set aside a photo.

I picked it up. It was larger than most I've seen from that era. But that hadn't stopped the paper from yellowing, eroding the contrast. It showed a group of men and one woman in front of a car parked by the covered entry to what might have been a theater, since the bit of the sign that showed said "reopening," "show," and "tonight." The faces were blurry.

I flipped it over. Nothing on the back.

When I looked up, Doug had a folder open and flipped past a sheet with rows of names. "Wait. What's that?"

"List of donors for the headstone."

I'd hoped he'd say a list of suspects. It would have given us a place to start our digging.

I recognized a fair number of names on the list. Mostly because the most frequent last name was Kielwegen, with a few Vittlows.

"That's an awful lot of Kielwegens donating for the headstone. Does that strike you as odd?"

"No. A lot of them lived in the area of the cemetery." He looked over my shoulder. "And look at the amounts."

He resumed sorting papers and I didn't interrupt to concede he had a point. Even allowing for a century of inflation, they were small donations, some *really* small. But the ones from the Vittlows and the Zweydorfs weren't a lot bigger.

"*Hah*," Clara said in triumph.

"What?" Doug and I chorused.

"Oh, sorry. Nothing for the investigations. It just confirms something I told Sheila. These are some of your grandfather's notes about what people said they saw or heard the two nights before Jane was found. Most said they didn't hear anything, but a few said they heard the haunted hearse. And it had become an automobile. See? I told you," Clara said to me.

"But you said when you were little, your neighbor first talked about the old horse-drawn hearse. And that was way, way after ZigZag Jane was found or you are astonishingly well-preserved."

She lightly smacked my shoulder with a rolled-up paper, but chuckled. "It was way after. But the old lady who lived behind us, must have reverted to what she'd known from her childhood until my logic jolted her into keeping up with the times."

"I'm sure that made her fond of you," I said absently, continuing to read.

"Don't think she was fond of anybody."

I'd found something.

"Or maybe it wasn't a haunted hearse the people near the cemetery heard—horse-drawn or otherwise. Listen to this. A witness said he saw a new Packard Twin Six—wasn't a Packard a kind of car?—on the road that night. Said the engine noise woke him, because it sounded powerful and he was curious and he saw it slowing to make the turn near Gackle Creek outside their house."

"That's where the hearse appears," Clara inserted.

"Said it was black and didn't have its lights on, but he was sure it had Kentucky plates. They had license plates then?"

I received shrugs in answer.

"He sounds like a great witness."

"I remember Grandfather telling me about that." Doug pointed at the final line of Douglas Vonner's notes. "He was ten years old and all excited about what happened, thinking it was like the movies. He wanted to be in the newspapers the way my grandfather had been."

AFTER A COUPLE hours, all of us were yawning.

Back at Clara's house, we sorted dogs and cars, then Gracie and I went home.

I moved around the house restlessly. At first, Gracie followed, clearly hoping this was the rather boring precursor of some fun game. Then she flopped down, watching me when I came in view, but not bothering to lift her head to keep me in sight when I walked away.

Was I thinking about ZigZag Jane or Doug Vonner's grandfather or even Berrie Vitlow's great-great whatever, ZigZag John?

No.

I was thinking that I was pretending I'd never been the person I'd pretended to be for a decade and a half. Plus, there was the person I'd been for the first twenty-one years of my life. The *Abandon All* author used parts of that person. This me—Sheila—held far more of them.

But sometimes it got confusing over which pieces went where.

But that only affected me.

Kit scoffed whenever I'd raised the broader issues. "Don't worry. I've written a full account of our dealings and left it with my lawyer, to be released in the event of my death."

"Kit, don't make me wish for your death," I'd said.

She laughed. Most people wouldn't, but that was Kit.

"You're protected legally," she said. "My lawyer set it up so you— as your legal name—were authorized to sign in that author name on behalf of the corporation. So you don't have to worry about fraud."

"I never worried…" But I had. And now I worried how our charade might affect Teague.

In the first heady, whirlwind years of our charade, I focused on giving Kit the mega-bestseller experience she'd always deserved, even if it was half a step removed.

When the whirl began to slow, I'd worried she would miss it, regret its passing. More recently I realized she not only didn't regret the slide toward relative obscurity, she welcomed it.

One snowy Sunday night, sitting with slippered feet aimed toward a toasty fire, eating roast beef sandwiches and coleslaw from our favorite deli, she'd said, "I wrote the book I wanted to write, the way I wanted to write it. It became a huge critical and commercial success. It earned more money than I ever thought I'd possess, giving both of us fat nest eggs for the rest of our lives. Doesn't get any better than that."

"But wouldn't you want to be acknowledged as the author of *Abandon All?*"

"And go through all the nonsense you've gone through? Absolutely not. Besides hating that sort of folderol, I wouldn't have been able to write nearly as many books these years if I'd been dragged into being *Abandon All*'s author. This way I kept writing, while you were being the public author. Pass me the wine bottle."

With Kit so much on my mind, I shouldn't have been surprised when the phone rang and identified her as the caller.

✧ ✧ ✧ ✧

"HAVEN'T HEARD FROM you in a while," her familiar voice said without preamble.

"You must not be on deadline or you'd never notice."

"I'd notice. I'd bury it until the book was done. What are you up to? You and that young man of yours."

"I'm not sure he's—"

"He is. I hear it in your voice. And since your reluctance was always the stumbling block with anyone you met in New York, I'm satisfied it's mutual."

I slid past that. "He's been busy. Teaching and with his job at the sheriff's department. But, as a matter of fact, Clara and I have been busy, too."

"Hah! Another murder. I knew it. And you weren't going to share?"

"Not sure you'll be interested."

"When am I not interested in a murder?"

"This one's a hundred years old. In fact … Kit, among all your many, many contacts, do you know any DNA-testing facilities that might help pro-bono?"

"You have DNA you want to test?"

"Not exactly. Not yet, anyway. That's some of the pro-bono help we'd need—getting the body exhumed to see if it's possible to get DNA."

"Take it from the top, Sheila."

I did.

At the end, she expelled a breath through her teeth. "That's asking a lot more than running a DNA sample. If the community's against it—"

"Clara's going to work on that. If we can get the community's support…"

"I'll put out feelers, but I'm not trading any favors I have in the bank until—unless—I know where it stands on your end."

"That's fair. Thanks, Kit."

In practical assessment, she said, "If you had a name, you could check the census. That could give you multiple places to explore. An address, when the person was born, maybe where."

"Thanks for reminding me of everything we don't have. If we had her DNA … But that relies on relatives of hers happening to put their DNA in databases. And *that* relies on her having living relatives. Yet it didn't seem like anyone looked for her. What if she's always been alone."

"She hasn't been alone. That young man who found her cared so much that he not only searched all his life, he enlisted his grandson, and now *he's* enlisted you and Clara—"

"And you."

"Keep trying angles. Come at it sideways. See where that gets you. You're a long way from done, toots."

Despite my gloom, I grinned at the nickname.

"Thanks for letting me vent." She seldom had this much patience with lamenting.

As if she'd heard my thought she said, "Now, get to work."

I SAT AT the computer.

Not to write on my wip—work in progress.

Not to sort my thoughts about telling Teague my past.

The wild hare that came into my mind was likely an effort to avoid those things, brought on by a collision of Kit's words about the census and Clara's about Berrie's ancestors.

Come at it sideways.

We couldn't look up ZigZag Jane in the census, but I could try to find the other ZigZag.

ZigZag John.

CHAPTER THIRTEEN

UNLIKELY ZIGZAG JOHN would have welcomed a 1920 census taker to the woods he'd roamed, but Urban said he was 27 at the time of his death in 1922. That meant he should have been counted in earlier censuses.

And there he was in 1900.

Or *maybe* there he was.

There was a family named Kielwegen near Bowling Green, Kentucky, with a son named John of the right age.

If I knew more names from Berrie's ancestry—I stopped that wish before it finished forming. If I asked her, I'd have to listen to a lot more than the answers.

I tried to check for the Bowling Green family in the 1890 census and hit a major obstacle.

Most of that year's national census records were lost in a fire in 1921, leaving scattered pinpricks of information, none of those pinpricks in Kentucky. There were other Kentucky resources, but first, I'd continue with readily searchable national censuses online.

The Bowling Green family showed in the 1880 census, but only as husband and wife, well before ZigZag John was thought of—assuming the kid named John Junior in 1900 in Bowling Green ended up being ZigZag in the early 1920s in North Bend County.

I started to go back to 1870, to look for the parents of that 1890 Bowling Green family before marriage, but stopped myself. I wasn't trying to build Berrie's distant family tree. I wanted information on

ZigZag John.

In 1910, I found the mother from the 1890 Bowling Green group, now listed as a widow, and living in Stringer. That certainly put them closer to ZigZag's hangout, as well as to Berrie's branch of the family tree. But the only person listed living with the mother was her oldest daughter, apparently unmarried.

Where had John—aka ZigZag—gone?

Urban Parhem said the story was that he was a World War I veteran, but that war didn't start until 1914, even if he got involved before the United States entered in 1917.

I kept searching. Widening location, adding other years.

No other Kielwegens.

Kit's voice sounded in my head. Something profound from a previous conversation about not being defeated if you refused to give up.

I checked the box on the online form to widen my search to variants of the last name.

I got a backache, a crick in my neck, a sore index finger from scrolling, but nothing even close until a listing for a Louis Kiel in the 1910 census in Covington, Kentucky, which is east of North Bend County, along the Ohio River, and across from Cincinnati.

In the area, but ... *Louis Kiel.*

I clicked on the listing and found Louis Kiel was married to Florence, with three young children.

And then one more listing.

Only the initial J.

My heart *ka-thumped* before I saw the designation for male. For a second there, I totally forgot I was tracing ZigZag John.

Then came recognition of the unlikelihood that ZigZag Jane had a real name starting with J.

This J. was described as a nephew.

A smaller *ka-thump* of my heart.

He was the right age for J. to be John of the Bowling Green family. If Kiel was a shortened version of Kielwegen, it could make sense after his father's death for John to move to the city—which Covington was compared to Stringer—to live and work with a relative.

I needed more. Could I tie J. and Louis to the Bowling Green group.

There'd been no Louis in that household. But that had been John's immediate family. Louis's birthdate made him a generation older than the younger John. In fact, a bit older than John's father. I needed a generation back.

I went to the 1870 census, looking for ZigZag's father, John Senior.

Got him.

Living at home with his parents and a slew of siblings … including an older brother named Louis.

ZigZag John had an Uncle Louis Kielwegen according to the 1870 census. J.'s uncle was Louis Kiel in the 1910 census. The same two people?

Next, trace Louis Kielwegen going forward.

He remained with his family in 1880. No 1890 records and he'd disappeared in 1900. To become Louis Kiel? He wouldn't be the first to shorten his name.

Already knew where he was in 1910, so I skipped to 1920.

There he was, in Newport, Kentucky, the next town east from Covington.

No J. in the household now.

I reminded myself it didn't mean J. went to war, survived, came home, had a breakdown and, by 1920, roamed a certain section of North Bend County.

What to check next?

I'd barely asked myself the question, when pounding at my back door sent Gracie sprinting downstairs, barking vociferously. By the time I followed, the tenor of the barking switched from *Who the heck's there* to *Oh, boy, oh, boy, look who's here.*

I swung open the door to pale and goggle-eyed Clara Woodrow.

"Did you hear?" she demanded, half stumbling as she came inside. I sat her at the small table built into the kitchen wall.

"Hear what?"

"A body was found at ZigZag Cemetery."

I bit back the temptation to say there were lots of bodies at ZigZag Cemetery, what was the big deal about finding another one?

Because I could tell from her expression there was a big deal.

"I hadn't heard."

"A woman. She committed suicide. And her name is Jayne. With a *y*, but still. Another Jane."

CHAPTER FOURTEEN

"RECENTLY?"

"What do you mean, recently?" Clara's pitch rose. "We were there yesterday and there wasn't a body of a woman who'd committed suicide or we would have noticed." Her certainty wobbled. "Don't you think?"

"Yes." As I got each of us a glass of water, I thought about the monuments there, cutting off lines of sight. I also thought about my not wanting to look at anything too closely. "Probably." And the fact that I, for one, had not entered the cemetery, much less examined nooks and crannies. Nor had anyone else that I saw. We all stayed outside the main gate. "Maybe."

Her eyes widened, as I set down the glasses and took the chair opposite her. "You think her body could have been there and we missed it?"

"I don't know. It's definitely a recent body?"

"You mean—You think ZigZag Jane? But—"

I held up a hand to stop her ghost stories. "Tell me from the beginning. How did you hear about this and what do you know?"

"We covered the beginning. Party noise, police sirens, lights, walking LuLu over there, seeing Teague."

"The party? What does that have to do with it?"

"The woman who got in trouble for the party is the one whose body was found at ZigZag Cemetery today—Jayne Ulysee." She brightened. "So, actually, her body couldn't have been there when we were yesterday, because she was alive and at that party on the street behind us last night. Oh, and her car was at the cemetery, parked by the gate, and that *definitely* wasn't there yesterday. It makes me feel so much better that the poor woman wasn't there, dead, while Henderson Nickell and I wrangled."

I didn't remind her that a significant number of people *were* there, dead, listening to her and Henderson Nickell wrangle, not when she was feeling better.

"Right. What came after the party?"

"First, I have to tell you Teague didn't tell us anything, either, so don't think he shared with us and not with you. If I left that impression—"

"Let's get to the body found at the cemetery."

"Okay, okay. She rented the house and this shows exactly why nobody wants short-term rentals."

"Because she died there?"

"I hadn't thought of—I don't know, but—"

"Hold on, Clara, go back to Halloween night. This Jayne, who ended up dead at ZigZag Cemetery—I mean the recent one—rented the house in your neighborhood where the party was that deputies were called about?"

"Right, but—"

"Let me get this part straight first. She was from out of town?"

"Not *really* out of town. Stringer. She's why people were so upset the county commissioners allowed short-term rentals. People like her, I mean.

"But that party was worse than I told you about, because I didn't know the whole story. I heard more today. People from that so-called party were using drugs. A lot of drugs. Probably that guy who knocked over Eloise Gareer. Did I tell you they got him in custody when they broke up the party. Also, some of the people were underage and of course there were noise complaints and way, way too many people in the house. Then, today I heard about drugs. Though that might be a rumor. Because there was also a wild tale floating around that someone famous was there."

"Get back to Jayne whose body was found at the cemetery."

"I never met her, so I don't know much. Except she's risen fast since she was hired for some office about two years ago. PR or marketing, something like that. Her family moved to the area from Oklahoma when she was little. She lives in a two-bedroom apartment in a *very* nice complex in Stringer."

"What? You don't know how many cavities she had?"

"Do you think that's important?"

"No. I was making the point that you know a lot about someone you said you never met."

"Just the ordinary stuff you hear about somebody. Well, except you. You were definitely a mystery woman when you moved in." She grinned as if that were an amusing fluke and not intentional.

The grin faded as her eyes widened.

"Oh. *Oh.*"

My breath caught and I'd swear my heart did, too.

"You *and* Teague. We hardly knew anything about either of you. I wonder if that's why you're such a good couple?"

Breath and heartbeat came back in a rush.

I said, "They should test for that on all those online dating apps— Do you maintain an air of mystery by not sharing how many fillings you've had? Now," I continued over her genuine chuckle, which is one of the nicest things about Clara Woodrow, "about this woman—"

"Jayne Ulysee. She committed suicide and they found her at Zig-Zag Cemetery." Clara released a shuddering breath. I reached across and cupped her shoulder.

"We have to investigate, Sheila."

"But a suicide…"

"We have to. If not for us she might never have—"

"No, no. Don't say that. It's not our fault. She got in serious trouble about that party. That must have upset her. And if she was drinking or taking drugs, she could have been unbalanced."

"You're absolutely right."

Her about-face caught me completely off guard. "I am?"

"Yes. It's not *our* responsibility. It's mine. I'm the one who per-suaded you. I'm the one—"

"Don't say that, either. We do these things together. I could have said no to talking to Doug Vonner, to looking into ZigZag Jane."

"I kept after you. You did it for me. Plus, I was on TV—"

"At my suggestion."

"—trying to raise interest in ZigZag Jane, raising the profile of ZigZag Cemetery, reminding people of all those suicides," she said bitterly.

"You didn't mention the suicides."

"Maybe not. But it is my responsibility to figure this out."

Her dignity cemented what I'd known all along.

"Not your responsibility, Clara … *Ours.* We'll figure this out."

CLARA LEFT TO get ready for dinner. She and Ned were to meet Teague and me at our favorite local restaurant later.

I decided to shower and change right away.

It was going to be interesting to see when Teague arrived here.

He could come straight from teaching, which would produce his earliest arrival, almost any minute.

He could stop at his apartment not only for Murphy, but to change from his teaching clothes, which would produce a medium arrival.

Or, he could come here after spending time with his now-colleagues at the Sheriff's Department, which would produce his latest arrival.

If Teague came later, I'd have time after getting ready to do more research … of one kind or another.

An hour later, I was at the computer when Gracie lifted her head sharply, gave a yip of pleasure, and raced downstairs. Above her yips and yaps, comingled with Murphy's, I heard Teague call, "Anybody home?"

He didn't have a key, but I left it open when he was expected.

"Upstairs. Computer," I called back.

Gracie and Murphy raced ahead of him, circled around each other in my small office, bumped me with their noses, then ran back to Teague. From the noise, they nearly upended him on the second cycle of their rinse and repeat, but he recovered enough to reach the office and plant a kiss on the top of my head.

"What're you doing?"

"Sneaking up on me is getting to be a habit, O'Donnell."

The glint in his eyes said my hiding what I was looking at was also getting to be a habit. Usually my attempts at writing.

This time, I'd switched screens as he entered, from census material to blank, having closed the Internet search on Jayne Ulysee—the bare fact of a woman being found dead as an apparent suicide at ZigZag Cemetery—when Gracie lifted her head, announcing his arrival.

But that wasn't the only glint. He was amused at the notion of his dog-announced arrival qualifying as *sneaking up*. As I'd intended.

"I was a detective remember? *Am* a detective." Did he know how his eyes lit when he said that? Or how that made my insides flip to see him so happy … and then sink. "Approaching without calling attention to yourself is an important skill for a detective."

Equally deadpan, I said, "I'll remember that."

His expression shifted. "Researching ZigZag Jane?"

"Grasping at straws." No need to detail how tangential from Zig-Zag Jane those straws were.

"You and Clara—"

I interrupted him. "Are being careful and discreet. And it was a hundred years ago. Stop lecturing."

"Is that what I'm doing?"

"Yes. I watch those police reality shows where they sound like they're talking to backward three-year-olds. Okay, some of the people they pull over *act* like backward three-year-olds. But not all, yet even with reasonable, adult people, some cops—ones like Deputy Eckles—" I'd named my least favorite member of the North Bend County Sheriff's Department. "—get this sing-song tone and keep saying,

'Okay?' and if it were me they were talking to, I'd say, 'No, it's not okay. Why do you keep asking me if it's okay? Is that supposed to make me feel better? Or are you hoping it will make *you* feel better?' "

He stared at me a moment. "I'm going to say this, but notice it's not a question, it's an acknowledgment of hearing what you said. *Okay.* I'll also say, I hope you don't ever get pulled over by Deputy Eckles, because I don't think that response will go over well."

"Does anything go over well with him?" I grumbled.

"And that's what else I'm going to say. Don't dismiss him. Homicide might not be his forte, but he knows his county. Now, mind if I wash up and change?"

"Not at all." I waited a couple beats. "Teague?"

He turned back from the doorway, leaning against the frame.

"Want to trade Janes?"

"You know about that, do you? Figures. As tempting as that might be," he said wryly, "I do want to change. And there will be no talk of either Jane, or anything murderous or murder-adjacent at dinner, or Ned and I walk."

CHAPTER FIFTEEN

I WENT DOWNSTAIRS and turned on the TV.

I rarely watch TV until after dinner, yet here I was, tuning into the predinner local news for the second time in a week.

Being found dead in Northern Kentucky or Indiana mostly took a back seat on Cincinnati's TV news to any death in the city. Then again, major national and international news took a back seat to a dramatic fire, a shooting attempt with a juicy angle, or a city political dispute.

But being found dead in a cemetery where you were not already an official resident nudged up Jane Two—Jayne Ulysee—even when that cemetery was in Northern Kentucky.

Interesting they hadn't mentioned the two-Janes angle. I could imagine Kit's commentary on that failure to connect.

Then they flashed a photo on the screen.

I grabbed my phone, but Teague, with his canine outriders, jogged down the stairs at that moment.

No time.

CLARA AND NED had staked out a tall pub table in a corner of the bar at the Historic Haines Tavern. Locals tacked on the "historic" or paired it to the Tavern to distinguish the restaurant from its namesake, the town.

The restaurant tables were doing a brisk business. The bar area became even more cozy than usual with the overflow. Didn't bother me the least to be squeezed in hip to hip with Teague. And I could tell Clara and Ned weren't suffering, either.

Before I declared an urgent need to use the ladies' room (in the case of this small facility, call it lady's room) and suggested Clara accompany me to that one-person facility, she said, "I told Ned about the party woman killing herself at ZigZag Cemetery. Don't frown at me like that, Teague. I know we can't talk about that here."

"Or anywhere," he grumbled.

She pretended not to hear him. "But there was a rumor someone famous was at the party. Surely you can tell us if that's true."

He looked at her without answering.

Clara tipped her head, neither intimidated nor put off. "Was there?"

He relented. "Not by my definition of famous."

"In other words, not an athlete or super model," I said.

Teague considered. "Not sure I'd know if a model was super or not. Much less if a super model was famous or not."

I suppressed a chuckle. "But an athlete of any sort would qualify." Truth be told, I didn't mind his lack of expertise in the matter of models, super or otherwise.

"Oh, yeah. And not only was this guy none of the above but he wasn't even there."

Clara slumped slightly as the wait person arrived with glasses of ice water.

Ned said cheerfully, "Let's order."

With that taken care of, I caught Clara's eyes for long enough that she knew something was up and asked—silently—what it was.

"I'm going to the ladies' room," I said deliberately. "I'll be right back."

A beat later, Clara said, "I think I'll go with you, Sheila."

Teague looked from her to me, but before he could do more, Ned caught his attention with a question comparing the Cincinnati Bengals and Kansas City Chiefs offensive lines. *Thank you, Ned.*

Down the hall leading toward the back of the building, Clara said,

"What's going on?"

"Wait. Just in case."

Finally, with both of us inside the ladies' room, I showed her the screen of my phone, displaying the news station's online photo.

"Meet Jayne Ulysee," I said. "Well, you can't meet her, because she committed suicide at ZigZag Cemetery, but you already did sort of meet her yesterday when she introduced Henderson Nickell."

Clara tried her best, pasting both hands over her mouth. Still, a high-pitched sound escaped her that would have put Ned and Teague on alert if they'd been around to hear it.

But she kept her voice low when she spoke. "That's … that's the same woman … Jayne—the second Jane—was the woman at the cemetery with him, with Nickell. She's the same … Oh, my God. Oh, my God. But it can't be, because—No, no. It *can* be. Because I never saw the woman in charge of the party. She was inside with deputies when Ned and I got there, and I *never* saw her."

She'd just answered several questions, some of which I hadn't even formed yet.

"But why would she commit suicide?" Clara went on. That was one question I had formed and couldn't answer. "I don't think I've ever seen anyone less likely than her to kill herself."

An impression I shared.

"We can't stay in here long or they'll wonder," I said. "But you can stop thinking your being on TV about ZigZag Jane inspired her to use that spot, since she saw it for herself."

She shook her head. "But she wouldn't have been there with Henderson Nickell if it hadn't been for me being on TV talking about the cemetery. That's what made him see the opportunity to get himself on the news. It's a step removed, but still, if it weren't for me, she wouldn't have killed herself—"

"But as you said, why would she? Despair over getting in trouble for the party? Really? Does that match the woman you saw at the cemetery yesterday? It sure doesn't match the one I saw. There's something else I can't pin down, but here's what I think—rather than blaming yourself for giving her ideas, we should first be sure she committed suicide."

She nodded decisively. "Right. That's what we'll do." Her tone shifted. "Only we won't mention it, not tonight with the guys."

"Agreed."

After that, the conversation never came close to murder-adjacent or suicide-adjacent.

And it stayed that way until the next morning, because Teague and I had other things to do that night.

THURSDAY

CHAPTER SIXTEEN

"YOU AND CLARA are not going to that cemetery."

I didn't pretend I didn't know what Teague was talking about when he said that abruptly over coffee the next morning. "You didn't object before."

"It wasn't a police scene before," he said sternly. "Under the sheriff department's jurisdiction."

"So, not a *crime* scene."

"I'm not quibbling with you, Sheila. You and Clara stay out of that cemetery. I'll suggest anyone who finds either of you there charge you with obstruction."

I grimaced at him.

He kissed the top of my head again. "Besides, you and Clara are looking into that poor woman found a hundred years ago, right?"

"Right."

AFTER RELAYING THAT exchange to Clara during our dog park foray, I added, "You might have noticed that while Teague was issuing orders, he did not say anything about ZigZag Trail. In fact, he specifically said *in* the cemetery."

"You want to go to the cemetery?" Clara asked in surprise.

Want to? No.

Especially on a day like this.

Gusts of wind kept the clouds moving and that meant the rain could not make up its mind. It would sprinkle. Stop. Gush. Turn to blue sky. Sprinkle. Hit double-time. Stop. Gush. On and on.

We'd been fortunate to have only sprinkles so far as the dogs ran and played. At the moment we even had a slice of blue overhead.

I didn't answer Clara's surprise directly. "We both have doubts about Jayne Ulysee committing suicide."

"But she *was* hanged from a tree branch by her scarf."

Startled, I said, "How do you know that?"

"Evelyn Dermotte from TV called this morning and told me and she said the body was on the ground, with a broken branch nearby and her scarf still tied to it. Though she said not to tell anyone. She also confirmed Jayne's car was at the cemetery. The sheriff's department has it now."

"She hasn't used any of that on-air," I said after speed scrolling on my phone. "I bet that means she doesn't know for sure. Besides, there's Teague's reaction. Not only does he not want us there, but his saying he'd tell others to charge us might mean they're leaving someone there, unless he said that to scare us off."

"That would make the cemetery a crime scene?"

"Yeah. Outside of it isn't, though."

Clara's phone rang. With a quizzical expression, she answered. I moved away to give her privacy and to check on our three-dog pack, who'd oh-so-casually trotted down into the area called Las Vegas.

"Sheila," Clara called to me after a moment. "We have to go. Get the dogs."

I whistled, which they might have responded to, but I also jogged toward Clara, and that they couldn't resist. They chased after me joyfully. Less joyful when they were hooked to leashes, but not resisting as a burst of serious rain hit us in the parking lot.

Many dogs didn't mind rain, especially water dogs like lab mix Murphy. But Gracie does not care for that wet stuff falling willy-nilly from the sky. She was fine this summer with a sprinkler she could predict. And she likes snow. But rain? No way.

Don't entirely blame her. When a collie has a bad hair day, it's a *lot* of hair to go bad.

As we tumbled the dogs into her SUV, Clara's only explanation for the pre-rain urgency was that Ruby Zweydorf said to get to the post office right away.

AFTER WE'D PARKED in town, Gracie objected to exiting in the rain. I overruled her objection, because Ruby adores my dog and if the postal worker had something significant to tell us, I didn't want to take any chances annoying her.

I prevailed, though Gracie made her point by shaking herself vigorously all over me. Repeatedly.

As soon as we walked in the door, she stopped shaking. She and LuLu pranced over to Ike, who petted one with each hand and issued a low-pitched coo. Murphy pressed against his side and look up adoringly.

Ruby's expression didn't change as she talked with a young man at the counter, but her eyes lit at seeing the dogs and—especially—Ike's pleasure.

"Oh, Clara, Sheila, come meet Noah Canepa," she called out, as if passing off an awkward attendee at a social gathering. "He and Jayne Ulysee worked together."

Ruby had just handed over the best gift ever.

"I remember you." Clara latched onto his arm with one hand and pumped his hand with the other. That turned him partially toward her. With the dogs and me between him and the door there was nowhere for him to go in this small space.

"I don't know you," he said ungraciously.

"Oh, yes," she continued with an air of delight. "You were at the party Halloween night. I recognized you from earlier in the day with the TV news at ZigZag Cemetery. You and Jayne Ulysee were with Henderson Nickell."

That rattled him, but was it her reference to the party or the cemetery?

"My husband and I came around the block because of all the noise from the party and you were over by the corner of the house away from the driveway."

"I left early."

"You were there when the neighbor called the sheriff's department and still there after the deputies arrived."

"I was about to leave. It wasn't like there was anything I could tell the deputies. I saw the kids streaming out the back, but I didn't see the old woman get knocked down or anything."

She shook her head. "That was a terrible thing, wasn't it?"

"Yeah, yeah. Look, I have to—"

"You said you saw kids streaming out back, getting away from the deputies?" She didn't wait for him to confirm it. "You must have seen what happened when Jayne realized the deputies arrived."

A reminiscent lift of his lips was more sneer than smile. "She was crazy angry. Second time that night. Thought she was going to burn right up. Or go after that old lady who called the cops. Then she tore into the house. Have to wonder what was so vital for her to do."

He paused, making sure we'd caught the implication that she could have been flushing drugs or otherwise destroying evidence.

Satisfied, he continued. "When she came back out, Jayne had calmed down. She usually went all gooey and Little Miss Innocent when Henderson was around, although that night…"

"So Henderson Nickell shows up and—"

"He didn't show up. He was on the phone. I knew it was him from her voice. She could switch it off and on. Just like the other guy she got so angry at before the cops came. With him she started off normal, then about ten seconds of listening to him and she was a shark, chewing into him."

"Do you know who it was?"

"No."

He had a guess, but he wasn't sharing.

"Tell us about her."

"Haven't you ever heard about not speaking ill of the dead?"

Which meant there was ill to speak, and I suspected Noah Canepa wanted to speak it.

"On the other hand," I said quickly, "it's important to tell what you know when there's an investigation into a death."

Flimsy as it was, it was the moral cover Noah sought. Clara cemented it with, "That's a really good point."

"It is," Noah said with passable solemnity. "Okay, I'll tell you the truth, but I'm not talking to the cops or anything."

"We understand."

I meant that in all honesty. We did understand he didn't intend to talk to the cops. The sheriff's department would talk to him anyway and likely learn whatever he knew. Especially if Teague did the questioning.

If Deputy Eckles interviewed him, all bets were off.

"Jayne was rising fast. Real fast."

Clara nodded. "That's what we heard. Advancing fast in the office."

"Yeah." Clara looked startled at the bitter sarcasm in his tone, then deeply interested. "And you could say she employed all her ... uh, assets ... to accomplish that."

I probably never could have gotten him to spell out his meaning, but Clara's wide eyes and hanging-on-every syllable rendition of "You mean...? You're saying..." did the trick.

"She was sleeping her way to the top."

"But ... who with?"

I'll admit it. I nearly did a double-take at Clara's confusion. A short one though. She knew what she was doing.

I prepared to sit back and listen.

"Who do you think? The boss. Who else would she sleep with to try to get to the top?"

He had a point.

"Oh, my. And he's married with children, isn't he?"

"He's married, yeah, though ... As for kids, his son's in college.

Can't imagine having him around looking grown up would go over big with either of the parents, but especially Henderson. Hard to be the young up and comer when your son's existence screams you're not so young." A thought struck him. "That could've been part of Jayne's appeal. She looked younger than she was, so he might have hoped it would rub off on him."

"That's a really smart observation. They must have kept it very secret. Although…" Clara turned a look of awe on him. "You knew about it. Did she tell you or … Did he?"

He snort-chuckled. "Jayne or Henderson *tell* me? No way. They *tried* to be secret, but they weren't exactly world-class spies. Besides, I notice things."

"That's obvious," she said with admiration.

"I can't help it. Like when Jayne was spitting mad at him last week and for once actually let him see it. She said she did all the work and he raked in all the money."

"In the Drain Commissioner's office?"

"No way. Nobody's raking in money there. It must've had something to do with their extracurricular activities. At first, I thought it was all … you know. Horizontal. But over the last few months I've heard the m-word—money—spoken between them several times. Less and less lovey-dovey recently, too."

"You must be *very* sharp to have picked up on things when they didn't want it known. I don't imagine anyone else could have possibly known."

I looked at Clara from the corner of my eye. Yeah, her face was as innocent as her voice.

I switched back to him in time to see a crafty expression.

"Well…" he drew it out. "I've thought Krystal had to know. That's Henderson's wife, Krystal Nickell. She doesn't miss a thing. I mean, a *thing*. And she came in one Tuesday around lunchtime, which was one of their regular, uh, getaway times. Tuesday lunch and Friday after work—suppose you could call it their happy hour."

Clara chuckled without making it sound like an obligatory response.

"There were other times, too. For a while, they were at it like rabbits. Like in the restroom. The noises and banging against the door or the walls—people would have to wait or go next door. At least that stopped when they had to replace the sink because it came off the wall.

"Although, lately..." He gave a good imitation of someone who had pulled himself back from the brink of saying something he shouldn't have. Except for the sideways look to see if Clara and I had caught the implication that Henderson and Jayne had cooled off.

She sucked in air. "You don't think he could have—? Or his wife? I mean, something triggers a suicide, right?"

"I don't see how they could have. They were both at a party one of their cronies gave to raise money *for the cause.*" His ironic twist of the phrase didn't entirely cover what seemed like a whiff of disappointment that his boss and his boss's wife had alibis.

And wasn't that interesting ... Alibis for a suicide?

But was that really his reaction? Or was it me seeing things through murder-colored glasses?

"Anyway, one Tuesday a few months ago, Krystal came in, went right back to his office, and looked surprised to see it empty. One of the longtime employees got flustered—Mrs. Nickell has that effect on some people, even people who didn't know her husband was screwing Jayne Ulysee at the moment—and started babbling about taking a message for him and having him call her as soon as he came back from lunch.

"Krystal gave this sharp little shake of her head, like someone else might thump the heel of their hand to their forehead, you know?"

Clara nodded earnestly.

"And then she muttered something and I'd swear, absolutely swear, it included *of course* and—" A dramatic pause, then almost triumphantly, "*it's Tuesday.*"

We both nodded solemnly.

"Noah, you said when the deputies arrived was the second time Jayne got really angry that night. When was the first?"

He looked at me blankly for a second. "Oh, yeah. The phone call. Someone called and she got really pissed. It was like I said, one minute all smiley, the next about to tear out your throat with her teeth. Whoever called got that treatment big time."

"Do you know who it was?" I asked again.

"No," he said again. But with little attempt to make us believe it.

"What did she say?" Clara asked with her flattering interest.

"Other than swearing like I've never heard, even from her, she said to stay away, she wasn't giving him any more, and she *might* be in contact when it was convenient for her. And then she went back to swearing about what she'd do if the person didn't obey."

"Could she have been talking to Henderson Nickell?" I asked.

He gaped. And in case we didn't get the point, he said, "No way."

CHAPTER SEVENTEEN

HE HAD MORE to say, but it was about how his talents weren't fully appreciated or rewarded in the Drain Commission office.

Clara commiserated. I shifted from foot to foot.

Finally, with a pat on his arm, she slightly rolled her eyes toward me, letting him know it was all my fault that we had to go now, but she hoped they could talk again, because he was so perceptive.

He reflexively checked the time and said, "Oh, my God. I have to go. It's only twenty minutes until the news conference."

He started out, then looked back toward Clara with something like longing. He clearly didn't get an audience like her often.

It was a little sad and even more creepy.

It also meant he'd welcome our—at least her—return. And that could only be good for our inquiries.

Clara and I didn't even have to look at each other to know where we were going next.

Apparently Ruby didn't, either.

"News conference is at the courthouse," she said from behind the counter. "Figured you'd be interested in this Jayne's death along with researching ZigZag Jane. Have a nice time, girls. You can leave the dogs here."

THE COURTHOUSE STOOD at right angles to the post office on the Haines Tavern town square ... which was rectangular. The courthouse and Historic Haines Tavern occupied the long north and south sides. The post office and library on the west and the town's two oldest churches on the east got the smaller ends.

Rather than turning left out of the post office to follow Noah's path to the courthouse, we went counterclockwise, to not look as if we were following him.

"Did you really see him at the party?" I asked her.

"No. But it seemed a good bet he'd have been there." Clara grinned with satisfaction. "Easy pickings, huh?"

I started laughing. "You are a dangerous woman, Clara Woodrow. A very dangerous woman."

She smiled a smile the Mona Lisa would envy. "I know."

Not only could the woman act, but since she was truly sincere about most things, you tended to more readily accept all of it as sincere.

"What did you think about the *Although lately*, followed by a pregnant pause?" I asked her.

"Saying the relationship was on the downgrade," she said promptly. "Though I did wonder if he'd thought that through before he said it. Because if Henderson Nickell was the one behind the downgrade, that might strengthen Henderson's motive to kill Jayne. He wanted her gone and she wasn't going. And if *that's* true, Noah Canepa could be out of a job."

I pointed at her. "That's good. I bet she never knew he was eavesdropping on her phone conversations, hoping to pick up anything he could use against her."

"Obsessed," she repeated thoughtfully.

"Yeah. I agree. He's a possibility. If it wasn't suicide."

"What do you think about what he said about the wife?" she asked me.

"Fifty-fifty. Could have been the truth. Or he could have realized that him being the only one who knew or suspected Jayne was having a thing with Henderson Nickell could put a spotlight on him, considering his jealousy over Jayne's advancement, which I'll bet anything he hasn't hidden. Decided to foist some of the spotlight onto the wife under the theory that a shared motive makes him look less guilty."

"So after this news conference, we go talk to the wife, right?"

"Let's learn more about her first."

She gave me a questioning look, then seemed to read the answer. "Dog park?"

"Dog park," I confirmed. "Tomorrow morning."

We both understood that meant when Donna was there.

In the meantime, we had a news conference to attend.

HENDERSON NICKELL SMILED. And smiled.

I could hear the line in my head from Hamlet—not the cheeriest of Shakespeare's characters, but his words might fit in this case: *One may smile, and smile, and be a villain—At least I am sure it may be so in Denmark.*

Hamlet might have said in North Bend County, Kentucky, too, if it had been around then and if Will Shakespeare had seen Henderson Nickell in action.

The publicity pros I'd worked with during *Abandon All*'s greatest fame would have gnashed their teeth to nubs watching him.

I nearly did, too.

Those smiles—mostly sad, some nostalgic, a few caught up in a happy memory until the abrupt and shattering recollection that all that was gone with the snuffing out of a young and beautiful life. Yes, he said that.

And a lot more.

Over and over.

I wondered if part of Jayne Ulysee's job had been to stop him talking into eternity. Noah sure wasn't performing that task, though he looked as bored as Bianca Abernathy, Evelyn Demotte, their crews, and a couple other media members.

Krystal Nickell wasn't there. Just as well, since we hoped to talk to Henderson afterward.

Clara and I agreed beforehand to wait out all members of the media, both so Nickell wouldn't be eager to move on and so our questions wouldn't be overheard.

His droning on took care of that. Techs started to pack their gear while he still talked. When he finally took a breath, everyone left in a hurry. Even Noah disappeared.

"Henderson? Henderson Nickell?"

He turned, another sad smile already in place.

As she had with Noah, Clara took his hand to shake and held onto his other arm. Except he did the same thing to her, leaving them in a sort of deadlock.

"We met the other day. I'm Clara Woodrow and this is Sheila Mackey." She showed no sign of recognizing the awkwardness of their mutual grip. "We're so very sorry for your tragic loss."

"Tragic, tragic." He shook his head. "To think my wife and I were at a party together while this tragedy unfolded. It's one of the blessings of our marriage that we enjoy going to such events together. Because there are so many such events in our calendars. My position, of course, our business, and my wife's charity work."

"You don't do charity work?" Clara asked in her sweet voice.

"Oh, well, some, of course. But my wife is so devoted to it and so effective, I hate to even mention my paltry efforts in the same breath."

A fine example of the non-humble humble brag. Not to mention emphasizing his wife and marriage like someone who wouldn't consider fooling around with a younger woman.

"Was the party you were at that night a charity event?" she asked.

"Not that one." He chuckled lightly. "One night of the week, just for fun, you might say. Especially for Halloween."

Maybe it wasn't entirely a lie. I wouldn't be at all surprised if he considered fund-raising for his ambitions a lot of fun.

"Were you and your wife together the entire time?"

"Sure. We were at the same party you know." From patronizing, he turned brisk. "And it wasn't that big an event where you might enter together and never see each other again. Not like an inaugural ball."

A number of interesting elements in that. Including that his thoughts—ambitions?—went to inaugural balls. And the hint that at big events he and his wife might enter together, then not see each other again, presumably until it was time to leave. Some couples stayed together, even at inaugural balls. Apparently not Henderson Nickell and his Mrs.

"Was it a costume party?" Clara asked brightly.

Early on in our acquaintance I'd have accepted that bright cheeriness as part of her natural bright cheeriness. Now, I detected a different quality to it. Like she'd bit into aluminum foil as she said the words.

"No. Strictly business casual. That crowd's not the kind to wear costumes." Back to patronizing. "Anyway, an entirely different kind of event from what I hear Jayne got up to that night." He shook his head. More in disapproval than sorrow or anger. "If it hadn't ended so tragically for her, I'd really be disappointed in her."

I thought I heard Clara grinding her teeth. Or maybe that was projecting my reaction. I stifled it to ask, "You hadn't seen any behavior from Jayne that matched throwing a party like that?"

"Not at all." He breathed in deeply through his nose. "Though, I really didn't know her. So there could have been signs I missed. Especially in her personal life. Sorry, I do need to talk to other people now."

Because everyone wanted to spend time with the star was the implication.

Except there was no one else there.

AS WE LEFT the courthouse, Clara said, "One good thing about Jayne Ulysee dying."

The words snapped my head around to her because she didn't usually take an upbeat view of people being murdered. It was one of the reasons we got involved in these things. She wanted the guilty caught and punished. I did, too, but I would have been okay if someone else did the catching.

"She didn't have to endure Henderson Nickell's disappointment in her, which he so nobly withheld," she said.

"Why Clara Woodrow, I do believe you just snarked. Very well, too."

"I'm nice, but some people get under my skin. And that guy's the human equivalent of the itch mite."

"Do I want to ask the human equivalent of the what?"

"Probably not, but you did," she said cheerfully, as we started down the steps. "I saw a nature special on them. They're microscopic. The females get under the skin and live there and lay eggs. The males make tunnels under your skin."

"Yuck. Thanks for that image."

"It fits." I couldn't disagree. "You don't get them from animals. Not directly, but from dirt they've infected. Or from skin-to-skin contact with people who are infected."

"Clara," I protested.

With no effect.

"The difference is, the human itch mite can be cured with topical medicine. Henderson Nickell not so much."

I acknowledged that with a *Huh*, then quickly took the conversation another direction. "Why'd you ask him if it was a costume party?"

She looked down, but not before I'd spotted her sly smile. "I hoped it was, so I could ask if he went as a horse's rear end."

CHAPTER EIGHTEEN

"Clara."

The urgent whisper-shout on the heels of her words made us both jump and turn around.

It was Noah Canepa, coming toward us from the courthouse.

After the first breath-held instant, I realized he hadn't overheard us. From Clara's expelled breath, she came to the same conclusion.

"Do you know who that is?" He stopped a few feet away and whispered from the side of his mouth.

We looked around.

"Don't look," he ordered us. "He'll know I told you he's Jayne's ex. Willie Foglestedt. Over there, by the fountain. He's the one she argued with, earlier in the party. I thought you'd want to know."

And he thought telling us—Clara—would get him more time in her ego-stroking company.

She said, "Thank you for telling us, Noah. Thank you so much. Now you better go before he sees us and thinks we're together."

"Right. Right."

He hurried away.

I caught up with Clara, advancing fast on the young man lounging by the fountain.

He hadn't wasted money on shampoo lately. Or laundry detergent, because the hem of his too-long jeans held rings of sediment that surely could have told scientists of all his recent travels. Or not so recent travels.

Clara employed the same hand-outreach she had with Noah and Henderson. But this guy not only didn't grab her arm back, he didn't even meet her handshake.

That didn't stop Clara. She gripped his arm. His jacket wasn't any more familiar with laundry detergent than his jeans. But Clara looked only into his eyes.

"What the hell," he said.

"Willie Foglestedt, it's so good to see you home, even though it's under such tragic circumstances. I remember you as a boy, and now to see you back here, stunned by the death of Jayne Ulysee, I can only imagine how heartbroken you are."

"Yeah. That's it. I'm heartbroken. Broken. A broken man. A broken shell of a man. Broken all right."

We got the gist.

"Of course you are."

"Here I came home like I always told her I would, getting closer to being ready to start our lives together like we talked about from when we were kids, and this is what happens. My girl kills herself."

This guy made it sound like Jayne died for the sole purpose of inconveniencing him.

"Maybe she'd lost hope that you'd come back," Clara suggested.

"Nah, that wasn't it, because she knew—"

He broke off, looking off to his side, as if the founding churches of Haines Tavern fascinated him.

She knew...

He was in town.

Had to be.

"When was the last time you talked to her?" I asked.

He licked his lips, then a light came on in his eyes. He thought he had an answer that would serve him well.

"Got into town the other day, as a matter of fact," he said with would-be casualness. "Called her. She told me about the Halloween party and I went over to see her."

Someone called and she got really pissed ... said to stay away and she'd be in contact when it was convenient for her.

"Did she invite you to the party?" I kept it neutral.

"She didn't know I'd be in town. How could she?"

"When you called her, that day, did she invite you?"

"No reason for her to issue no glit-edged—"

"Gilt-edged," Clara murmured.

He heard her, but settled for a glare as he continued. "—invitation. She's my girl. Always has been."

"How long have you been away?"

"A while. Man needs to make his mark in the world."

"Did she know you were coming back?"

"Wanted to surprise her."

"What made you decide to come back now?"

He glared. "Told you. Wanted to surprise her."

"When did you talk to her before the night of the party?"

"I didn't keep a spreadsheet or anything."

"A week?" Clearly more than that from his eye-shift over my shoulder. "A month? Over the summer? Last spring? Anytime this year? Last Christmas, maybe? No? Okay, so we're talking a year—" I raised my eyebrows at him. "Or more. But you expected her to wait around for you."

"Told you. She's my girl. Always has been. We planned this for a long time."

"Plans change," Clara murmured.

"What does that mean?" he demanded. "You can't go accusing me of stuff. I don't have no reason to be guilty."

Sorting through his double negatives, which meant he *did* have reason for guilt, I also realized he'd taken Clara's correction to *gilt* as *guilt*.

"Were you aware Jayne was working, uh, closely with Henderson Nickell?"

"So? She had a lot of jobs. Didn't settle in like a robot. We were alike that way. Wanted our freedom, ya know. From the man," he added hurriedly. "Not from each other. From bosses and stuff."

"What did she say when you called her?"

"Said she was real happy—thrilled—to hear from me." He smirked. It faded as he added, "But she had this party gig for work she had to finish. We'd get together after."

Not bright of him to tack on that last part, since it might make him the last person to see her alive.

I tipped my head slightly. "You do know her end of the conversation was overheard, don't you?"

Clearly, he hadn't.

He backtracked, defensive all the way. "She was stressed. That party was a big deal for her work. She said it was going to make it so nobody could treat her like a flunky anymore."

"Did she say she'd meet you someplace later?"

"Not exactly."

"At all?"

He didn't answer, his ego blinding him to the fact that *not* meeting her would be fortunate for him.

"That's why you went to the party," I said.

"I wanted to see her. It'd been a long time," he grumbled. "So shoot me."

He started to turn away, had a delayed recognition that Clara's grip on his arm was the holdup, jerked away as she released him, then stumbled three steps before he shuffled off.

"Nice bluff about him being at the party, Sheila," Clara said.

"I've learned from the best. Did you know him as a kid?"

"Nope."

WE RETRIEVED THE dogs from the post office and thanked Ruby and Ike.

On the way out, I said, "We do appreciate the call, but what made you decide to give us the heads-up?"

"Dead body at that cemetery? Of course I called."

The weather had not improved. If anything, the clouds were thicker.

We picked up food—it was far too late to call it lunch, but it didn't qualify as dinner—at a drive-through that dispensed dog treats, as if they needed more after Ruby and Ike. We ate in the car, paying tolerance tolls to the dogs with French fries flipped back to them.

After a short discussion, I texted Deputy Hensen and Teague, saying Jayne Ulysee's one-time boyfriend had been in touch with her, showed up at the Halloween party, and was in town now.

Hensen texted back, "Interesting. TY" for thank you.

Teague texted back, "Really?" He wasn't questioning our information, he was questioning the universe allowing such things as our acquiring this information to happen.

Clara giggled over that.

She was completely serious, though, when she asked, "What next? We don't have anything set until we go back to Doug's tomorrow."

"We could always postpone that if—"

"No. We're not going to drop ZigZag Jane even if my talking about her gave Jayne Ulysee ideas about hanging herself from that tree. Doug and his grandfather and ZigZag Jane, all of them got snatches of attention, but never enough to settle her once and for all. It's natural we're interested in Jayne Ulysee and we have to talk to people fast, because it's just happened. But we're not going to let everybody forget ZigZag Jane again. We're going to follow through. We can zigzag ourselves, from one Jane to the other, but we're not forgetting the original."

I heard all her words, but some snagged on something that had been lurking below the surface of my mind. Then it clicked. The niggle in my head. The tendency to frown whenever someone said Jayne Ulysee committed suicide.

Clara said, "You went really quiet for a while."

I wasn't conscious of the gap in time. "Sorry—"

"Don't apologize. Just tell me what you were thinking about."

"Remember what that place was like?"

"What place?"

"The cemetery. The only tree close enough for Jayne Ulysee to have hanged herself and be found inside the cemetery was that spectral white one. Do you think any of its branches would hold a body long enough to kill somebody?"

"I don't know," she said slowly. Then she shifted to warp speed to add, "We have to check, Sheila. We have to check right now."

CHAPTER NINETEEN

THE DIFFERENCE BETWEEN driving on ZigZag Trail from Sunday to today was the difference between day and night.

Or the difference between a sunshiny day and a gloomy, rainy, foggy late afternoon sliding toward night.

If Clara had tried to bring me down this road in this weather the first time, I never would have heard about ZigZag Jane, Jayne Ulysee, or any of this, because I would have exited the SUV.

As Clara said, ZigZag Trail zigged and it zagged. That meant the headlights pierced the gloom straight ahead, while we zigged to the left. Almost before the light caught up, we zagged to the right. Again, the headlights illuminated where we weren't going.

I might have explored how that reflected our investigative process, but not while concentrating on blanking my mind to our surroundings.

"Sleepy Hollow's known for fog, but, boy, this is bad," Clara said. "Must be coming off Gackle Creek. You know, that's where the hearse most often appears."

Making me feel, oh, so much better.

Yes, there was fog. There was imminent darkness. There was also a sliver of a moon that would show from behind clouds when you least expected it, then disappeared like a malevolent hand switched it off.

A sheen on the road surface from today's rain made it seem darker. And there was wind. Can't leave that out. Especially the sound.

I wouldn't mind sighing wind so much, but the moaning got to me.

First, I told myself it didn't sound like a hearse. Then I realized I didn't know what a hearse would sound like.

Clara drove past the cemetery and parked around the nearest bend.

It wasn't much of a precaution, since any deputy left there would have seen us go by and had a good look at the vehicle, but as it turned out, even that precaution wasn't needed.

Yellow police tape, a sparkling new padlock on the gate, and an official sign saying to stay the heck out—in somewhat more formal langue. But no deputy.

Still, in case they sent periodic patrols, we did not go to the cemetery's main gate, but made our way around the perimeter through the brush. Clara found a sort of a trail, about the width of a bicycle, which helped. From the deer poop on it, I suspected it was made by Bambi and friends, not BMX riders.

It cut through brambles. Burrs hitchhiked on our clothing.

"Sure am glad we dropped off the dogs," Clara muttered from in front of me as we emerged into the rough semicircular clearing between the white tree and its darker backdrop of live brush. "We'd be combing them for days."

I grunted agreement. My focus was elsewhere.

You know how they say it's hard-wired into our brains to see human faces in all sorts of things, from the surface of the moon to the side of a mountain to a plate of spaghetti? They call it pareidolia. I know of a case where a piece of lumber was identified as looking like a hobby horse.

But in this case, it was my brain hearing words in the wind.

Like *Go back, go back.* And *Are you crazy?*

Okay, now I missed the words, because that last sound was a scream. "Did you hear that?" I demanded of Clara.

"Huh," she grunted with mild interest. "Don't usually hear that this time of year."

As relieved as I was that she'd heard it, too, I tested further by asking, "Hear what?"

"Fox. Females do that during the mating season, which usually happens well into winter. This is awfully early."

I did not share my theory that the female fox might be practicing early to scare me or wasn't really a fox … because we'd reached the tree. And I could only focus on one eerie thing at time.

"We can't try any of the branches that reach over the cemetery," I reminded Clara.

"Right. No compromising the crime scene. Besides, we can't reach them from here. We'd have to go inside the cemetery, so how about that branch instead." She pointed to one sticking out to the side as if reaching for its next victim. "It's a little bigger around than the biggest one that leans into the cemetery."

"Good choice. Let's get started."

Plucking burrs and brambles from the surface of her backpack to clear the way, she extracted a flat-knit scarf of fine gauge.

We'd discussed this. A rope would have been easier to toss over the branch, but we theorized not as reliable a test, because a rope would concentrate the force more and make a branch more likely to break than a scarf would.

We could have researched it. Or taken the quicker route of calling Kit, who would almost certainly know from the number of people she'd hanged over the years—all fictionally.

But we couldn't afford any delay. We needed to act before this soggy day wrung out its last bit of daylight. Neither of us considered waiting until tomorrow.

She tossed one end of the scarf up toward the branch. It slid off.

She tried three more times, once using a stick from the ground to try to encourage the end of the scarf over the branch. Each attempt fell back to the ground.

"This is hard and this branch is lower than that big one Jayne would have had to use. You try," she suggested.

I had no better success until my fifth attempt. The scarf topped the branch and extended a few inches on the far side. Using the stick, we gently tugged it to even the ends.

The next part we hadn't discussed.

"She would have had to tie a noose, then toss that over the

branch," I said.

Clara groaned. "You mean pull it down and start over?"

"No, you're right. We can test by tugging on it with a little jump to simulate a person…" I didn't spell it out.

"You do it. You're about her size."

"Okay." I took the two ends of the scarf in one hand and tugged lightly. Nothing.

"You said a jump," Clara prompted.

"Right." Reaching up a couple feet on the scarf's ends, I wrapped my hands around them, hopped, and let myself drop with gravity.

For a slice of a second I thought there'd been a shot.

That was before the falling branch nearly brained me.

When it gave way, I landed on my feet—I'd only been a foot off the ground. But to avoid the branch, I tumbled sideways.

"Sheila? Are you okay? Are you hurt? Did it hit your head—?"

"I'm fine." I scrambled to my feet. "I hardly put any pressure on that branch. Let's try another one."

The next one was thinner than the first yet still thicker than the newly broken-off one reaching into the cemetery. It came down even more easily. This time I was prepared and ducked out of the way faster.

Clara and I looked at each other.

"Jayne Ulysee did not commit suicide," Clara said.

"Certainly not by hanging herself from a branch of that tree."

BACK AT THE road, we spent several minutes plucking off burrs from our own clothes, then each other's where we couldn't reach, like chimpanzees grooming their fellows.

"Let's get going," I said despite more burrs left to go.

Might have had something to do with the fact that Teague messaged that he'd come over tonight. Or with the gloomy light fading toward twilight.

"Because of the cemetery?" Clara glanced over her shoulder toward it. "I wonder why people are afraid of cemeteries."

She truly was wondering. Not in any way mocking or teasing me.

I stated the obvious. "They're filled with dead people."

"But it's not like death is contagious—oh, unless, it is. Like the Black Death."

I side-eyed her. She didn't notice. "I don't think my dislike of cemeteries is related to the Black Death. They're innately spooky."

"Maybe the killer—killers—brought the Janes here because they felt the same way you do about cemeteries?"

If they did feel the same way I did, they would have picked somewhere else. Aloud, I said, "I think the second one was more likely opportunistic. He—or she—had a dead body on his or her hands. Where better to dump it than a cemetery? Especially one already associated with a Jane. Blends in, sort of.

"And that means the killer almost certainly knew Jayne Ulysee. At least her name. Otherwise why take the trouble to come here? It's not the sort of place you happen to pass on your way home from getting takeout."

"That's such a good point, Sheila. I was so focused on Jayne Ulysee going to the cemetery to kill herself because of me being on TV talking about ZigZag Jane, but since it's not suicide, the killer had to know about that and know Jayne Ulysee's first name."

TEAGUE KNOCKED ONCE at my back door, then entered with a warm "Hello," but paused by the hooks where my most-in-use outerwear hung.

Being legally blind in one eye didn't stop him from teaching, doing fine carpentry work for me and others, or from consulting with the North Bend County Sheriff's Department.

And now it didn't stop him from spotting a burr I'd missed on my jacket.

He picked it off and held it between his fingers, studying it as he said with a sitcom lilt, "How was your day today, dear?"

I couldn't take the suspense. I said, "The branches on that big white tree couldn't support a body."

He dropped the burr in the sink, then slowly turned to me. "How do you know that?"

"Well, *know* might be a little strong. Especially in the sense of absolute certainty. But looking at that tree, it seems pretty obvious."

"Does it?"

"It does," I said firmly.

"Did you have anything to do with freshly broken branches off that tree?"

I'm lying by omission to this man in a lot of ways, which is for his own good. But I wasn't going to add commission. "Yes."

"Sheila—"

"We never went inside the police tape, we never went inside the cemetery."

"You broke off branches of the tree where it appeared Jayne Ulysee hanged herself."

"On the opposite side of the tree. Away from the cemetery. To be found in the cemetery the way she was, she'd have to have hanged from a branch extending into the cemetery. And the point is, Teague, they cracked off with hardly any effort at all. There's no way any of those branches could be strong enough to—" I broke off, narrowing my eyes at him. "*Where it appeared* she hanged herself. You said *appeared.* You know it wasn't suicide."

"Not in the sense of absolute certainty," he parroted back to me with a glint in his eyes. The glint dimmed to seriousness as he added, "We have a lot more evidence to gather before we get around to *knowing* things."

I parted my lips to try another approach.

He didn't let me.

"And in the meantime, I'm not sharing the thought processes of the North Bend County Sheriff's Department with you, Sheila." Slightly less sternly he added, "I will point out law enforcement has a number of tools available to assess if someone hanged herself. And they're a heck of a lot more scientific and reliable than testing the weight-bearing ability of the branches of a dead tree."

I got it. Our little experiment looked silly against the breadth of forensic tools available to law enforcement.

"You have her car and you're processing it, right? Because the car being there doesn't mean she killed herself there. She could have been driven there by the killer or killed somewhere else and taken to the cemetery. Of course that means the killer needed a way to get away from the cemetery. A ride from an accomplice or—"

"We're doing our jobs, Sheila. We're working the case. Do you trust me to do a good job?"

"Of course I do."

My immediate and sincere response sparked heat in his eyes. I put my arms around his neck.

He met me for a kiss that curled my toes.

Deliberately, I uncurled my toes to go up on them in order to deepen the kiss.

Accomplishing the same goal much more effectively, he wrapped his arms around the back of my waist and hauled me up against his chest.

When oxygen played the spoilsport, we separated our mouths enough to suck in air and grin at each other as we maintained all the other contact.

There was no more discussion of the death of Jayne Ulysee that night.

FRIDAY

CHAPTER TWENTY

I WOKE TO the sound of Teague in the shower.

He wasn't teaching today, but he was—surprise, surprise—working for the sheriff's department.

Usually, I'd roll over and go back to sleep—the life of a would-be writer is great for a non-morning person. But, unrelated to any of the thoughts uppermost in my mind—all associated with Teague and many of them centered on last night—an idea occurred to me.

With a reluctant groan, I climbed out of bed, pulled on sweats under my nightshirt and a sweater over it. I was not used to the chill at this hour. It was way too early even to intercept Donna at the dog park, which Clara and I had on our agenda for the day.

"More straw-grasping?" Teague asked from the doorway of the office.

He was dried, dressed, and groomed. And I hadn't heard any of it, so I must have been deeply absorbed.

Unless I fell asleep sitting up.

Nah. My hands were on the keyboard and there were results on the screen from my latest search.

"I've moved onto chasing wild hares," I said. That oblique confirmation that what I was looking into connected to ZigZag Jane and not Jayne Ulysee eased his stance, which I hadn't realized held tension until it didn't. "Have to see where they lead now."

"I know how that works. One thing leading to another. Don't know when or if I'll get a break today…"

He bent. I tipped my head back. "I know how that works, too," I murmured just before we kissed.

"I'll call when I can. Stay out of trouble."

I widened my eyes. He didn't understand that I was the sane one. "Of course."

MY SUBCONSCIOUS MUST have mulled over ZigZag Jane while Clara and I tracked information on Jayne Ulysee yesterday.

The wild hare that took up residence while I slept was to go back to Louis Kiel in the census, this time looking beyond J.

In 1910, Louis Kiel was listed as married to Florence with two sons and a daughter.

By 1920, the wife's name changed. Now Zelda. And she'd been born nine years later than Florence, so not a name change. The three kids had grown by a decade, as expected. A fourth—a boy named Ray—was listed at eleven months old.

Could that explain the absence of J.?

In 1910, he'd been a teenager. By 1920, he was probably on his own, possibly starting a family.

You have to know what I did next. You'd do it, too, I'm sure.

I looked up the 1930 census.

Louis Kiel was at the same address as 1920, with no J. listed and no children at home—not even the little one, who would have been around 11. Just Louis and yet another new wife, Mildred.

The man did run through wives.

I broadened my search for J. Kielwegen and Kiel. None with those spellings. And none of the sometimes wildly distant phonetic spellings of the last name fit with the age of the J. living with Louis Kiel in 1910.

Then I searched for Florence Kiel—and, for good measure, Kiel-wegen. Did the same with Zelda. Nothing.

Could one of those two previous wives be our Jane? No, not ours. Doug Vonner's. And before that, Douglas Vonner's.

Probably not the 1910 wife. By 1920, she'd be at least thirty-five.

Unless the authorities of that time were off by more than a decade in estimating ZigZag Jane's age.

But the wife listed in 1920 fit the right age.

Still it was quite the leap to think she could be ZigZag Jane. Not finding her in the 1930 census wasn't definitive. She could have remarried or gone back to her maiden name. Plus, people died younger then. Especially women of child-bearing age. And why would she be in ZigZag Cemetery?

Though, it was interesting.

Oh, hell, it was more than interesting. It was exciting.

I CALLED CLARA first.

She was exultant. Certain we'd solved the whole thing.

I had to reel in her enthusiasm with the cautions, even as I enjoyed it. All done via speaker phone as I let Gracie out, then fed her.

Next, I called Urban. Mostly because I wanted to check if there were flaws in my thinking, fact-gathering, or conclusions.

He was … intrigued.

That was his word. "It's certainly intriguing. I also don't believe anyone ever researched a potential connection between John and ZigZag Jane. Though it would require considerably more substantiation to accept it as *fact*."

"Of course." I tried to keep my grin out of my voice.

Because he was already talking about sources he wanted to check against the information I'd found. Marriage certificates, death certificates, church records, surveys of veterans. Urban was on the job.

And even more grin-producing was that he wasn't saying anything I'd found *wasn't* a fact, nor that how I'd put it together made no sense.

Next, I called my great-aunt.

I laid it all out for her, while I put on dog park clothes and did the minimal personal care required for that outing.

I heard myself repeating to Kit all the caveats I'd been telling myself about how it didn't mean J. became ZigZag John and Louis having three different wives in three decades didn't mean the middle wife was ZigZag Jane.

"Good to stay skeptical," said my skeptical aunt. "But it also doesn't mean she's not ZigZag Jane. It's a *possibility*. What I'd want to know is what happened to her child?"

"He wasn't there in 1930, so..."

"Dead's not the only answer. Living somewhere else with his mother. Abroad. At boarding school, because of a new stepmother being there," Kit went on. "If his mother did die or leave, the child might be with another relative—hers or his father's. Or—"

"I checked under the Kielwegen and Kiel names in 1930 and no one who could be J. from 1910 or Ray from 1920 fit."

"Or," she repeated, "he could have been missed by the census-taker. It happens. Happened then, happens now. What you want to do now is—"

"Check 1940," I said.

"And 1950, for all those people," she confirmed.

Over the next twenty minutes, we had computers going in two states completing dueling census searches.

Louis Kiel did not show up again.

His wife from 1930 did show up as a widow in 1940, then she disappeared, too. Perhaps into the anonymity of another married name.

We found possible adulthood tracks of the two boys from 1910, one in New York, one in Arizona. No trail for the girl, but—again— that could be disappearing into a married name.

As for eleven-month-old Ray from 1920, nothing. Same for his mother.

The upshot was we knew where Wife 2 and Child 4 *weren't* after 1920. But that lack didn't prove she *was* in ZigZag Cemetery. Plus, where was the child?

When Clara arrived, I called her upstairs while Kit and I wrapped up, then showed her the new results, with significantly less enthusiasm than our earlier phone call.

"But why aren't you excited?" she asked me.

"We're not a lot farther along."

"Of course we are," she said. "We know a lot of things that aren't so and we know a lot more that could be true. This is great, Sheila. Really great. Or is this about Teague? Did you guys…?"

"We didn't have a fight. But…" I told her what we'd said, focusing first on the *appeared* to hang herself, and finishing with, "I bet that means she was strangled. Strangulation could require more examination to know for sure if it was murder or suicide. Although maybe smothering…"

"You went through that with Teague?"

"No." I told her what else he and I said. "But it's not a matter of my not trusting the sheriff's department to do their job."

"Well, it is a little bit and I can see how it might look like that to Teague," she said.

"I trust *him* to do a good job—a great job. But he might not have all the information we do about Jayne Ulysee and certainly not all we have about ZigZag Jane. Because he doesn't think they're connected."

She sucked in her bottom lip. "Maybe they're not."

"They are. They have to be. At least to the extent that—" I broke off.

Clara exhaled loudly enough for LuLu to turn toward her. "To the extent that I gave someone the idea to murder Jayne Ulysee at ZigZag Cemetery."

"*You* didn't. The news story about the anniversary and the coincidence of the name, maybe." I tapped my pen against the stack of as-yet unread articles Urban gave me. "And it doesn't have to be that she was murdered there. She could have been dumped."

"True. That would match what they believed about ZigZag Jane, too."

I looked down to see ink pinpricks on the top article because I'd tapped the tip end against it.

And then a word near my ink-pricks caught my attention.

A word.

A sentence.

A fact.

"Clara. Look at this." I stabbed my finger to what I'd seen in the now marked-up article.

Clara read, then looked at me with brightened eyes. "That's interesting."

"Especially since Urban Parhem didn't mention it."

"You think—?"

"I don't think anything. Except that we're going to ask him. Right now."

CHAPTER TWENTY-ONE

"YOU DIDN'T TELL us everything you know about ZigZag Jane and the investigation."

Urban looked around from his desk at the historical society, mildly surprised. "My knowledge is limited. Doug Vonner's the living expert on the subject."

"You know all the material you gave me. This article—" I waved it at him. "—says they found a ticket stub to a theater in Newport in the pocket of her dress. But you said before that she wasn't from around here."

He snorted a rendition of *Is that all?* "In that day, Newport wasn't *around here*. It might as well have been New York City or Paris."

"I know transportation wasn't as fast back then—"

"It was more than that. Newport was a different world. You know it was Sin City before Las Vegas was thought of."

It sounded like a quote. "Newport? Sin City?" I repeated. "The Newport right across the river from Cincinnati?"

"That's the one. From the time the Army put a fort there in the 1790s to guard Cincinnati, the Newport area drew a lot of—shall we call them services—for the soldiers. Especially women and alcohol."

"But I thought the Army built Fort Thomas as its facility."

"Not until after more than a century of being routinely flooded in the 'bottoms' of Newport. Finally got the idea in the late 1880s to move the fort up to what's now Fort Thomas, so they'd stop having the Ohio River as a frequent uninvited guest."

"Did the *services* move to the heights, too?"

"They pretty much stayed put in Newport. More elbow room and less oversight. Really took off as a center for criminal activity when Prohibition came into force, a little over a hundred years ago."

He didn't emphasize the timeline. He didn't need to. Clara and I both got the connection to when ZigZag Jane was found.

"Crime was Newport's growth industry. It was a center for bootlegging, with local speakeasies called tiger blinds, but also helping supply Chicago and points in between. As for the women…

"Have you heard of 'day houses' and 'night houses'?" He waited for us to shake our heads. "Had to do with traffic patterns. Brothels on the main one-way street leading toward Cincinnati were 'day houses,' open morning and afternoon for those heading into the city. 'Night houses' clustered around the main one-way street catering to customers traveling from Cincinnati to Kentucky.

"Later on, there were fancier establishments, including casinos, as the criminal element used gambling to replace income lost with the repeal of Prohibition. At the time ZigZag Jane was found, though, the general feeling was if she came from Newport, she most likely worked day houses or night houses."

"So they didn't investigate her murder?" Clara demanded indignantly.

He looked over the top of his glasses at her. "They must have done some or there wouldn't be any files. There's another story that says they checked with the movie theater, but no one there had anything to add. A dead end. You must not have read that one yet."

I ignored that mild gibe. "If there's a history of the theater—"

"It was torn down in the Thirties. People weren't preserving a lot of history at that point. They were more concerned about surviving the Depression."

"Was there anything in these records—" I patted the folder. "—or anywhere else about a child being found around the same time? Maybe they didn't connect it to Jane."

"Ah. You're thinking of that eleven-month-old in the census. You are rather jumping to a conclusion that his mother, Louis's second wife, might be our ZigZag Jane."

"Not a conclusion, but something to explore."

He looked thoughtful a moment, then a glitter entered his eyes. "Not an area I have examined extensively, but I do have an idea to pursue…"

We left him with a heartfelt request to pursue his idea.

Outside, I said to Clara, "We need to ask Doug if his grandfather could have found the child. Maybe it was hushed up?"

"I suppose we do, but…"

Not fun. I already knew that. I said, "But first we go to the dog park before Donna leaves, to talk to her about Henderson and Krystal Nickell."

ONE DOES NOT go to the Torrid Avenue Dog Park in Haines Tavern, Kentucky, without a dog.

At least one does not do so if one does not want to get side-eyed by every human and dog in attendance … and a lot worse when one gets home and one's dog sniffs out the evidence of what one has done.

Despite our tight timeline, Clara and I did not take that risk. We picked up our dogs. We also picked up Teague's dog.

Their bliss—already intensified by being together—became specific when we pulled in to the parking lot.

"Donna's," Clara said over the din with a nod toward a mud-splattered vehicle. "She's still here."

After that, all conversation was devoted to sorting the three dogs and proceeding to the entry gate.

That gate opened to a smallish area with four more gates off it— two to large dog enclosures, two to small-dog enclosures. With a collie (Gracie), Great Pyrenes mix (LuLu), and lab mix (Murphy), we naturally headed for the large dog enclosure—and Donna.

I had no idea how much her gracefully aging golden retriever, Hattie, knew of the inner workings of North Bend County, but Donna knew a lot.

"What do you want from me this time?" she demanded immediately.

Equally blunt, I said, "Henderson and Krystal Nickell."

That raised her eyebrows. "That young woman's suicide at ZigZag Cemetery? The one from his office." Her brows crashed down into a frown. "Or was it suicide? No—Don't tell me. You don't know yet or you wouldn't be asking me questions. But good dog almighty—" Her way of swearing. "—you're biting off a lot to chew this time, especially with Krystal. The only reason Henderson Nickell isn't drooling in a corner and sucking his thumb is Krystal.

"He's capable of charming people." Clearly not her. "He's also fully capable of putting his foot in his mouth, letting his—" She eyed us. "—male appendage lead him, and screwing up royally. I wouldn't be at all surprised if Krystal ran the business of the Drain Commissioner's office to the extent that long-time staff members don't run it."

"You know the staff? Do you know Noah Canepa?"

"By sight. Thinks he's smarter than anybody else, including the people who've been running the place for decades."

"What about Jayne Ulysee?"

"She didn't do any work. My friends tell me Noah Canepa does some when they can get him rolling. A great pair—him a know-it-all, her a do-nothing."

"How long had Jayne Ulysee worked in the office for Nickell?"

"Exactly? I couldn't tell you." But even as she said it, her head-shake slowed to a stop. "Although, let's see… Yes, I think it would have been at least two years ago because Hattie was just back on her feet after surgery on her paw."

Some people might think it's strange to use dog events to segment time, but Clara and I nodded our complete understanding.

"I'd heard about Jayne and Noah being brought in by Nickell from my friends. The next day, I met Jayne, because a puppy she was supposed to be caring for got away as they left Zepke's."

That was a pet store, not far off the town square.

"A number of us tried to direct the puppy off Beguiling Way, so he wouldn't be run over and here the young woman responsible for him kept blithering on about how she'd gotten this new job at the Drain Commission and her boss was dreamy and she'd never been happier.

"And then Krystal Nickell emerges from the yoga studio and Jayne turns white, red, then white again. Krystal doesn't even look at her. She grabs an empty box from the flower store near the yoga studio, drops it over the puppy, then walks away, leaving the rest of us to scoop him up. Because Jayne was completely useless."

She shook her head.

"Good luck with that one—Krystal, I mean. She's a force all her own. Don't show any fear. And don't try to make an appointment—it would give her a chance to say no. You'll have a better chance just showing up. C'mon, Hattie. It's past our time to leave. Don't want to wear you out."

The dog plodded after her, passing close enough that Clara and I could each put down a hand to stroke her back as she went past. Old dogs have their tricks.

Clara looked over at me. "Krystal can't be that bad if she saved a dog from being run over on a busy street."

I was almost sidetracked by her describing Beguiling Way as a busy street. But I'd realized not long after arriving here that life in Manhattan had not prepared me for what North Bend County locals considered traffic.

"Oh, yes, she *can* be that bad, considering Donna—Donna, who's afraid of no one—said to show no fear and wished us good luck with her."

WE DIDN'T RUSH the dogs, possibly to put off taking on Krystal Nickell.

As we led them from the gate toward the SUV, a sheriff's department vehicle entered the parking lot, pulling up uncomfortably close.

The driver's door opened and Deputy Eckles emerged.

He was solidly built, determined to do a good job, not overly blessed with insight, and devoid of humor.

He also didn't like dogs and had not covered himself in glory during our first encounter, which involved a death here at the dog park.

Staying behind the open vehicle door, as if for a shootout but really to avoid dog cooties, he said in a loud voice, "You two have gone too far this time. You can't go around poking into an active investigation and asking people questions."

"We can, actually. They don't have to answer, but—"

He wasn't listening. "It's against regulations. You *and* O'Donnell. He can't act like regulations don't apply to him and tell civilians that someone was back in town when that woman killed herself just because he's sleeping with them. That's—"

I stepped toward him. He stepped back.

"First, he wouldn't. Second, he didn't. *We* found out Willie Foglestedt was at Jayne Ulysee's Halloween party ourselves and informed the North Bend County Sheriff's Department of that fact. Ask Deputy Hensen. Third, don't throw around pronouns carelessly. Teague O'Donnell is not sleeping with *them*—plural—he's sleeping with *me*. Singular. And fourth—fourth, you owe him a groveling, on-your-knees apology, you ... you ... *Deputy*."

I turned on my heel. As I did, Gracie's leash went taut. I glanced back to see her glaring at Deputy Eckles. For a slice of a second, I thought she might—But no, of course she didn't.

She did, however, give him a single, sharp bark usually reserved for reprimanding a bumptious dog who'd gone way over the line. Then she turned to follow me, bouncing on her toes, her head and tail held high.

That'd show him.

Clara and Lulu caught up with us in a couple strides, to the sound of the official vehicle's door being slammed.

"You were magnificent. Both of you! I can't wait to tell—"

"You do not tell Teague about this. Not ever. I probably shredded his relationship with a colleague."

"Bah. Who'd want a good relationship with Eckles?"

"Teague's there as a part-timer, under unusual circumstances. He's going to have enough to fight against without…"

Me.

Who had *not* committed fraud—according to her great aunt—but still had big secrets and who now had torn into Teague's coworker.

Clara patted my shoulder, almost as if she knew my regret, worry, and guilt—even though she also had not received the truth, the whole truth, and nothing but the truth from me.

"C'mon, Killer. Let's go get you and Gracie your respective treats of choice—LuLu, Murphy, and me, too, while we're at it. Teague will be fine."

CHAPTER TWENTY-TWO

KRYSTAL NICKELL WAS the tall, angular woman who'd been at her husband's news conference. She had what I'd call a blade of a nose, except it was knobby, rather than straight.

She walked with her shoulders and head back, peering down that nose at the rest of humanity.

Right now, Clara and I represented that looked-down-upon population.

How much worse would it have been if we hadn't taken time to shower and change after the dog park.

Her house was imposing, with mixes of stone, brick, and siding that felt jumbled to me. It was located in an area of equally massive houses called Manor Cove that backed up to Clara's neighborhood, divided by a strip of woods.

"Yes?"

The syllable had a lot of subtext. Like *what are you doing here, who the heck do you think you are to ask for me,* and *I could think of a hundred better things to do with my time than talk to you two.*

"Hello, Mrs. Nickell," Clara said brightly. "I'm Clara Woodrow and this is Sheila Mackey. We were hoping to talk to you to—"

"I know who you are." That was not said the way most people would say it, as a response to Clara's introduction. It was more an auditory nod to her own thoughts ... which left it unclear if she'd heard anything Clara said.

That uncertainty stymied Clara into a drawn-out, "Um."

I edged forward, Clara followed, and Krystal Nickell allowed us into the entryway. Marble floor, clustered columns, and a large stone and gilt table that brought to mind the word baroque were meant to impress. And they did. They also didn't make me want to see any more of the house.

If design was supposed to reflect the owner, this succeeded.

"I'm right." Krystal's short, emphatic nod accompanied that statement. I had the feeling she said it a lot. To herself and everyone else. "You were on TV. Talking about that woman who died a hundred years ago. Like it makes any difference who she was. She was nobody then or someone would have been looking for her and she's less than nobody now." She huffed air out through her nose. Possibly her version of a chuckle. "She's dust."

"So's everybody after a hundred years."

At that retort, she turned her looking-down gaze full on me. "Some people leave a mark."

"Long-time residents remember ZigZag Jane and now everyone who watched that TV news segment knows." Maybe *nah, nyah-nah, nyah-nah-na* intonation leaked into my response.

"Doesn't mean they care. Even the few who have as good a memory as I do. Because I sure don't care. If you're here to try to get me to give money for whatever it is you're trying to do about her, the answer's no."

"We're not asking for money, Mrs. Nickell," Clara started again.

Clara's sweetness works wonders with many people. This woman wasn't one of them. "We're here to ask you about Jayne Ulysee, who worked in the Drain Commission office, with your husband."

"For my husband," she corrected instantly.

She intended to leave it there. Less from design than surprise, I said, "That's it? A young woman from your husband's office commits suicide—" I paused, then deliberately added, "—appears to commit suicide—and that's all you have to say?" Before she could say yes, I hurried on. "Did you know her? Were you aware if she was troubled?"

She didn't take that invitation to say heck, yes, Jayne was troubled and that's why she killed herself. Instead, she huffed through her nose, a sound as sharp as that facial feature.

"How did she do at the office? Was she a good worker?" Clara asked.

"No."

"So, you were aware of her standing at your husband's office, but—"

"Her *standing*?" she mimicked with apparently dark humor. "Oh, yes. Though standing wasn't her usual position. I told her at the start it wasn't a good fit for her. Told Henderson, too. They didn't listen."

I reeled from the implication—from tone and manner layered atop the words—that this woman was telling us she'd advised her husband and his would-be mistress not to get involved because they weren't a good fit.

Consider my mind boggled.

"You told… You said they shouldn't get together?" Clara stumbled, but she got words out, which was more than I could at the moment.

"Get together?" She clicked her tongue. "For the office. A poor fit for the *office*, where she sat around on her brains." She bit it off, but we could all hear the mental *stupid* at the end of that, addressed to Clara, but surely covering me, too.

Before I could adjust—she hadn't meant the relationship between her husband and Jayne—she threw another curve ball by adding, "Why would I get involved in the other aspect?"

It felt like that curve ball hit me in the head. "Because he's your *husband*," I blurted out.

"Yeah, and I'm his wife."

Was she saying what I thought she was saying? That she fooled around, too, and her husband knew it and didn't care?

Clara turned to me and I saw she was asking the same questions, but there was no time to consider, because Krystal was talking again. "There's business and there's sex. Both are fun but only one matters. And that's the one to keep inside your marriage."

I started, "You didn't feel Jayne was a good fit for your husband's business—"

"Our business."

"—office staff at the Drain Commission." I didn't know how to address her taking partial possession of her husband's elected position.

"She was a terrible fit. Not all her fault. He's a filthy boss."

Her flat delivery indicated she didn't recognize the potential double *entendre* in that description of her husband. Add lack of self-awareness to her personality.

Skirting issues of his filthiness and her personality, Clara managed, "In what way was she not a good fit for the staff? Did she think she knew everything?"

"That would be annoying." The woman said that without the least bit of irony. Oh, yeah, self-awareness did not mix into her makeup. "She didn't do that. Then again, she didn't do much of anything. At least not for the Drain Commission."

Again, the implication *seemed* clear, but with this woman I really couldn't be sure.

"How did her, uh, employment come to happen when you'd expressed, uh, reservations?"

"How do you think? They didn't listen. If people listened to me, they'd be a lot better off."

"It can be difficult to change people—"

She cut off Clara's gentle introduction. "Too many people whine about how you can't change others. They're too lazy to try."

Honestly curious, I asked, "Have you had success changing people?"

"Not as many as should have changed. And then the problem is staying away from them so you don't whack them upside the head to drive home sense."

If Henderson Nickell weren't such a jerk, I might have felt a flicker of empathy for him. Instead, it felt like the universe had gotten this one right.

Kit had been known to say that one nasty person could spoil a couple. With these two it was not only an even match, but being married to each other meant they didn't spoil any other couples.

Asking her about Jayne and Henderson felt like trying to swim in mud. I made a sharp turn and hoped it would take us to clear water. "Were you with Henderson on Halloween night?"

"I'm not with him many nights."

After all the full-frontal remarks, that one she sidestepped?

"That night?" I pursued.

"As a matter of fact, we were at a party. That's not to say we were in each other's pockets the entire time. We double our reach by circulating separately. Make more connections."

I tried to imagine how effective she would be in gaining political allies with her approach to interpersonal relationships.

As far as I could tell, she either didn't read a room well—and the people in it, such as Clara and me—or she didn't care. Or both.

Unless … she'd made the instant decision that Clara and I weren't worth any effort, while she was an ultra-smooth schmoozing machine with useful connections.

Hard to imagine, though.

"I don't have any more time for this." She hadn't closed the door. Now she opened it wider, directing us to leave.

"The party you were at Tuesday night—"

"Adrian Jemson's house."

The door snapped closed behind us.

Clara and I looked at each other. We'd wrestled an alligator and survived, even if we did forfeit some skin.

CHAPTER TWENTY-THREE

FROWNING, ADRIAN JEMSON answered the front door of a house with jutting angles and aggressive glass expanses on the edge of the same neighborhood as the Nickells'.

Like the Nickells' house, the Jemsons' made up in size what it missed in taste. It was like the builder said, what style do you want? And the owners said, make it bigger.

After looking up Adrian Jemson and getting a campaign ad-ish headshot and list of accomplishments along with his address, which was also in Manor Cove, we'd come straight here in case Krystal called him to say … What? Be discreet? After her performance?

Clara introduced us.

Adrian Jemson clearly didn't recognize our names. But he didn't turn us away, either. He looked us over.

A woman started to come down the hall toward the door.

He waved her away. "Never mind, Priscilla. I've got it."

"We're trying to straighten out some questions about tragedies from right here in North Bend County," Clara started. She wove together selected excerpts of ZigZag Jane's story and Jayne Ulysee's story so quickly and with so many oblique references that I couldn't follow it.

He couldn't either, and he didn't care, what with trying to peer down Clara's top for a personal viewing of her chest.

She foiled that with adroit shifts, then finished with, "…so you'll understand why we need to ask you—even though we know you're such a busy and important man—if Henderson Nickell was at the fabulous party you threw on Halloween night."

He chuckled and I thought Henderson might have learned the art of condescending chuckles from this man. Unless it was a natural talent.

"I suppose you want to check his alibi, like those plodders from the sheriff's department. Preposterous. But fine. Yes, yes, he was here. The entire time. That was the whole purpose of the party. Get Henderson to meet some important people who were in the area. And for them to watch him in action. He's good with people."

I thought of Henderson Nickell's smiles and suppressed a shudder.

"Why, I remember when he was starting—I was his mentor from the start—and he had issues with personnel in the office. People who'd been around forever with set ways of doing things. He said he couldn't communicate with them, couldn't get them to buy into his vision. I told him what he needed to do was schmooze with them."

Schmooze.

"Now, that boy could teach an old dog like me a trick or two on schmoozing. You should have seen him, talking to those party leaders. Even tromped into the muddy garden to pick a leaf for one of the ladies who wanted to know if it was a something-or-other or a something else. Hell if I know. Especially with her talking Greek all over us."

"Latin," Clara said. "Plants are often referred to by their Latin names."

"It's all Greek to me." He laughed heartily at his own repetition of a joke that must have been old when that civilization was young. "All I know is my wife had the landscaper put in a bunch of plants that cost a fortune when we built this place and we're still paying a fortune. Doesn't seem like any survive. And that's despite spending enough on watering them to float a couple yachts."

I could hear Kit's voice in my head, gleefully speculating that the wife was having an affair with the landscaper. I tuned out that voice to tune back in to Jemson.

"That's how Henderson's shoes got muddy during that leaf-picking episode. All the watering turns it into a bog back there. Told Henderson when I took him into the mudroom to scrape off his shoes that I admire a man who never thought he'd gone too far with a gesture. He almost had to use a pair of my son's shoes that are littered all over the mudroom. Henderson was grumbling and swearing then, but back to all smiles after he cleaned up enough to present the leaf to that gal like some knight from the old days. Didn't hurt that I went and got him a Scotch that could also float a yacht while he was cleaning his shoes."

He chuckled more at his own humor.

"So, yeah, Henderson Nickell was at the party I gave Halloween night and he made the most of his time with movers and shakers, like he always does. That young man's going someplace, let me tell you. And there's something else I'll give you for free. Some say Krystal's the power behind the throne. She certainly has a lot on the ball, but people underestimate Henderson. Oh, not at the beginning. When they first meet him, they overestimate him. Most with experience or insight or both get past that, only they can swing too far, get caught in underestimating him. Only a few see that's also a mistake."

He clearly counted himself among the perspicacious few.

"Just look how calm he was when the rumor started circulating at the party."

"No one really believed the rumor, though, did they?" Clara asked, drawing him out at the same time masking that we knew zip about a rumor.

Brilliant. I limited my mental applause, though, because Jemson was answering.

"Some probably did, with the detail about her working in Henderson's office, because people knew that was true. And somebody did confirm the sheriff's department was called to that house, plus talk of underage drinking, drugs and all—probably why she killed herself, getting caught in a mess like that, even if the deputies didn't arrest her on the spot. The stuff about her running parties for him? Some people jump on believing the worst. But it was clear he wasn't involved in *that* party, since he was here, and it was *that* party where she went way over the line. Nothing to do with him at all.

"How did the rumor start?" I asked.

"Messages. Most of us got them. Her name, the address of where the party was, the sheriff's department called, accusations of drugs, the whole nine yards. Of course I showed it to Henderson right away so he knew what he was fighting. He said straight out that he'd had nothing to do with that party. That young woman from his office did it all on her own. Nobody could deny he handled it cool as a cucumber. Never turned a hair. Said the situation was deplorable and he'd let her go the next day at the office. Guess someone else saw to it that he didn't need to do that."

"Thank you, Adrian," Clara said with her eyes-so-wide expression. "We appreciate your sharing that so much. There are a few other things…"

But she'd lost him.

A tall, sullen-looking boy in his mid-teens walked across the hall-way behind him, yanking Adrian Jemson's attention to what was in the house, instead of Clara on his front step. At that moment, we also heard a woman's voice inside, calling to Jemson.

He jerked slightly.

"Have to go now. We could get a drink—?"

The female voice called again. He closed the door on us.

CLARA SAID SHE'D meet me at Doug Vonner's house later for our appointment for more file-diving.

She had another errand to run. She'd collected leftover Halloween candy from her neighbors and me for an after-school program.

I passed on her offer to accompany her to drop it off. Getting the candy out of my house was hard enough. No sense testing my willpower.

My willpower flunked as I considered reading the rest of the articles from Urban or writing.

I did neither.

I called Kit.

She had less of a reaction to the death of Jayne Ulysee than I'd expected, though she muttered *good*, when I explained why Clara and I doubted it was suicide.

But I could hear her typing as I finished, so how interested was she?

"Are you taking notes, Kit? You can't use this in a book. It—"

"Not taking notes. Refreshing my memory. Here it is. Two women, from the same place in England, each 20 years old, go to dances the same date—May 27—and are found murdered in the same spot. The suspect in each case is a young man each young woman danced with that last night by the last name of Thornton."

"Serial killer?"

"Not without supernatural powers. The murders in Erdington were more than a century and a half apart—Mary Ashford in 1817 and Barbara Forrest in 1974. Found in the same area, though it wasn't a cemetery."

"That's ... that's spooky. But at least the victims didn't have the same name and weren't found in the same cemetery."

"There's more. Both Thorntons were tried and acquitted for lack of evidence. The 1974 Thornton is unlikely to be a descendant of the 1817 Thornton, though, because the first one left for America. Any of your Kielwegens marry a Thornton?"

"I haven't noticed any, but I wasn't looking."

Which led to explaining Berrie's connection. I also told her about the Newport theater ticket found in ZigZag Jane's pocket.

She aligned with Urban's skepticism. "Or she was passing through and went to a movie."

"You're full of good cheer. Next, remind me she might not have any family now, which would make the DNA quest hopeless, even if she is exhumed and we can get her DNA."

"They can track quite distant relations."

Happy to change the subject, I said, "Speaking of relations, we met

Jayne Ulysee's boss's wife." I described the encounter. "If I say she swung her hips, that could be misleading, making you think slinky or sexy. It wasn't that. It was a loose-legged gait that made me think of a gunslinger from TV and movies."

Kit snorted. "TV and movies have no idea how real gunfighters moved."

"It's her eyes, always gauging her target," I said, still on gunslingers. "With her head back—"

"To look down her nose," Kit said immediately.

I uh-huhed and kept going, "—and her legs in front of her hips. All loose."

"*Arrogant.* That's what makes you think of gunslingers, Sheila."

"Yes. Arrogant and icy. It amazes me she wouldn't realize how she comes off to other people. She's otherwise clearly an intelligent woman."

"Don't assume she doesn't realize it. Some people do the calculus that being thought of as not likable is worth the benefits."

"What possible benefits are there to not being liked?"

"A lot. You don't have to worry about staying in anyone's good graces, so you don't have to think about how others will react to what you say or do. Only how it feels to you. It's quite efficient."

"You're not saying you're like that, because—"

"Only on deadline. But I admit I've recognized the potential benefits."

"Kit," I expostulated.

"All right, all right. I've also realized the drawbacks. Which is why I don't do it unless driven into a corner by deadline." She paused a moment, then added, "Or insufferable people."

"Speaking of insufferable, remember I said we talked to her ex-boyfriend yesterday? You have all those connections from the series you wrote with the trumpet-playing detective, and I hoped you could ask around, because the ex-boyfriend says he's a musician."

"You don't believe him," Kit said.

"I have no reason to not believe—"

"Yes, you do. Only you know what reason or reasons, but you have them. Otherwise, you would have said he's a musician, not that he *says* he's a musician."

In the face of Kit's flat certainty, I ran through my memories of our conversation with him.

"Yeah. I think you're right."

"No. *You're* right, Sheila. You picked up on something. I'll check around, but even if I don't get outside confirmation, listen to your gut." Without a pause, she pivoted topics. "Speaking of listening to your gut and the matter of Teague O'Donnell…"

I groaned. It didn't stop her.

She said exactly what I would have predicted, which was why I'd let more time than usual go by between calls until ZigZag Jane entered our lives.

"Sheila, you have to share some of yourself to really know someone."

I bit my tongue to keep from asking if that's what she was doing with the widower in the Outer Banks, because if so, why limit her time with him so strictly, not introduce him to her family, not get involved with his family. Then I exerted more teeth-to-tongue pressure as I recognized I mostly would have asked that to deflect from my situation.

"I don't want to put any of that burden on him—not that those years were a burden to me, Kit. I don't mean that. Not at all. But with his position, working as a detective again…"

She huffed out. "By protecting him, you're taking choice away from him, along with any chance the two of you could be something more. Maybe you tell him the truth and he ends it right then. Is that worse than not telling him, letting him wonder what's missing—if he's smart, which it sounds like he is—and the whole thing withering away?"

"I honestly don't know. I—Kit, I have to go. A call's coming in from Clara. I have to take this."

I didn't care if the call was about how many chocolate bars Clara gave out.

It wasn't.

"SHEILA, CHANGE OF plans. I need you to meet me at the café right away. Before we go talk to Doug again."

"Urgent need for dessert after inhaling chocolate fumes on the way to the after-school program?"

"I wouldn't mind some dessert after giving away all that chocolate. But you need to be there because we're going to meet with one of the people who works in the Drain Commission office. She knows Donna and she was here today, helping out, because her daughter runs the program. We got talking and…"

CHAPTER TWENTY-FOUR

YAKIRA LOOKED A lot like my mother's friends, with short brown hair, sensible glasses, and a warm smile.

"Were you at the party Halloween night that Henderson and his wife went to?" Clara asked her as soon as we settled at a table with pieces of pie—pumpkin for me, cherry for Clara, and key lime for Yakira.

"Me? At Adrian Jemson's? No chance."

"Adrian Jemson said Henderson had difficulties with personnel in the office at the start."

"More the other way around." That level of honesty surprised me, especially talking to a stranger.

"Four of us had been there since the beginning of time. Knew how things ran and kept it humming no matter what new nincompoop the electorate foisted on us. Drain Commission's not real high profile, but the commissioner gets to vote on things. Politicians like Jemson think it's a place to test their flunky candidates, make sure they're loyal and all." She huffed indignantly. "We've had some real doozies. But Henderson's a new level of idiocy."

"That sounds miserable," Clara said.

She met the sympathy with a matter-of-fact, "Working around them's part of the job." Then she asked abruptly, "You said a party at Adrian Jemson's right? That explains a lot."

"Oh?"

"Yeah. Another nincompoop. At least he's not running for offices anymore. Only reason he ever did was to be in a position to vote in measures that benefited him. Basic ethics would be a big improvement for that one. If someone cared to look, he must have broken laws, left, right, and center.

"Now he backs young idiots following in his footsteps like Henderson, making life a misery for those actually doing the work. I'd wager he's the one who put the bug in Henderson's ear to take us to dinner one by one. On our own time, of course. Except Jayne." She looked at us closely. "You know about that, I take it? She got special treatment. And wasn't Noah fit to be tied over that? Jayne didn't make my heart sing, but Noah ... Everything she did or got, large or small, it all drove him mad. Tried to keep him busy so he didn't have time to be petty, but it didn't always work, like when he'd put through calls from her ex-boyfriend."

"Willie Foglestedt?"

"That's the ex-boyfriend?" Yakira asked.

"Not ex according to him," Clara said, "but that is his name."

"Is that so? Because I heard her telling him she didn't care what he'd heard about how she was rolling in money, not only wasn't she giving him more, but she never wanted to see him again. Couldn't have been more ex than she sounded."

"When was that?"

"A few times, actually. Last time? Let me think ... A week ago today. He called just before she was getting ready to leave for the weekend—hours before the rest of us. Noah told her the call was for her and the way he said it caught my attention. I listened in right along with him. Might've been wrong, but I did. It went sour from the second she heard who was calling. Then she said what I told you, about not giving him money, never wanting to see him again. She even hinted about her and Henderson, but said he wasn't going to boss her around anymore. Glancing toward the rest of us now and then—as if we didn't all know from the start. Then she said she had important things to do next week—that was this past week—because she was working on a *project*—on her own and nobody could hold her back."

"Do you know what that was?"

"Those parties she and Henderson cooked up, I'd imagine." She rolled her eyes. "The whole office knew about those, too. Beforehand, when they were deciding which of Henderson's properties they'd use, and after, when the two of them totaled the take like a couple of Scrooges."

"Do you think Krystal knew what they were doing?"

"Hah. She probably planned it. Can't imagine Henderson or Jayne initiating that sort of thinking. Henderson sure wasn't the brains behind the county allowing short term rentals. That was Krystal all the way."

"Did you get the impression the thing between Henderson and Jayne was over?"

"On the outs, for sure. Whether that could change again?" Yakira lifted one shoulder. "Can't say I was interested enough to pay close attention to them. Anyway, back to Henderson and his great campaign to become boss of the year by taking us to dinner. Of course, he picked the place—took a vegetarian to a ribs joint, the idiot. And no matter the restaurant he spent most of the time chatting up the waitstaff. Needed a bib the way he drooled over one young thing where we went.

"What on earth he thought he'd accomplish, I couldn't imagine, but if Jemson gave him advice on managing people, that's the answer."

"DO YOU THINK Noah sent the messages about Jayne's party to the people at Jemson's party?" Clara asked on our way to Doug Vonner's house.

"Oh, yeah."

She sighed. "Now if Nickell were the victim…"

"Oh, yeah. Long line of suspects. Plus, more on Noah's plate, I'd say. Anticipating the conversation between Jayne and Willie because he let Willie know Jayne had money? Then there's Jemson giving Henderson schmoozing advice—"

"I could feel executive coaches all over the world shuddering at Jemson's suggestion."

"And at Nickell's implementation. That episode also suggests he's suggestible."

She side-eyed me. "You're thinking Krystal got fed up and was too smart to do the deed herself, so she manipulated Henderson into killing Jayne?"

"I wasn't thinking anything that explicit, but now that you say it, it's an interesting idea."

✧　✧　✧　✧

CLARA DROVE A different way to Vonner's house and a lightbulb went on.

"That's the entry to where the Nickells and Jemsons live?" I asked as we passed a stone and lumber edifice holding a large sign announcing Manor Cove.

"The main entry. We went in from the other side before." She was already turning onto Doug's street.

"The party house from Halloween night is through those woods? Someone could get from Manor Cove or this neighborhood to the party house by cutting through the woods?"

She frowned, but said, "A jogging path that goes from Manor Cove, touches this neighborhood, cuts through the woods, then comes out at the clubhouse for my neighborhood. It goes right behind the house where the party was. But you can't think—"

"Just gathering information. That's all.

"As a native, would Willie know about it?"

"Probably. Why—?"

I exited the vehicle before she could ask more.

"You did come," Doug Vonner said when he answered his front door.

Clara shot me a look, underscoring that I'd raised the possibility of not keeping this appointment. "Of course we did," she said to him.

"News has a way of wiping out interest in ZigZag Jane." He stated the fact, not feeling sorry for himself.

"We're still on it," Clara said.

"In fact, we have a question, Doug," I said. "Did your grandfather ever mention anything about a child in association with ZigZag Jane?"

"A child? I don't understand."

Was that the truth?

"A child went missing around the same time your grandfather found Jane. A boy, a little over two years old. Did your grandfather ever say anything or did you see anything in the files or..." He was shaking his head. I wasn't ready to let it go. "Or accounts of a child found. Anywhere in the area."

"I don't remember Grandfather ever ... But it's not just that. I've been rereading things as I've made you copies and haven't seen anything about a boy. What does this have to do with ZigZag Jane?"

Ignoring looks from Clara screaming *Tell him! Tell him!* I made vague references to wide-flung research, possibly leaving the impression Urban did the research and we didn't know details.

I finished by suggesting we dive into those files. "And the list of donors, can you get me a copy of that?"

"Sure. A paper copy he typed later or a photo of the original?"

"A photo of the original would be great." That jogged a memory. "As long as you're at it, a copy of the photo that was with it, too? The people leaning against a car."

"Oh, yeah, that one." He went to a file and pulled one out.

"This isn't the same—No, wait. It is the same scene but the other one was bigger. An enlargement of this one?" If so, it had been reprinted around the time the original was taken, based on the aged and yellowed paper.

"Yeah. I remember a bigger version. I'll look for that."

The three of us settled to work through more of Douglas Vonner's files.

He had lived these files and Doug Vonner had grown up on them. Wouldn't they already have found what there was to find?

I reminded myself this reflected eighty years of a man's life. That demanded respect and attention. Even if it didn't advance us.

Now and then conversation arose.

Looking at a newspaper clip with a photo of a thirty-something Douglas Vonner, Clara asked about Doug's family.

"My grandmother died when I was young, as I said. A lot of cancer on that side of the family. My dad died of it when I was fifteen. I was already close with Grandfather, but after that..." He shrugged. "Father figure, I guess."

"Following your father's interest in it, too?" Fern said the Vonner monomania skipped that generation, but I was curious about Doug's take.

"I guess he was interested when he was young, but as far as I knew first-hand, he thought the whole thing was stupid—this quest of his father's. He resented it. I heard him telling Mom once that even when he worked with Grandfather he was sure he kept secrets from him, like his dad didn't want to share all of ZigZag Jane with him.

"But Mom encouraged me to spend time with Grandfather after Dad's death. She had to work to support us and with all the changes ... Hard not to take advantage of the free after-school program her father-in-law provided, even if it did end up at one cemetery a lot.

"I asked her—not many years ago—what she thought Dad would think of me carrying on what Grandfather started. She said she thought he'd understand now. I don't know if that's true, but I sure appreciated her saying it."

"She's a great lady," Clara said.

Was Clara's regard for Doug Vonner's mother a thread Urban tugged to get us involved in this?

"She is. She's supported all my efforts." His face darkened. "Although she's upset about the young woman found at ZigZag Cemetery."

I was conscious of a prickle up the back of my neck. Not necessarily at what he said, but at the surfacing of a thought.

"Did Jayne Ulysee ever meet her, Doug?"

Clara shot me a look at the question. I kept my focus on him.

"Not that I know of."

"But you went to Henderson Nickell's office where she worked and confronted Nickell at the cemetery."

"I told him he'd never get ZigZag Cemetery closed, that's all. She wasn't there, just some young guy. Do you think it's connected somehow? Why she killed herself there?"

"*If* she killed herself," Clara said.

He blinked hard. "What?"

"There's good reason to think it was murder, not suicide." Leaving no time for his gasp to fade out, she added, "Sheila's so smart. She recognized immediately that finding the second Jayne's body at ZigZag Cemetery means it couldn't be a stranger-on-stranger killing. The killer had to know—"

"Probably knew," I inserted.

"—Jayne Ulysee or at least her name. That was the reason to take the body there, since it's not on the way to anything."

"Not anymore," Doug said. "But it used to be on the way to a ferry. A long time ago. A lot of people figured that's where Jane— ZigZag Jane—was heading when she was killed."

"I remember Gran telling me about the river changing its course bit by bit and then a big storm wiping out the ferry landing."

They talked more about changes brought on by the power and persistence of the Ohio River, I took a break from file-diving to check messages.

One from Teague said he was going to be tied up tonight and all day Saturday, but hoped to have a few hours free for a planned brunch Sunday at my house with Clara and Ned.

Next was a message from Urban, urging us to come to the historical society office at our earliest convenience.

CHAPTER TWENTY-FIVE

THINGS WERE HOPPING at North Bend County's former courthouses, leaving no parking near the Old Old Courthouse.

Clara dropped me off in case Urban had something urgent, while she searched for a spot. I suspected she hoped to trim exposure to his tales.

If so, I foiled her by telling him to wait until she joined us.

In the meantime, I said, "Clara told me tribal grounds are all over the county and no one knows their locations."

"True. In addition, some early settlements disappeared. After a couple generations, no one remembered where their old plots were." As if I were an interesting specimen, he asked, "I never took you for the superstitious sort, Sheila. Would it bother you to know your house was built on a burial ground?"

"Yes." Suspicion crashed over me. "Was it?"

"It's the cycle of life. Someone's great-great-great-great uncle might be the reason your roses bloom well."

"I will never look at roses the same way."

Unperturbed, he said, "Someday that will be you—and me—fertilizing the roses."

"My house—?"

"I know of no lost cemeteries or native burial grounds under your house. On the other hand, should a dog dig up a bone at the dog park, I wouldn't assume it was recent.

"Ah, here's Clara. Now we can attend to why I asked you to come.

Birth records in Kentucky were kept for a time in the 1850s, but stopped in the early 1860s."

Not helpful for us.

With no sign he sensed impatience from his audience, Urban continued, "Formal keeping of birth records resumed in 1920."

The youngest son, Ray, was listed as eleven months old in 1920. My hopes deflated as I remembered the July 1920 date at the top of that census sheet. "According to the census sheet, Ray would have been born in August 1919."

"Yes. However, that is not definitive. Sometimes the sheets are wrong. Sometimes the enumerator got the wrong age. Sometimes records were kept before they were mandated."

Each *sometimes* pumped air into my hopes.

"I checked for such records," he said. "I found nothing."

Hopes flattened in a *whoosh*.

"However, churches also kept records."

"But those records…" I prompted, expecting to hear they stopped the day before we needed them, counted everyone except people named Ray, or were lost in an unprecedented lava flow in Northern Kentucky.

This research was not for sissies, and I was getting pessimistic.

"Are at the Diocese of Covington. One must go there to access them," Urban said.

I raised one eyebrow. Surely, he'd jump at doing in-person research.

He shook his head.

Before I could begin to contemplate spending hours of my inexpert time going over the records, he added, "However, I have a colleague with access to the records who owes me a favor."

If he used the favor this colleague owed him, I'd owe him a favor.

This was no time for haggling.

"Done," I said.

"Very well." He added a solemn nod. "I will inform you when there are results. In the interim, let me say that you two young ladies have me digging into a most unpleasant character who is not even a resident of our county."

Earnestly, Clara said. "But it might help discover the story behind a piece of county history—ZigZag Jane."

"You do not need to persuade me again. But allow me the pleasure of complaining."

"Sorry." Clara fought a grin. "Go ahead, complain."

"You've taken the bloom off the complaint now. It's like wheedling a compliment from someone. It never satisfies." His gravity disappeared as he added, "Although I *have* found intriguing tidbits. First, I spoke with a colleague with a special interest in the lawless history of Newport. He was quite familiar with Louis Kiel—also known as Louis the K—and pointed me toward useful sources."

"Louis the K?"

"The K did not stand for Kindness," he said dryly. "He was known as Louis the Killer, though presumably not to his face."

I whistled. "Uncle Louis, Uncle Louis."

Did that contribute to no one acknowledging ZigZag Jane? If she was connected to Louis Kiel—Louis the Killer—could they have been too concerned about surviving to identify her? Could they have known about connections between ZigZag John and ZigZag Jane—contributing to her being called that—but kept quiet.

"With your finding young J. in his household in 1910, one has to wonder what he was exposed to even before going to war. Yes, I confirmed John Kielwegen Junior served in World War I, with an honorable discharge. He participated in extremely difficult fighting.

"As for the rest—" He placed an open hand on the folder, which he slid toward me. "—this is also intriguing. Read the top sheet aloud for Clara."

It was a copy of a newspaper called *The Steamer*, dated January 17, 1922, centered on a column under the byline *A.N. Observer*. As I started to read about a wedding, I noted it used no names. Only initials, each followed by a dash, so if I'd been a wedding guest, I'd have been included as S—M—Which meant a reader had to already have a notion who was being talked about to make sense of this.

From Clara's expression, she shared my confusion.

"Third item," Urban said.

I gladly left the wedding mid-description, skipped to what I saw was the shortest item, and obeyed.

"It is whispered into A.N. Observer's ear that Mr. L—K—will soon be wifeless again. As with his previous wife, the current Mrs. K— is reported to have changed her address from our environs to Reno, Nevada, some months ago.

"As with the previous wife of Mr. L—K—, it is also reported that she intends to remain in that vicinity after the legalities are complete, severing ties to this community."

I looked at him. "Did you sense a sinister vibe or is it only me from hanging out in cemeteries?"

"I often frequent cemeteries," he said simply. "But, yes, there is an undertone that could be called sinister. Certainly the writer comes across as skeptical of the information whispered into his ear. I wonder how much of a risk he—or she—took by writing it. I would imagine contemporary readers would have picked up on that as well as more."

"Like the first Mrs. Kiel didn't come back from Reno because she couldn't?" Clara asked. "Because that was the agreement? Because that was his order? Or ... something more permanent."

"That is an area my colleague interested in Newport is exploring. He also pointed me to accounts when Louis Kiel was convicted—"

"For murder?" I interrupted eagerly.

"—for tax evasion, in the mold of Al Capone. Louis Kiel was sent to prison and died there in what might have been the precursor to curbing Newport's lawlessness. Although, there is a tidbit you both might appreciate. Here. Read this."

The news article seemed quite straightforward, though in a some-what more florid style than we were accustomed to. Kiel was found guilty. He was sentenced immediately—no delays for mitigating or aggravating factors. The defense attorney said it was a travesty, *blah, blah, blah.* The prosecutor said it was a fine day for justice, but instead of adding *blah, blah, blah* from the lawyer phrase book, the prosecutor was quoted as saying:

As a fisherman, I'm delighted that one of the benefits of Louis Kiel being off the streets, besides making those streets safer, is that the Ohio River will not be nearly so clogged up with dead bodies of those associated with him.

Clara whistled softly.

"He didn't convict Louis of murder, but he got his digs in." But I was thinking how much better it would have been if the prosecutor said Louis Kiel was known for dumping bodies in cemeteries. "This— all of it—is terrific work, Urban. I can't tell you how much we appreciate it. We'd never have found it in a million years."

"There. Was that so hard? I barely had to wheedle that compliment out of you."

I grinned at him.

Then I stopped grinning. "But does this mean the church records won't help? Considering his criminal activities, would Louis the K have his children baptized?"

"My source on the early days of the criminal network in Newport said they were active in churches of varying denominations. Perhaps to present a front of rectitude or perhaps hedging their eternal bets. It is worth investigating."

The image of that photo of the three men and a woman by a car in front of a theater marque popped into my head. Could that be Louis the K? Was that too much of a stretch to hope for?

"Urban, that movie theater that was torn down in the 1930s, can you check if it opened or reopened around 1920?"

"I can try," he said cautiously. "Why?"

Instead of answering, I added another question. "Did Kentucky have license plates on cars in the 1920s?"

"Yes. Started in 1910."

"You know that off the top of your head?"

"Yes."

I chuckled. "Of course you do. Can you look up a license plate number from the 1920s and find out who owned it?"

"Smart, Sheila," Clara said.

Urban wasn't as impressed. "It might take considerable checking to know if it can be done at all. And that will need to wait until Monday when state offices are open."

"But first thing Monday you will check, right?" Clara gazed at him.

Urban folded. "Yes."

I READ THE rest of the files in the original folder Urban gave me that night.

Nothing new.

SATURDAY

CHAPTER TWENTY-SIX

I EYED THE pickup two spots closer to the gate in the dog park lot than where Clara pulled in.

It was familiar.

"Just a minute," I told Clara. "I want to take a picture of Gracie. They're taking submissions for the annual collie rescue fundraiser calendar and she looks particularly good."

"She always looks good," Clara said loyally. "She should be on the cover."

I couldn't disagree.

Though I wasn't sure this shot would make the cut. I maneuvered her in between the two vehicles, stood on the running board and angled to catch as much of the pickup bed as I could, which meant only a slice of Gracie's butt, along with her inquisitive nose as she lifted it to see what the crazy human was doing, remained in the photos.

Maybe the Collie Rescue and Pickup Enthusiasts Calendar would consider it for its cover.

I clicked a couple more times for good measure.

"Get a good one?" Clara asked as we walked to the gate.

"I'll check when we get inside."

❖ ❖ ❖ ❖

THE RIOT OF noise that greeted us as Clara and I prepared to let

Gracie, LuLu, and Murphy into the large dog enclosure came from the small dog enclosure.

It originated with Marcus, a member of Berrie Vittlow's crowd of Boston Terriers. I don't know if he was the oldest. He definitely was the acknowledged leader.

Whither Marcus barked, the other BTs barked, as they all did at the moment.

Marcus didn't bark at our three dogs. He regarded them through the gate that separated him from the sort of foyer where we stood with supreme indifference, which they returned in full measure. Though I had the feeling Murphy would have clamped a palm over his ear if he'd been capable of such a thing.

Marcus barked at me.

With all the indignant, piercing, shriek of which he was capable. Which was plenty. His fellow Boston Terriers provided full-throated support.

"Control your dogs!" came from Berrie in the exact register used by Marcus and in complete defiance of logic, since all three dogs sat silently at the large-dog gate, waiting for Clara to get the sometimes recalcitrant mechanism to work.

She opened the gate, gave the release word, and our dogs shot inside.

"If you had any idea of training, your dogs wouldn't start a ruckus every time they came in this dog park," Berrie shouted over her dogs' noise with her still some distance away from the gate because her dogs kept shooting off in different directions in front of her.

The instigator's frenzy of sound reached a new height.

"Marcus, sit."

I did shout it. I had to in order to be heard over his racket. But it was a command, not a temper-lost scream.

He sat.

The dog and I stared at each other, apparently both of us taken aback.

"Good dog," I got out.

Berrie bustled up, with Boston Terriers preceding her like heralds, but—for once—with their trumpets silenced. "How dare you shout at my dog."

I opened my mouth to lambaste her … and laughed instead.

After a beat, Clara joined me. Then more laughter from the large dog enclosure. Followed by laughter from the small-dog enclosure.

Though that died an abrupt death when Berrie spun around toward the laughers.

Her other dogs milled around, but Marcus still sat.

"May I give him a treat?" I asked.

"No," Berrie snapped.

As if he understood, Marcus stood, gave Berrie a dirty look, and toddled off in the canine version of a penguin walk. Some of her dogs trailed him.

Berrie's mottled red face did not bode well for her blood pressure.

Clara—bless her—stepped into the breach.

"We're so glad to see you here today, Berrie. We hoped to talk to you about the death of that young woman who was found at Zig—at the old cemetery. Since you know so many people and always have your finger on the pulse of what's happening." Truly, Clara's acting skills are impressive. "Just let us get these guys in and unleashed."

Clara didn't even glance at the other woman, as if there were no question she would stick around. I did steal glances while we moved to a spot along the fence.

If Marcus had still been carrying on, this was when he would have quit. As if Berrie felt that wiped out the ignominy of her dog obeying me and her ill-tempered refusal to let me give him a treat, she joined us from her side of the fence.

Or maybe she didn't want us joining the other humans in the large-dog enclosure and risk stirring more laughter.

"I hadn't known Vittlow was your married name, Berrie," I said. Possibly not the wisest way to start this conversation, but I wanted this moment. "And you were born a Kielwegen."

"Yeah? What about it?" Her bravado didn't mask how much she

hated that I knew.

That was enough for me. I said mildly, "Interesting role the Kielwegens played in the county's past."

It lit her ever-short fuse.

"I know you two are poking around trying to find out about the ZigZag hermit."

Figured Berrie had it wrong. Neither of us wasted time denying it. Berrie wouldn't have heard.

"You better not make him out to be a monster. He wasn't. Or crazy. People around here treated him that way. It was like that guy in that book. Everybody was scared of him, but he was even more scared of them, only a few people said to leave him alone and not tease him, but not many listened. And in the movie he never says a word, but he's played by that guy who played that lawyer guy in the *Godfather* movies."

I doubt I could have untangled that without the head start of *Abandon All* being praised as this century's *To Kill a Mockingbird*.

Clara's expressions said she got it with the *Godfather* reference and worked backward from there.

Berrie meant Boo Radley, played by Robert Duvall in the movie *To Kill a Mockingbird*. He later played the lawyer/consiglieri in some of the *Godfather* movies.

"Interesting you brought up movies about the mafia," Clara said. "Louis Kiel—"

"Rumors. Nasty, nasty rumors. That was after so-called upstanding citizens killed John Kielwegen and pulled out every excuse in the book to justify what they did. People tormented and persecuted that poor guy. That's what my grandma told me and when I was old enough, I looked it up and she was right. And I don't care what the Vonners say then or now. John Kielwegen had nothing to do with ZigZag Jane ending up in the cemetery."

"I don't think they ever accused ZigZag John of—"

"Don't call him that. They killed him for no reason and—"

"Well, he *had* killed someone. Zigzags carved in the neck," I said.

Berrie's face turned purple.

"And I'll tell you another thing," she said in a classic change-the-subject-because-I-don't-like-this-one diversion. "You know why that cemetery's in such bad shape? Because Henderson Nickell votes against funds to maintain it every darn time. Gets his cronies to vote the same way, too, and that blocks it. He wants to close it to make money."

"How would he make money from it being closed?" I asked.

"Don't ask me," she snapped. "But he manages to make money on all sorts of things. Nothing would surprise me about him."

"He made money when the old schoolhouse was torn down a few years back," Clara said.

That stirred a memory. "You mentioned that on TV, Clara. What was that all about?"

"I don't know the ins and outs, but he owned property nearby and when they tore down the schoolhouse, that let a project go through that made his property more valuable."

"Exactly," Berrie said with as much triumph as if she did know the ins and outs. "If he hadn't fought against the funds to maintain the cemetery, he wouldn't have been on my radar. But now he is. Him and that wife of his. And you mark my words, he's up to no good. Not that he'll get what he wants. Because, like you said on TV, he has to get permission to close that cemetery for the descendants and I'm one and I won't give my permission, not ever."

With a would-be flounce of triumph—flounces are hard to carry off in dog park boots and an old field jacket—she pivoted away from us.

Clara rolled her eyes, then turned to watch the action in our big dog enclosure. I was about to follow suit when I noticed Marcus wandering along the fence line, coming toward me, but as if that were an unintended consequence of his heading somewhere vitally important.

"Marcus. Marcus, come," Berrie called from halfway across the small dog enclosure.

He gave no sign of hearing. Unless his making eye-contact with me was a rebellious sign of it. I swear a moment of communion connected us.

At that moment, a whirlpool of Boston Terriers whipped up in frantic noise on the far side of that enclosure.

The instant Berrie turned toward them, a treat dropped out of my pocket and through the mesh to Marcus' side of the fence.

Without ever looking at me—or Berrie—he marched to it, ate it, and walked on.

It was, after all, his due.

CLARA AND I headed to our favorite picnic table. A couple other dog park regulars were already there. We all sat on the table's top. Only newbies sat on the seats, which were favorite targets of leg-lifting male dogs.

Clara chatted with them, while I checked the photos on my phone. Eureka.

Into a pause in the conversation, I inserted, as casually as I could, "Have any idea who drives the gray pickup a couple vehicles from Clara's SUV?"

Apparently not casual enough, because Clara gave me a sharp look, then spun around to look toward the parking lot.

"You mean the ratty one pulling out now?" asked one of the older dog park regulars.

I, too, turned. "Yeah. That one."

"Not sure of the name, but it's a young guy with a hound mix. Friendly enough pup, but the guy has no idea how to handle it. Repeating commands a dozen times—and that's when he doesn't alternate them, so the animal doesn't know if he's supposed to sit, lie down, come, or stand on his head."

CHAPTER TWENTY-SEVEN

"**WHAT WAS THAT** about with the pickup?" Clara asked as soon as we were back in the SUV. "Were you really taking pictures of Gracie?"

"No." I explained and showed her the photos of junk loose in the truck bed, including another container of brake fluid like the one that hit her roof.

"If he hadn't run away, I'd give him a piece of my mind for nearly causing an accident at the drive-through."

"Which raises the question *why* he nearly caused that accident."

She blinked at me. "He didn't want to wait behind the other car?" Her voice made it not only a question, but a question she was questioning.

"Most people would have honked the horn."

"True. I should have thought of that."

"You had adrenaline going through you to avoid a pickup that came flying at us out of nowhere, then to keep from slamming into the wall of the building, then the jolt of the Good Samaritan at the window, telling us about the potential damage from the brake fluid. I didn't think about it, either. Not until I described it and Kit's question was why."

'I described it, too—to Ned—and I still didn't wonder."

"I bet you and Ned focused on potential damage to the SUV."

"Yeah, after the potential damage to you or the dogs or me."

"That's because you have a kind and good heart. With my aunt, the first thing that came to mind was what could the guy be trying to hide."

She chuckled. "I can't wait to meet Kit. The way you talk about her, she sounds like a lot of fun."

I dearly loved Kit. She *was* fun. She also thought first of murder and nefarious motives, which could be rather disconcerting until you got used to it. And when you got used to it, that was disconcerting because you wondered when did you start thinking of murder and nefarious motives first?

✧ ✧ ✧ ✧

AS WE PARKED around the corner from the yoga studio—so we could stop at the café for a post-class pick-me-up—we spotted Noah Canepa coming out of it.

He practically melted at the sight of Clara.

She chatted to him for a moment, while I barely contained myself before saying abruptly, "What do you know about ZigZag Cemetery?"

"You mean like why Jayne killed herself there?"

I didn't correct him on the method of death, focusing on the location. "Yes."

"I don't know. Unless…"

"Unless what, Noah?" Clara asked with fascination.

"Well, Henderson was trying to get it closed. I do know that. He had me go out there with him to take pictures. He pointed to things that were wrong and I took the pictures." He frowned. "Jayne seemed mostly angry about their relationship cooling. But maybe the cemetery meant something to them?"

"Why didn't he take the photos himself?"

He snorted. "There's no filter strong enough to fix his messes."

"What sort of things did he have you take photos of?"

"Where the fence was mostly down, the broken lock on the gate, stones tipped over, long grass and stuff. He had a list Krystal gave him."

"Why?"

"No idea, although … he did talk to some people about a business opportunity and one time Krystal heard him and told him to shut up. Oh, and that guy showed up and yelled at us for taking the pictures."

"What guy?"

"The cemetery guy. The one obsessed with some woman buried there. He'd been to the office before, trying to get Henderson to stop blocking funds to maintain the place. He and Jayne sort of got into it—she was still in her nobody-dare-criticize-Henderson phase."

Could that be anyone other than Doug Vonner?

"At least that guy didn't bring a pack of yappy dogs like that woman who screamed about the cemetery another time."

Berrie Vittlow. It had to be.

"But he was way angrier at the cemetery than he'd been at the office. Thought he was going to punch Henderson. But he didn't."

He sounded slightly disappointed.

"Do you know anything about messages sent to people at Adrian Jemson's party about Jayne's party?"

His eyes went improbably wide. "No. How did that happen? What did they say?"

Clara didn't answer, saying we needed to get to yoga.

Out of earshot, she said, "He sent those messages for sure. And Krystal knew all about the cemetery."

"Yup and yup. Krystal seems to have some business interest in it. And Doug Vonner confronted Henderson Nickell—more than once."

Clara clicked her tongue, dismissing that point. "C'mon. We need to get there to get our spots."

THE GOOD NEWS was Berrie was not at this yoga class.

"...to bring your mind here, now. Inside the four corners of your mat," the guest instructor said.

If I brought my mind to inside the four corners of my mat, I'd notice it could use a good scrubbing—the mat, not my mind. Besides, I had better things to think about.

Like murder.

Unless we were wrong about Jayne committing suicide. But ZigZag Jane … that had to be murder. Unless … That tree or its predecessor could have been strong enough then for a woman to hang herself.

But she was found on the ground.

What if she wasn't, though. What if she was found hanging. By Douglas Vonner or by someone else before he came. That someone— ZigZag John?—took her down, untied the scarf, laid her out, covered her with a blanket of leaves and—

"Thoughts may come, but let them go…" the instructor said.

I didn't want to let my thoughts go.

Okay, the one about scrubbing the mat could go, but those others might lead somewhere.

We were instructed to stand at the top of our mats, then forward fold and dangle. As I folded, the front two corners of the mat came into view.

I'm a good dangler. Not a whole lot else I'm good at in yoga, but I can dangle.

With my head upside down and my face toward the back of the mat, I saw the other two corners.

Four corners of the mat…

Were there four corners involved in figuring out who might be a murderer?

"Straighten halfway—flat back—and fold again. Maybe a little deeper."

My head dangled even lower.

With the blood rush came the three elements frequently brought up in connection with crimes—means, motive, and opportunity.

A three-cornered mat? That would be weird.

…but was there a fourth element in figuring out who could be a murderer?

"Straighten halfway—flat back—and fold again."

Far more people had means, motive, and opportunity than ever committed murder—look at Jayne Ulysee. Several folks with means, motive, and opportunity. Not all of them killed her.

So yes, there had to be another element.

A willingness to let the motive drive you to use the means and opportunity.

"Straighten—slowly."

That last word was directed at me, because I'd popped up straight. I paid the price with dizziness, but I thought it was worth it for that insight.

Now, what was I going to do with it?

AS CLASS ENDED, I recognized a drawback to our spots at the back of the studio—Fern cornered us before we rolled up our mats.

"The sooner you two settle who did away with Jayne Ulysee, the sooner you can get back to what matters. ZigZag Jane."

"We're not ignoring ZigZag Jane, Fern. We're sort of zigzagging back and forth ourselves. But you're right, if we settle one, we'll have more time for the other."

"ZigZag Jane matters to you, Fern?"

It wasn't my most tactful, but it was genuine and she took it that way, nodding. "My momma talked about her. She remembered when Jane was found and it affected her strongly. Momma had a real sentimental streak."

Sentimental was not a trait I'd associate with Fern and from the oblique references to her mother, I'd wondered...

Fern lived in a historic house that she said belonged to her family for generations and that sat in the middle of an area once known for houses of a specific kind—those of ill-repute. Putting that together with a few other hints, I'd wondered—strongly wondered—about a possible family business.

"Anytime the topic came up, Momma would say that poor lost soul could have been one of her girls—" I clamped my teeth together to keep from repeating *girls,* maybe with mingled question marks and exclamation points. "—and then she'd hug me real tight."

Thank heavens for my clamped teeth. Fern's momma hadn't meant one of her *girls*, in the madam sense, but in the mother sense.

"She donated to the fund to get her a stone at the cemetery. She'd be real pleased you two were trying to get to the rights of what happened to ZigZag Jane.

"So, I'll tell you what I know to get you moving faster on the other one, so you can get back to the first. There's video of someone in a hoodie heading in the direction of the house where that Jayne had the party the night before she was found dead."

"How do you know that?"

"A friend's doorbell camera caught it just before the figure went into the woods. You know the ones," she said to Clara.

In an undertone, Clara reminded me, "Between Manor Cove and the back of my neighborhood."

I'd bet her friend's house was the one just outside of Manor Cove.

"Your friend should turn that into the sheriff's department," I said dutifully. "Deputy Hensen or Teague O'Donnell would—"

"She will. But first it'll be on TV news later today. And then it'll be all over the Internet. Told her she should watermark it with her name. Never know when a business opportunity might come up."

A septuagenarian entrepreneur at heart.

"Have you seen it?" Clara asked her.

"Of course." I almost grinned at her indignation. "Can't recognize the person, but can see somebody in the hoodie walk past a car, so real experts could tell how tall the person was from angles and measurements and all. But you can see it for yourself."

She pulled out her phone.

"You have a copy?" I asked.

"Of course," she repeated with the same indignation.

The video showed the shape of a small, dark car parked on the street. A dark figure appeared and strode from right to left, toward the end of the sidewalk and what I knew from Clara and maps was the direction of the back of the house Jayne Ulysee rented for the party Halloween night.

"That was quick," Clara said. "Could we see it again?"

Repetitions didn't help. Not even when Fern hit slow-motion.

I doubted we could have recognized the face even without it being shadowed by the hood.

"Don't look so disappointed," Fern said. "Told you, a figure in a hoodie."

"Did the figure come back?" I asked.

"No. Only thing caught later was what looks like a group of kids running away from the direction that house is."

I frowned. "What time did the figure in the hoodie go toward the house where the party was?"

"Don't know. My friend didn't set up the clock right on the camera thingy."

"But it was before the group of kids ran by in the opposite direction?"

"Yeah. I can tell that messes up something for you, but—"

"No. Everything helps. Really."

"—I also saw an encounter between Jayne Ulysee and Krystal Nickell that was like watching NASCAR."

Clara nodded knowingly and said, "Stock car racing."

As if that explained everything. Maybe I needed more forward folding to get this. A good rush of blood to my head couldn't hurt.

"How was it like watching stock car racing?" I asked.

"The two of them, going round and round and round, looking for all the world like they were just driving the track, but coming this close to tangling in the corner, then scooting away, then coming around again and you're sure *this* time, they'll lock bumpers but good."

Clara nodded again, sagely this time.

"They'd both showed up at the same class here, two weeks ago. It was dagger eyes with the blades sharpened and ready to skewer."

That I understood. My turn—finally—to nod. "Krystal gave Jayne dagger looks."

"Krystal Nickell? Not her. She swanned into class, took a survey of who was here, like she does, decided no one was worthy of her attention—including Jayne—and kept her nose pinned to the ceiling the rest of the time. You might think she was doing what the instructors say about keeping our minds within the four corners of our mat, but I say she can't be bothered with most people. No idea why she settled on Henderson of all people."

Reminded me of my thoughts about the four corners of someone becoming a murderer. But no time to consider that with Fern continuing.

"No, it was Jayne Ulysee. Face turned as purple as her yoga pants. Kept those dagger eyes on Krystal the whole time. One poor little thing kept scooching her mat back to get out of the line of fire, until she was practically in Berrie's lap. Of course Berrie didn't notice a thing. Anyway, if Krystal turned up murdered, it wouldn't need you two to figure it out."

"But with Jayne the victim, you don't think the motive works the other way around?" Clara asked.

"Nah."

CHAPTER TWENTY-EIGHT

"**YOU DON'T THINK** the figure in the hoodie could be the murderer, do you. What's bothering you about it?" Clara asked once we'd ordered at the cafe.

"It's most likely the figure in the hoodie was going toward the house when we know Jayne was alive."

"How could you know that, since Fern said her friend messed up the timer."

"Don't know for sure, but the most logical reason for the group of kids to be running *away* from the party house as deputies arrived. And that comes *after* the figure in the hoodie going *toward* the house."

"What if the figure in the hoodie stayed in the woods and killed Jayne after things calmed down?"

"Possible. But Henderson and Krystal were at Jemson's party and Noah and Willie were out front."

That left another possibility.

Before I could ease into it, though, Clara said, "What Fern said does take the edge off Krystal's motive. If Fern says she wasn't bothered seeing Jayne, you can bank on it. And that means the affair didn't bother her."

I mmm'd.

"Doesn't it?" Clara asked.

"Unless Jayne's reaction made her *more* of a threat. To make a scene, to hurt Henderson's political career, to possibly turn off the spigot of donations or..." Our gazes met. "...their source of income."

"Oh, that's good, Sheila, that's really good."

We ate in silence for a moment. Derby pie for me and blueberry cheesecake for Clara deserved that kind of attention.

After a swallow, Clara said, "I was thinking about Jayne Ulysee and how there was a lot of envy around her."

I turned to her. "And *that's* really good. What kind of person has a lot of envy around her?"

"Somebody who has a lot. Especially a lot of things other people want."

"You don't sound positive about that."

"Well, I was thinking of people I know who have a lot more than other folks around them, yet don't stir envy."

"I think it depends on both people. The one who has more and the one who doesn't."

She was nodding before I finished. "Absolutely. The one who has more can be a jerk about it and that can make people envious—or at least not like them—but the person who has less can be a jerk, too, and it wouldn't matter how nice the one with more is. And of course if that one with less got more he—or she—would still be a jerk, only with more."

I thought I followed that. Enough to "uh-huh" wisely, which satisfied Clara.

"So, what do we think about Jayne Ulysee? Was she nice, but the people around her were jerks?"

Her immediate frown said she agreed with how I'd already answered in my head.

"Can they all be jerks? Or sort of jerks, anyway," Clara said. "Because you can understand why a wife would act that way or an ex-boyfriend, even with no right to. Or, when you think about it, a fellow employee who's watching someone else get advancement. That's natural for—Look." Clara pointed out the window, where Willie shambled by.

She raised her eyebrows at me and I nodded. She hopped up, since she was in a better position to reach the door.

In pantomime, I saw her catch up with him, say a few words, then a few more that immediately overcame his reluctance.

Inside, Clara grabbed a menu as she directed him to our table.

"…just had dessert, but feel free to order a sandwich," she said.

He didn't need encouragement. He ordered two sandwiches, extra sides, and cherry pie.

"How are you doing, Willie?" Clara asked with sympathy.

"It's tough. Real tough."

Tempted to point out his bereavement hadn't hurt his appetite, I left it to Clara to gently draw him out with a combination of her acting skills and genuine compassion.

We heard how he and Jayne met in school here, dated for years, and how she totally, completely, and wholeheartedly supported his rise toward superstardom in music. Mostly we heard about Willie.

"She knew even as a major star, I'd treat her okay. It's really tough to lose her when I need her to help me over this rough patch. Don't know what I'm going to do."

Kit once commented how the first thought of some mourners was to talk about what *they* lost, rather than what the dead person lost. I've noticed it ever since. It didn't endear Willie to me.

Clara drew him toward more recent interactions with Jayne. It still came back to her bankrolling him.

"She had a regular job, some sort of extra gig on the side, too, making lots for doing practically nothing. I just need a boost. Hang in long enough that people see I'm the real deal. That's all."

"How did you know about her extra gig?"

"Somebody messaged me about it. I figured she would help me through this rough spot. All the great ones have spells like this. What matters is hanging on. I came back like I always told her I would. Just had to make my mark on the world first."

Not much of a mark from what Kit found out.

"Who messaged you?" I asked.

"Dunno. Maybe it was her from a different number."

"She must have confided in you about her hopes and dreams,"

Clara said.

"Oh, yeah. All the time."

I couldn't resist asking, "What were they?"

"Oh, you know. The usual stuff. Be rich, famous."

"We heard there was someone famous at her party," I said.

He brightened dramatically. "That must've been me."

Clara picked up before I could say more and tear the delicate rapport she'd built with him. "That's right, you said she told you the Halloween party was a big deal for her and she wouldn't be a flunky anymore. How was the party going to do that?"

"I don't know. She was going on, all talking money and renting and not sharing—oh, yeah—" A memory flickered across his face. "—and not taking orders from old people afraid of their shadows. I was with her there. For sure. But, really, it wasn't my thing. I'm an artist. Money, all that stuff is of no interest to me."

A MESSAGE FROM Urban Parhem came in with an attachment.

I left Willie in Clara's capable hands and checked what Urban said.

His contact at the diocese came through, he wrote. The attachment held a photocopy of handwritten records.

"Sent you these so you could look yourself," Urban's message ended.

He also forwarded his contact's note that said no Ray was listed for 1919 or 1920.

Darn.

In keeping with that news, Willie gave us nothing else of interest as he blathered on about his certainty to be a star.

We left him still eating. We paid the whole bill on our way out.

WHEN I GOT home, I found Doug Vonner had left an envelope in my door with a note.

"Wanted to get these copies to you right away. I should have re-membered the photo. It was there with the donor list and the notes Grandfather took when he talked to people. Hope they help. Let me know if you need anything else."

I pulled out the papers for a second look.

The photo still didn't show the name of the theater and mocked me with the license plate. The notes of what people saw and heard still pointed mostly to a ghostly hearse and not at all to a person then-living. The donor list still showed many names with amounts beside them.

I leaned forward to look at the small, neat handwriting more close-ly.

The first time I'd looked at this list, this entry hadn't made an im-pression.

It did now.

Louis Kielwegen donated five cents.

CHAPTER TWENTY-NINE

TEAGUE WAS WORKING, Clara and Ned were at dinner with his work colleagues. I was curled into a corner of the sofa, watching a TV mystery.

These I usually solved well before the end. Too bad Jane and Jayne weren't on TV.

Kit called.

I grabbed for the phone. Hoping for … something.

"Hi Kit. Wait a second. I'll pause the TV."

"One of those British mystery shows, huh?"

"How did you know that?" She was right, of course.

"This is the right time for one to be on. You like them. And I heard the accent."

Grinning, even though she couldn't see it, I asked, "Are you going to tell me whodunit, too?"

"Probably could. If there's an American character in it, it's the American. If there's more than one American character, it's the one played by a Brit. If there's more than one American character played by Brits, it's the one who wears white socks with black shoes."

I spluttered with laughter. There *was* an American character played by a Brit—I'd looked him up after a weird pronunciation—and I had winced at the white socks with black shoes. "They can't be that predictable," I protested.

"Sure they can. They think they're being subtle by not making the French person the murderer."

"Boy, I wish these murders were one of those shows with one American character so we knew who did it."

"Setback, huh? What's happened?"

I caught Kit up with what we'd added, including no Ray born in 1919 or 1920 and Louis Kiel—or Kielwegen—giving a nickel to provide ZigZag Jane a decent burial. "Looks like someone else filled in the w-e-g-e-n, so that adds to the possibility that some people did know who ZigZag Jane was at the time. She *must* be Zelda. He'd have no reason to be so dismissive of a stranger."

"Emotion can give you a place to start, but don't stop there. Look for facts. You said Urban Parhem from the historical society sent you the original birth records for the boy, Ray."

"Yeah. In the original handwriting, which would have been right at home in a Pharoah's tomb."

"Look at them yourself, anyway."

I gusted out a sigh. "That's what Urban said. *Take a look.*"

"Smarter than he sounds."

"Urban *is* smart."

"It's not a name I'd give a smart character."

"Apparently his parents didn't share your writerly sensibilities."

"Quit changing the subject. Read the records yourself."

"I'm not sure records are going to be the answer. I was thinking at yoga today—"

"Didn't know you were allowed to think there. Only breathe."

"C'mon, Kit. You know the benefit of movement—for your body and your mind. You always took a walk when you were stuck on a book. Even if you paced through the house because of the weather or the time of night. Gets your body moving, lets your mind find solutions."

"As long as you're not going to *namaste* all over me, go ahead," she said begrudgingly.

I told her my theory about a fourth element needed, along with means, motive, and opportunity.

"That's not bad, Sheila. That's not bad at all. There is that fourth element. That willingness to solve your problem by taking someone else's life. How do the suspects strike you on that dimension?"

"That's just it. All of them have that fourth dimension."

"What about Willie?"

"Definitely on the selfishness, though the money—Oh. You've got information on him already?"

"Yes. Took some doing. He's not exactly well-known. Had to go down several layers from the people I know, but they did it for me."

I grinned—glad we weren't on a video call where she'd strenuously object to my noticing her bit of snobbery.

"He knocks around with backup work here and there. Mostly there. Always moving on to someplace else. Might be partly looking for greener grass, but a couple of my sources indicated it's also a matter of each local music community not giving him ongoing gigs once they'd worked with him. He has to move on to where he's not known."

"Huh. So definitely not working his way up and just in a rough patch before he would have returned as the conquering hero to sweep his old girlfriend off her feet and claim her by right of success."

"Definitely not. Though where you came up with the idea of a male claiming a female by right of success—"

"Not me. Him. And he tried to sell it too hard."

AS A BEDTIME story, I looked over what Doug Vonner had left again, this time ending on the photo.

There was the car with the tease of a license plate. A modern license number could be tracked—if not by Clara and me, certainly by Teague and his colleagues. But I had to wait until Monday to even find out if one from a century ago could be tracked.

Kit taught me the trick of looking at the visual matter first, without reading a caption. No caption in this case, but drawing my own conclusions from the photo itself still applied.

A group gathered outside the theater. A corner of a marquee proclaiming an opening or reopening in the upper left. Six men and one woman arrayed in front of a shiny car parked right at the entrance.

The photo was not only grainy with age, but the area of focus appeared to be knee level of the people, further obscuring facial details.

Still, there were other tidbits to pick up, I realized.

The man at the center of the photo truly was at the center of the photo. With the others trailing off to either side like the wake left by a boat's prow cutting through water.

This man at the center wasn't the best looking, but there was an air of power about him that went beyond his position in the group or even that he was the only one leaning back against the car, though that did convey not only possession, but a familiarity with possession.

That thought made me look more closely at the sole woman.

The men all wore suits, topcoats, and hats.

She wore a long, clingy dress and nothing more.

The man at the center had his right arm around her waist, not tight, yet his hold shifted her waist closer to him in what couldn't have been a comfortable position. His left arm extended slightly, as if directing the photographer, and in his left hand he held what looked to be fine leather gloves. I looked from that glove-holding hand to the one showing at the far side of the woman's waist.

It might have been my imagination, but it seemed they expressed the same possession—gloves, car, woman. Not clutching tightly as if afraid someone might take them away, but easy possession because he was sure no one could.

I sat back, staring out the darkened window.

Aloud, I asked Douglas Vonner, the boy who'd found ZigZag Jane, "Why did you keep this photo? Why did you blow it up?" Or maybe I was asking the old man who'd tasked his grandson with carrying on the quest.

Neither answered.

SUNDAY

CHAPTER THIRTY

TEAGUE ARRIVED AT my house right after I'd put the breakfast casserole in the oven for our brunch with Clara and Ned.

After letting each other know what we'd missed since he left Friday morning, I whispered the non-sweet-nothing of, "Heard you got some video evidence."

He rolled his eyes. "Of course you did. Did you also see it first?"

"No." It was my best imitation of a teenager conveying the absurdity of a notion. "Did it tell you anything?"

"Nothing we're sharing with the public."

I didn't take the hint. "Did you do the calculations to know how tall the figure in the hoodie is?"

"No."

"But you eyeballed it as the figure passed the vehicle and you have a guess."

"How do you know there's a vehicle in the footage?"

My turn to roll my eyes.

"Grapevine." He didn't wait for me to confirm or deny. "We made no identification, if that's what you're asking."

"It's not. If you had, there'd be an arrest." Then I added, "Wouldn't there?"

"Walking past a house is no crime."

He expected me to argue. To bring up the hoodie and the way it masked identity. To point out that after the sidewalk ended there wasn't much of anywhere to go, except the path through the woods to behind the back of the house Jayne rented.

And the figure didn't come back.

I barely stopped myself from saying it aloud.

What if I was wrong about the figure in the hoodie?

What if it did lurk in the woods or elsewhere until it had the opportunity to kill Jayne Ulysee and drive her body in her car to the cemetery to stage a suicide?

That should eliminate the Nickells, who were at Jemson's party. Or so said Adrian Jemson.

I caught Teague watching me and blurted, "I have something to tell you."

"Oh?" His expression shifted. Interested, certainly, and something else? Sort of … deliberately laid back.

Although I'd blurted the words to stop myself from thinking and him from reading my mind, I'd planned to tell him soon. So, you'd think I'd have the dialogue written, revised, edited. Nope. And in this instant, no brilliant words came into my head. No unbrilliant words, either.

I continued blurting. "I'm writing. Stories. Books. Fiction. Trying to write."

He regarded me evenly. "That's what you want to tell me?"

"That's it." I managed a laugh. "I want to be an author, like my great aunt, and I'm trying to make it happen. Wild, huh?"

"Not really. How's it going?"

Somehow this wasn't the reaction I'd expected. Though I couldn't say what I *had* expected.

"Not well. It's a lot harder than it looks."

"I bet. What are you writing?"

"I wish I knew."

He chuckled at my morose tone. Suddenly cheered, I almost joined him, "No, seriously, I've tried romances, including a historical, and haven't finished anything. I get partway in, then I can't see a way out. Then I start something new."

"Isn't that what writers do? That's what they say in movies and books about writers. Either that or they sit around and think about writing without actually writing. What does Kit say?"

"I haven't asked."

Without raising his head, he looked up at me. "Because?"

"Because she doesn't know I'm trying to write."

"You told me before Kit?"

"Yeah. Clara found out sort of by accident, but no one else." I realized what bugged me about his reaction. "You don't seem surprised."

He turned back to his coffee. "As you said, you're writing—"

"Trying to write."

"—like your great-aunt. Not all that surprising that it might run in the family."

"You're right," I said with some relief. "Hearing her stories about the writing world was either going to make me want to do it or stay as far away as possible."

"Guess you tried that first." After a beat, he added, by way of explanation, which my expression must have told him I needed. "Teaching."

"Of course. Yeah. You're right."

"This is what you were going to tell me a while back before you broke out the champagne about me going to work for the sheriff's department?"

"Yes," I lied, at least partially.

I'd intended to tell him the entire *Abandon All* and Aunt Kit scenario, probably throwing in the writing somewhere. But with Teague officially connected to the sheriff's department, I'd aborted that plan.

"You aren't surprised?" I asked.

He closed in and kissed the top of my head, chuckling again. "I *am* a detective, you know."

"How did you know?"

"I didn't. I suspected."

"Fine. How did you suspect."

"Lots more time spent on the computer. Mysterious about all the time spent on the computer. Abrupt spells of distraction, followed by odd comments that sounded like you might be referring to something other than what we'd been talking about."

"I did that?" Kit did all the time. I didn't know if I was delighted that I might have at least one characteristic of a real writer or terrified I'd already started acting like Kit.

"You did. Also, hurriedly switching off your screen a couple times. But not quite fast enough. Ludovic? That's your villain?"

"Hero. Playing against type. But that was the historical. It died after three chapters. They all do."

"Why?"

"I don't know what happens next. And I don't know what the end will be, so I really, really don't know what comes between next and the end."

His expression grew solemn, but his eyes didn't. "Sounds sort of like what a detective does. Not knowing, but needing to keep going bit by bit, maybe trying a lot of things to see which one's a good fit for what's next, rinse and repeat, until you do get to the end."

He was exactly right. And I not only listened to Kit do that dozens of times over the years we'd shared the brownstone, but I did it with the mysteries Clara and I solved.

I could do this.

I threw my arms around his neck and kissed him.

"Thank you."

"Happy to help."

I kissed him again, with more *involvement* this time.

"Very happy to help," he said.

AFTER AN INTERLUDE during which he proved how happy he was, Teague helped me finish prep for brunch.

"Great. All set. Thanks, Teague. I'm going upstairs for just a minute. Will you please listen for the timer on the casserole?"

"Sure. Before you go, though, I meant to ask if you want a piece of my shirt?"

Confused, I stopped and turned back to him. "Why would I want a piece of your shirt?"

"I don't wear ribbons or scarves or leather gloves, which I'm told are the usual tokens of favor to bestow on a champion who defends your honor in the lists."

He'd heard about my run-in with Deputy Eckles. I felt prickling heat rush up my throat and into my cheeks.

"I told Clara not to—"

"She didn't. Not a word, not a hint." I opened my mouth, but he shut it with his next words. "Not Ned, either."

"Oh."

"Don't look concerned, Sheila. It's all good." He grinned, hooked his arm around my neck and drew me close. "As long as you didn't take a swing at him, it's all good. Honest." He nuzzled the hair at my temple, then kissed me there. "It wasn't necessary, but it's good to know you care."

The oven timer dinged.

He released me. "I got the casserole. You go upstairs."

From the corner of my eye as I turned toward the stairs, I saw Teague bend to ruffle Gracie's fur around her face. "You, too, girl. Appreciate you having my back."

CHAPTER THIRTY-ONE

NOT EVERYONE WHO has friends over for brunch shares a photo from a hundred years ago and asks their impressions. None of my guests appeared the least surprised when I did.

"Anything strike you about her position?" I asked when they'd all looked at it.

Clara immediately said, "She doesn't want to be close to that guy, but feels she has to be, so she slides her waist in his direction so he doesn't feel any resistance, but she holds as much of herself away from him as she can."

Ned did a doubletake, then whistled through his teeth. "That's my Clara. Wow."

"I agree," I said. "With her interpretation and that it's amazing. Teague?"

"Agree with the body language a hundred percent." That was muffled because he'd bent low for a closer look. "Mind if I look at this with my phone's camera?"

"Why would I mind?"

"It's old."

"It's a copy."

His head came up. "From where?"

"I don't know. Doug has this one and a smaller print of the same people in the same pose. I figured this was the copy—somebody, maybe Douglas Vonner, enlarging it to see better, only it sure didn't help with their faces."

"No," he said slowly, looking at the photo through his phone's camera, zooming in, out, then in more. "That's because the photographer was interested in something else. The license plate."

"THE PHOTOGRAPHER FOCUSED around their knees on purpose?"

"Can't know for sure, but my grandfather had a collection of photos by a guy who photographed Chicago mobsters' good times a lot, then slipped in ones that caught license plates or addresses or other identifiable information. Those went to law enforcement. I remember the weird focus around the knees or over people's heads or off to the side."

"Why did your grandfather have a collection like that?" Clara asked.

"He was in law enforcement." One side of Teague's mouth lifted. "You pick up odd interests."

Ned asked, "You're thinking these guys were mob?"

"I think the group around that Packard might have been of interest to law enforcement of the time," he amended.

"That fits what Urban—Urban Parhem from the historical society—said about Newport being a center for bootlegging during Prohibition," Clara said.

"Around that what?" I asked Teague, perhaps with some urgency.

"Packard. It was a kind of car."

"I know it was a kind of car, but you're sure that's what kind this is?"

"Look for yourself. It says Packard on the grill."

I'd overlooked that completely. "Is it a Packard Twin Six?"

He grinned. "Hey, I can read the insignia. I don't have old cars memorized." Then he turned serious. "Why?"

I explained about Douglas Vonner's notes from talking to a ten-year-old who swore he'd heard a Packard Twin Six the night before ZigZag Jane was found.

"There's something else." I pulled out the donor list and pointed.

Clara spotted it first. "Louis Kielwegen. *Five cents.* What a jerk. Worse than a jerk. I'd call him a son of something, but that would put the badness on his mother, when it was all him."

"Look at his name."

They all squinted where I pointed.

Ned said, "He didn't write out his whole name."

"No, he didn't. It looks like one handwriting wrote Kiel and another—I'd guess Douglas Vonner's from the other samples I've seen—added the w-e-g-e-n. Because that's how he was known around here. As a member of the Kielwegen family, no matter what he called himself in Newport."

Clara looked up, her eyes glowing. "This should convince county officials. The family connections, the census, ZigZag John's history, living with Louis in Newport, Louis's wife disappearing at the right time. This has got to be enough to get them to go for DNA."

"So that ends the whole thing," Ned said.

I shook my head. "We still have a lot to figure out. For starters, we can't know if Douglas Vonner recognized the man in the photo in front of the theater as Louis Kiel who donated a nickel to Jane's headstone, but it is suggestive that he kept the photo with the donor list."

"Why didn't he act on it if he suspected?" Clara asked.

"Might have been scared—with good cause," Teague said. "The gangs running Newport were not nice guys. This was early, but the Cleveland mob came in, along with others."

"That raises the question of whether other people around North Bend County—especially officials—truly didn't recognize her or pretended ignorance out of fear that Newport wasn't nearly as far away as it needed to be before they'd cross Louis the K," I said.

"But she was strangled, right?" Ned asked. "You'd think an organized crime type would use a gun."

"Or weren't they organized enough then to be called organized crime?" I tacked on.

Teague said, "They were plenty organized enough to terrorize and kill people, in between stealing from them. Don't go getting romantic ideas about Prohibition and criminals."

"I only have romantic ideas about part-time detectives."

He grinned at me. "Glad to hear it."

TEAGUE WENT TO work.

Ned left to help a first-time-homeowner friend prep for winter.

Clara and I stayed to clean up.

The second the door closed behind the guys, we turned to each other.

"I've been thinking," she said.

"Me, too. You go first."

"About the hoodie. *If* it was Henderson or Krystal in the hoodie— and I know your reasons for doubting that, but let me follow this through for a second. The question is where did it come from? Kept one in the car?" She shook her head before she'd finished the words. "They're not the types. But there were hoodies in the Jemson mudroom and Henderson was in that mudroom, while Krystal also had access to it."

"Absolutely agree, Clara. And—"

"Wait, there's more. Not as upbeat. Because if Henderson or Krystal used the hoodie to go to the party house, they couldn't have killed Jayne then. Because they were back at Jemson's party *after* the texts about the deputies closing down Jayne's party and she was still alive then. That hoodie goes to Jayne's party at the totally wrong time for murder. But could they have used that time to talk to Jayne to set up a meeting later?"

"Not only is that great thinking, Clara, but it links with what I was thinking, including that we need to talk to Adrian Jemson again. I'll tell you more on the way."

"The dishes—"

"Can wait. I'm a great believer in soaking."

CHAPTER THIRTY-TWO

THE WOMAN WE'D seen down the hallway on our first visit to Adrian Jemson's house answered the door in a dark tunic and knit pants, somewhere between scrubs and a maid's uniform.

She turned and started toward the back of the house, apparently viewing us as accepted guests since Jemson chatted with us last time.

Without a word, she gestured toward a side hallway and peeled off to our left.

Hearing Adrian Jemson's voice from the side hallway, we followed her halfhearted invitation.

"—and wear one of your other sweatshirts if you can't find that one."

A young voice, impatient with adult stupidity said, "I need the black one."

"What did you do with it?"

"If I knew that I wouldn't need a new one, would I."

On that line, delivered in classic teen sarcasm, Jemson and the sullen-looking teen we'd seen before emerged from a wide doorway and into the hallway.

The teen had to be Jemson's son. Not because of a strong family resemblance, but because of the interactions.

"Uh-oh, lost something?" Clara asked with sympathy.

Despite a championship quality slouch, the young man was a head taller than Jemson, who vented his exasperation with, "He's always losing things. It's probably in there somewhere."

His wide-flung arm gave us an excuse to advance forward to peer into the cavern of a mudroom. The thing was nearly as big as my kitchen and had more conveniences. It also had more stuff in it. Mostly clothes and most of that, clearly, the kid's.

"Did you even look," Jemson grumbled. He sounded like a top winding down.

And the kid knew it. "Yeah, I looked. Tell Priscilla to get me a new one. Fast."

"What did you lose?" Clara asked.

"Hoodie," the kid mumbled without looking at any of the adults. "Priscilla knows what to get. Just tell her." Presumably that order was for his father.

"Wellington—"

But the kid was gone.

I might have been, too, if my parents named me Wellington.

Grumbling, Jemson went in the other direction, but not far, before he bellowed to Priscilla with instructions about ordering Wellington a replacement hoodie. Express.

Clara and I exchanged a look. And not just in horror at imagining the express delivery charges. We agreed without saying a word. The one thing we'd lacked was leverage. Now we had it.

Jemson spun around and came back to us. "Sorry about that, but honestly, I have nothing else to tell you. Henderson was here for the whole party, talked to a slew of people, made a good impression with them. Now, if you don't mind—"

He flapped one hand in the general direction of the front door, though it was some distance away.

"It's interesting that your son's lost his black hoodie. You do know, don't you, that the sheriff's department has video of a tall figure—right about your son's height—wearing a dark hoodie, likely black, and walking toward where that murdered woman, Jayne Ulysee, was the night of the murder?"

Points for Jemson. He wasn't stupid. He saw the implications.

"My son lost his hoodie in that mess. He's always losing things.

Besides, if they have the hoodie, they'll know it's not his—"

"That's the thing. They haven't found it. Yet. But they're looking for it." If they weren't now, they would be when Clara and I told Teague and Deputy Hensen about this.

"When they find it," I continued, "they'll confirm the owner through DNA and other tests."

His gaze flicked into the mudroom. Had him.

The hoodie might not be the immediate answer we could have hoped for when Fern told us about the video, but it provided us leverage.

"In the meantime, the sheriff's department can't limit their inquiries to what they absolutely *know*. They have widened their questions to pursue all the possibilities. And since a murder investigation is followed so closely by the media…"

"Wellington had nothing to do with that woman or her death. He didn't even know her."

"Teenagers are known for going to parties they shouldn't and Jayne Ulysee put on a lot of parties. The one Halloween night had a number of underage kids in attendance. Apparently, a group eluded the deputies by going out the back and following a path that runs behind the house and comes out around here."

His face went slack, but calculations flew across his eyes.

He spoke slowly, almost reluctantly. "Henderson was here for the whole party. The only time other people couldn't swear to his being here was when he was in the mudroom and I saw him then. He never had enough time to get to that house, much less get back."

"Krystal?" Clara asked.

"I don't know the way I do for Henderson. But there was never a time I was aware of her not being around and a lot of time I was aware of her working the party. I'd be surprised if she left. That's all I can say."

"Wellington?" I asked.

His lips drew back from his teeth. "I told you. He didn't know that woman. He was in his room that night."

He didn't believe it any more than we did.

He wanted to protect his son. That added credibility to his statements about Henderson and Krystal.

"The sheriff's department will have to investigate," I said.

He knew that. That's why he'd told the truth that could be corroborated by other partygoers.

Wasn't about to tell Jemson that investigating the hoodie would be low priority if they saw the later video of the kids leaving and realized that set the hoodie-wearing figure video to way before the murder.

"I've told the truth, to the deputies and you. There is something else, though. When Henderson and I were in here for him to clean mud off his shoes from that leaf business, he asked to use my phone. I wondered why."

No, he didn't. He thought Henderson wanted to call a woman and not have a record of it on his phone. He was right.

"But it wasn't really any of my business. I gave him my phone and left him alone a few minutes—four, five at the tops. Not enough time to get to that house and back, that's for sure."

I returned his gaze sternly.

"We, most certainly, will share this new information with the sheriff's department."

He looked satisfied.

"WILL WE?" CLARA asked once we were in her SUV.

I knew she meant share Jemson's new version of events with the sheriff's department.

"Well, it's only fair to give him a little time to get there on his own."

She grinned. "I completely agree. What now?"

"Back to those dishes and review what we've got."

CHAPTER THIRTY-THREE

"**Henderson and Noah** went to the cemetery to take photos of the broken lock, fallen fence sections—from a list Krystal gave them. So she must have been there previously. All three of them knew they could get in there to dump Jayne's already-dead body or to meet her to kill her there."

"And Willie grew up here, so he'd know about ZigZag Cemetery, too," Clara said.

"Right. Next point. Henderson, Krystal, and Doug all live near the walking path that goes past the back of the party house, where Jayne remained after deputies broke up the party. Henderson and Krystal were even closer to it, being at Jemson's house for that party." I loaded a bowl into the dishwasher. "Willie and Noah are natives and were hanging around at that party, so they could have driven away from the front of the house for all the world to see, then known about that way to get to the back of the house."

Clara wiped a cutting board she'd hand-washed. "So that doesn't eliminate or point to any of them. But would Willie kill her when he needed her money?"

"Heat of the moment," I proposed. "Though I agree his mercenary bent casts doubts on his acting against his interests." As I said the words, I realized acting within his or her character also fed into that fourth corner, joining means, motive, and opportunity.

The last item loaded into the dishwasher, I gestured for Clara to join me at the little table and proposed, "Let's look at how this could have played out. Jayne's at her party. Henderson's at his. There's a rumor going around at Jemson's party about hers because of the messages—sent by Noah, we think. Henderson calls her on Jemson's phone and … then what?"

"Her having a party can't be enough for him to kill her," she said. "What if he was jealous? He might have seen her with another guy. Maybe Willie, her ex-boyfriend."

"But Noah only said she and Henderson talked on the phone. Nothing about him being there in person. Teague said the rumor of some local politician being there turned out not to be true, remember? Even if Jemson's lying—and would he at the expense of making his son more suspicious?—Henderson sure wasn't there when the deputies got there. Besides, if Noah's right, Henderson was trying to cool it. If it were the other way around, I could see Jayne being jealous, but…"

Clara grimaced. We both sank into silent thought.

After a minute or so, she straightened.

"Krystal heard the report about Jayne's party getting wild, too. Say she's the one who grabs the hoodie—she's almost as tall as Henderson—and goes to confront Jayne."

"That fits her personality." The fourth corner of yoga mat for murder, as Kit and I discussed. "She's smart enough to know that killing Jayne wouldn't bury gossip about Henderson and Jayne—in fact more likely to bring it to light, as we've seen."

"But maybe Krystal wasn't thinking things through at that point. Maybe she saw red and—No, you're right. She's not the kind to do that."

"I didn't say a word," I protested.

"You thought some, though."

I chuckled. Maybe I had.

"There have to be other suspects," Clara said.

"Doug Vonner," I said.

"Why would you say that?" she demanded.

Interesting that she asked why I *said* it, not why I would think it.

Which possibly betrayed her own wonderings.

"Because it's logical. You look at who benefitted and he's definitely benefitted."

"The cause to test ZigZag Jane's DNA, maybe, but—"

"What's nearer and dearer to him than that cause? As far as I can tell, he's living to fulfill his grandfather's quest. But there are other things, too."

"Like what?"

"The scratches on his face and neck when we saw him the day after Jayne died."

"He explained that."

"Weak story. No witnesses. Also, you said you were surprised he didn't answer your messages in the morning. Sleeping in after a late night of committing murder?"

"But *why?*"

"Henderson's trying to close the cemetery and Jayne was associated with Henderson. He might have thought she was more important to the effort than she was, for example thinking she was the one who had Noah taking pictures instead of Krystal. Everything we've heard says Jayne would make herself sound more important, too."

"That's—"

"Possible. He's a suspect."

She stared at her cup a moment. "If you're right and those scratches came from Jayne rather than the branch, they might get proof from under her fingernails, in which case forensics would solve this, not us."

"We would have helped. Also, the scratches might have been from the tree. Remember how the branch almost got me in the head. He might have had the same experience trying to hang Jayne's body from that tree to make it look like suicide."

She didn't argue, but she didn't like it.

"We're not done with suspects. There's Willie. Noah and Yakira said Jayne wasn't the least bit interested in seeing him again. We know from Noah and Yakira and Krystal that Jayne was fooling around with Henderson—even if he was trying to cool it. So Willie goes to the party and Jayne tells him to get lost, that she's involved with some-one."

"And he goes into a jealous rage." That prospect brightened Clara's mood considerably, presumably because it moved the spotlight away from Doug. "That makes sense."

"There's also Noah. As you said, there was a lot of envy around Jayne, including his. I saw some that day at the news conference at the cemetery. And it oozed out around everything he told us about her."

"How about what he said about Krystal? He tried to steer us her way."

"He did. And we can't ignore Krystal. I can see her doing it herself or manipulating Henderson into committing murder. It's the mo-tive ... Because she was fed up with Jayne as a ... rival? That's where it falls apart. I have problems believing Krystal saw Jayne as a rival or cared enough to do that," I said.

"Agreed. She wouldn't care enough about him or the marriage or even if their affair became known. But what if she saw Jayne as a threat to their business? What *is* their business," Clara added parenthetically, before resuming with, "Or his political future? Or both?"

I clunked my mug on the table. "That's good. In fact, that's great, Clara. What *is* their business? Krystal isn't wowed by Henderson's political future, but she does talk about *the business.*"

"I know he was involved in tearing down the historic schoolhouse and putting up shoddy houses, but I don't know details. I can ask around."

"Maybe we should go back to Yakira. Remember what she said about Adrian Jemson using elected offices to vote on things that benefitted him? And with Henderson apparently his protégé, maybe there's something in that. *Oh.* Berrie practically said it, too. She said Henderson and his group voted against funds to maintain the cemetery so they could close it and develop it. Heck, you said it, too, Clara. On TV."

"I didn't know anything specific, though. I..." Clara's gaze became unfocused. After a moment, she jerked slightly. "I need to make a phone call."

"Right now? Let's keep working on—"

"It can't wait." She gathered her things, not looking at me. "I'll call or message you or come back later."

"Okay," I said slowly, respecting her decision to leave. Wouldn't have done me any good not to respect it. Clara wasn't sharing or she already would have.

CHECKING MESSAGES, I found one from Urban, telling me to call.

I wasted no time and neither did he when he answered. "I could find no reference to the theater that ZigZag Jane had a ticket for in her pocket opening or reopening around 1920."

Darn. I deflated. I hadn't realized how much I'd hoped for that connection, how much I'd wanted to know that photo—blurry face and all—was of Zelda and that she was ZigZag Jane.

"My source on Newport's criminal past did find something interesting. A theater—not for movies, but for live shows of a rather risqué nature did open in early 1921."

"That's nice, but—"

"I haven't finished. It was owned by three men, one of them being Louis Kiel—Louis the K."

Whoosh. Those few words and I was reinflated. "That's great. Why didn't you say that right away? That could be him in the photo and that would make the woman Zelda and—"

"Or it could be one of the other owners or someone else entirely."

"Aren't you a bundle of cheer."

"Realistic. You can't build facts out of mights and coulds. You find the facts in the records, such as those birth records—" A not-so-subtle nag. "—and let their facts lead you to a conclusion."

THE COMBINED VOICES-IN-MY-HEAD of Urban and Kit pushed me

into the chair in front of the computer with the big screen to read the hieroglyphic birth records myself and shut them both up—for real and in my head.

An hour later, I arched my back and rubbed my neck with both hands.

No Ray.

No Kielwegen.

No Kiel.

No last name that started with K at all.

Right on the heels of that thought came the memory of the iron-work over the cemetery entrance.

I scrolled back to the top, assessing this handwriting. H, B, R, even a loopy P, could all be confused with a K. Or vice versa.

Hamburg, Barnes, Rickentoffer.

And then, there it was.

It looked almost exactly like the name over the cemetery entrance. Or that's how I saw it because of that ironwork.

Kielwegen.

In the worst handwriting ever, but still there. Not my imagination. The actual letters.

I slid past the first name—another scramble of indecipherable letters—saw it was the record for a boy, born in August 1919. Which made him eleven months old in July 1920, when the census-taker came by.

Back to the first name.

A first letter that was mostly flourish, then I was pretty sure "a-c."

Far too long to be Ray.

I zoomed in to see the handwriting better, comparing the letters with others I had more confidence in.

Back and forth, back and forth.

Not Raymond, either.

Next ... h or k?

And then the first-letter flourish resolved into a Z.

Zackarias?

No.
It ended with r-a-u-s.
"Ray-us," I said aloud.
Zacharaus.
Ray as a nickname for Zacharaus.

CHAPTER THIRTY-FOUR

Clara messaged she was coming over.

I met her at the back door, burbling about what I'd found.

Once she hacked through my incoherence, she was as excited as I was.

Until we recognized that it pinned down Ray's birth, yet gave no hint of what happened to him after the 1921 census.

Perhaps to cheer us both up, she said, "I have some news, too. About Henderson Nickell. When I said that to him on TV about wanting to turn the cemetery into a development, I must have been thinking of bits and pieces I'd heard from Gran, repeating what her friend who worked for the county said. Anyway, she said to tell you everything."

Connecting dots, I said, "Your grandmother who's retired in Belize with the boyfriend?"

"Right. I called her—it took a while because they were out celebrating. I'm not sure what. She doesn't pass up opportunities to celebrate. Anyway, I explained everything and she said to tell you. Though she said we should think about it, because it might come back to bite us in the butt—that's what she said. They can't give her trouble, but they could give us trouble. They—"

"Who's the mysterious *they?*"

She rattled off two names that were vaguely familiar as county officials, then—

"—Adrian Jemson and Henderson Nickell," she finished triumphantly. "Gran says her friend said that group pushed through regulations that help their businesses or their families—including approval of short-term rentals. And Gran said Henderson Nickell does have property near the cemetery, though nobody's supposed to know."

"If they find out your grandmother's friend told—"

"She's in Belize, too. And her county pension's ironclad."

"Okay, then. Let's think this through … If Willie and Noah were telling the truth—and if Jayne told them the truth or accidentally let it slip—that means…"

I saw pieces as if they floated in front of me, shifting around, connecting with another piece.

"What if … What if she was a front and … She *was* a front. Jayne Ulyscc."

"Yeah." She wasn't humoring me. She was trying to follow my point. It might be what I appreciated most about Clara. She always thought I had a point.

"A front for Henderson Nickell. To let him make money from those parties. Think about what Krystal said, about *the business*. We know she didn't mean a political future for Henderson. And she didn't mean the office he holds now, which does not pay anywhere near enough to support their lifestyle. I should have paid more attention when we went to their house and Jemson's. I let myself be distracted by not caring for the houses or the owners. I should have been asking the question all along."

"What question?"

"How do they pay for those places? Then add what Yakira said about Jemson using offices to vote on things that benefitted him. Jemson and—no doubt—his protégé Nickell."

"That's exactly what Gran said her friend said. But we agreed renting out here wouldn't make them much money."

"Not if they rented to respectable families here for a family visit or business. But they could charge a lot more for wild parties. That's what Willie said—in a roundabout way. Jayne was raking in money from hosting parties. Noah knew that, too. He messaged Willie to make trouble for Jayne and Willie came back because she had money. Plus, Yakira and Noah said Jayne and Henderson had a falling out to do with money. Willie said she had some big work thing she said was her chance to get independent. To *show him* what she could do on her own—not to show Willie, but to show *Henderson.*

"She rented the house—I bet it's one of the Nickells' houses. And she put on the party. Used what she'd been doing for the other parties. Only this time, she let it get wild.

"Noah sends out messages to people at Jemson's party and word gets to the Nickells. As soon as they hear the address, they know it's one of their houses. Henderson calls her on Jemson's phone, probably to say, *What the hell are you doing?* They set a meeting for later at the house."

Clara raised a finger. "If Krystal killed Jayne, she had to have been killed at the house, because why would Jayne go with her to the cemetery Halloween night? But Henderson could have killed her at the house or at the cemetery."

"Why would she go there with Henderson?" Why would anyone go there—ever—without being bamboozled by someone like Clara.

"It's romantic," my friend said.

"Romantic?"

Clara stuck to her guns. "He tells her he wants to make good what's been going wrong between them. But they need to be some-place where no one else will see them. He'll meet her there and then they can talk and really be together. Oh, yeah, she'd fall for that. So, if she was killed at the house, it could have been Krystal or Henderson. If she was killed at the cemetery, it was Henderson. He lured her there, then killed her."

I wasn't totally sold, but one aspect struck me.

"If Henderson lured her there and they met at the cemetery, that resolves one big issue—how the killer left. He just drove off in his car. But if Henderson and Jayne went to the cemetery together, with her alive or dead, did someone give him a ride back, leaving her car to be found there?"

Clara flicked that away for a bigger issue. "But, Sheila, which one of them is the murderer? Henderson or Krystal?"

"I DON'T KNOW. In fact, I don't know that it's *not* one of the other people. Any of them might have an accomplice we don't know about yet to pick them up at the cemetery. Or they took that long, long walk back on ZigZag Trail."

"You're saying Noah or Willie—"

"Or Doug."

"Okay," she said slowly. "Then we keep investigating. And so will the sheriff's department. Maybe that doorbell video could be enhanced the way they do on TV. Or forensic evidence—"

"DNA," I murmured.

"Right. They might find DNA and—"

I interrupted her. "They're making great strides with DNA testing these days. So much so that most people don't know exactly what can and can't be found with it. We don't have to actually be able to prove DNA is there. We just need to have the murderer *think* we can prove it."

She pulled in a breath in obvious delight. "You have a plan."

CLARA THOUGHT MY plan was brilliant.

We split up to spread the word, with a place and time for us to rendezvous.

I told Fern, Ruby, and my neighbor Amy, along with instructions to share widely. Clara passed the word to Donna, a group of friends of her late mother-in-law, and many more people than I would ever know in North Bend County.

Fern canted her head to one side after hearing the request. "Imagine you want that old boyfriend of Jayne Ulysee to hear this. The Nickells, too? Noah, who works in the same office. Anybody else?"

I looked her straight in the eye. "Doug Vonner."

A flash crossed her face, then was gone. "I'll make sure he hears. To prove you wrong."

"I'm not saying—"

But she was gone.

What were we spreading around Haines Tavern at the speed of gossip?

That I was going to gather DNA from the tree at ZigZag Cemetery to prove Jayne Ulysee hadn't hanged herself. The story went that I had connections who'd do a super special test to tell who had been around that tree at the right time to be a murderer.

That touched on my biggest concern with my plan. Doug Vonner might know that one area where DNA didn't shine was in telling *when* a sample was left.

Still, worth a try.

Clara added one more piece to the plan and she would not budge on it.

As soon as she finished her rounds and headed for the rendezvous, she was calling Teague. She'd try to persuade him not to come in with lights and siren, but that would be up to him.

With a much shorter roster of people to tell, I finished well before our appointed time and headed to the designated meetup spot ... despite it being ZigZag Cemetery.

I passed Gackle Creek and I'll admit I listened carefully. But no sign of a tailgating hearse reached me. I parked in the spot Doug Vonner's car occupied a week ago, got out, then hesitated only a moment before going in.

I wanted to see that Z carved in the headstone near where Jane— or could we say Zelda now?—was found.

Might as well use the enforced timeout in one murder investigation to review the other.

I walked—briskly—to the farthest corner, pausing only for a quick nod to ZigZag Jane's headstone. *We're working on it, Jane. Or Zelda, if it is you.*

By the fence, a headstone from the 1840s showed a Z on the front, beside the word *Beloved* on the inscription.

The Z stood out strongly, even a hundred years later. John must have worked very hard to create that Z to lament his beloved.

I traced the indentation with my finger. From zigzags to the letter Z—

In that instant I knew.

ZigZag John never carved zigzags, he carved Z atop Z.

Zelda and Zacharaus. Z and Z. Connected. Forming a zigzag.

But when he carved this single letter, he lamented only the death of Zelda. He didn't yet believe the second Z had died. Zacharaus, son of Zelda.

CHAPTER THIRTY-FIVE

AFTER A FEW moments of letting the pieces of that sad story settle into place in my mind, I pulled out my phone to call Clara.

No signal.

I jogged out of the cemetery. If the connection I'd had here on Halloween when Urban messaged me was only because of the news crews, I was out of luck. But if it was spotty, going back to my spot outside the cemetery and a little distance away, might do the trick.

I paced across the area, head down, watching for bars. A couple popped up. I sent Clara a message.

"Waiting for somebody?"

The male voice behind me made me jump, but I held onto the phone long enough to tap the icon to use voice text. I slid it into my pocket before I turned.

"What are you doing here, Henderson Nickell?"

"Why are you talking so loud?"

"I'm not. What are you doing here?"

"What do you think?"

Falling into a trap … that wasn't ready to be sprung. He was here too early.

"Get inside the gate," he ordered.

"You want me to go inside the cemetery?"

"That's what I said. Go on, get in there."

Women are told not to let an attacker get you in a place he controls.

Not sure anyone giving that advice expected it to be a cemetery, but still…

I could have the showdown right now, try to escape before he herded me into the cemetery. But would I succeed?

On the other hand, the cavalry was coming. I knew it was. Even if Clara couldn't reach Teague or anyone in the sheriff's department to come immediately, she'd come herself.

That thought caused a burn in my chest. What if I got her killed, too. He took care of me, then shot her as soon as—

No. Stop. Think.

He didn't have a weapon or he'd have used it already.

But he hadn't needed a weapon to kill Jayne Ulysee. He'd used his hands to strangle her.

So maybe the most important thing was to stay out of his reach. Even if that meant backtracking into the cemetery.

I backed up a step. He advanced one.

"Didn't hear your car at all."

"Parked and walked up the hill."

He did sound a bit winded.

Another step for each of us.

"I understand you have property around here."

He frowned fiercely, then it cleared just as fast. He'd decided it didn't matter what I knew because I wouldn't be around to share with anyone else.

More steps.

Thank heavens he seemed in no hurry to close the gap. Though if that reflected a confidence that he could handle me as he had Jayne, maybe thankfulness was not in order.

"Get your hand out of your pocket." He sneered. "No calling for help."

I took my hand out. "Wouldn't think of it." Because I'd already hit send on whatever the voice text caught.

Please, God, don't let autocorrect mess it up too badly to be understood.

I stepped back and could only go half a step because my derriere hit the fountain. This was not good. Already halfway to the back of the cemetery. Unless he let me start doing circles around the cemetery, retreating was not a long-term solution.

I needed a new plan.

As I skirted the fountain, I caught sight of the ghost tree past the fence at the end of this path. The one where he'd hanged Jayne, trying to make her death look like suicide, only to have the branch break off.

"You've been doing well with short-term rentals on your houses, huh?"

I couldn't overpower him, but I could try to delay his overpowering me long enough for the cavalry to arrive.

I continued my retreat, around the fountain, then the main path.

"Yeah. Really well."

"Just bought one in Blue Grass Estates?"

"So what."

"It's already had problems with wild parties there. The neighbors are on alert."

He matched me step for step.

"Amateurs. Can make more without raising a red flag for everybody to see what's going on."

"And if anything does go wrong, you hold the properties through corporations in other states to mask your ownership—did Adrian Jemson teach you that?"

"I knew already."

Ah-hah. A little touchy about that.

"I bet you did. I bet you could teach him a thing or two."

"Yeah, I could. His big idea was to sit back and take the rent. I did better."

"You and Jayne put on parties, raking in entry fees, and selling, uh, extras."

"We had a good thing going."

"Until you tried to cool your relationship and she went out on her own."

"Like she thought she was in charge. Idiot." He added a rude word.

"She went too far Halloween night. Your parties stayed mostly under the radar until then, but there you were at Jemson's hearing about this blowout party the sheriff's department was raiding. You were understandably angry at her for jeopardizing everything."

He took an extra step forward. I shuffled back two.

"Was it greed on her part? Or was she trying to get you in trouble? Did she do it deliberately, reminding you that you couldn't break off with her so easily?"

"Enough of this."

Not yet, not yet.

I was almost to the fence, but needed to move more to the side … if I had the position right from that earlier glance. I couldn't afford another look.

And I couldn't afford for him to act on his obvious plan.

"How did you know I was here?" That question wasn't going to be enough to stall him long. "I was sure the word would never get to you before I did what I needed to do."

"You underestimated me. A lot of people do. I'm not stupid."

"Obviously. But how did you know I was here?"

"That woman with those little black and white dogs was at the house—my house."

Berrie. How did she find out so fast? Okay, we *had* told people to spread the word and she was a sure-fire way to do that. She must have gone straight to the Nickells' house.

I wanted to squeeze my eyes closed, but didn't. Of course she did. She wouldn't miss the opportunity to gloat that Henderson Nickell couldn't close the cemetery from behind bars.

I thought I heard a sound in the distance. I hadn't heard Henderson's vehicle from just a little farther away, in that back corner of the cemetery, but I'd also been lost in thought about Zelda, John, and Zacharaus.

Or was this sound what a tailgating hearse sounded like? Could it be chasing Clara? Or Teague?

"She was ranting about the cemetery and how I was going to get caught," he said. It took a beat to realize he was still talking about

Berrie—I'd almost forgotten about her. "I could hear her in the background when Krystal called me asking what the hell was going on. And I could tell Krystal *knew*. She *knew* and she said you were going to be here. Alone. So if I get rid of you everything will be okay."

"Krystal told you to get rid of me?" I shifted farther around. Almost there.

My question confused him for a beat. "No." He rallied. "But she didn't say not to."

He lunged toward me.

With both hands I grabbed the branch from the spectral tree I'd maneuvered under and jumped. I hoped it would swing me over the lowest section of the fence.

The branch broke off in my hands.

Change of plan.

I swung with all my grew-up-with-brothers might and skill and aimed for his head. At the last second, he put up one hand that blunted the blow.

The branch breaking in half also blunted it.

But the blow still stunned him momentarily.

I used the half of the branch still in my hands as a battering ram, right into his groin.

I heard his screech as he started to double over, but didn't delay to observe more. I spun around and ran. I was off the main path, needing to angle toward the gate.

I ran like a girl—the girl who'd grown up with those brothers.

I ran like I was in my hometown's Old Cemetery on Halloween night.

I ran like Bryan Ferris was chasing me.

And if something grabbed at me, I'd treat it the way I'd treated Bryan Ferris.

If I could get out of the cemetery and back to my car…

I'd nearly reconnected with the main path, several yards short of the gate.

Ahead of me was a headstone. Not a monument, thank heavens,

but about knee height. If Grandfather Vonner could do it, so could I.

I had to.

With long forgotten form, I led with one leg and pushed off with the other, clearing that headstone with ease.

And ran right into a body.

IT WAS AN upright, breathing body, which was some relief.

I knew immediately it wasn't Teague.

That would have been perfect, wouldn't it?

Far from perfection, it was Willie Foglestedt.

"What the hell?" he said. I had the feeling he asked that a lot in his life.

"Hold … onto … her. Don't … let … her … go," Henderson shouted from behind me. Each word came as a pant. How much from my blow to his privates and how much from his running, I didn't know.

I tried to jerk away, to resume my run, but Willie held on.

Pulling, I half-dragged him around and I could see the open gate ahead.

I stopped pulling.

"You. It was you in that pickup."

Willie turned and looked at the truck he'd left outside the gate. So that was the sound I heard. Not a tailgating hearse, but a beaten down pickup that I'd seen before at the Jolly Roger drive-through pharmacy lane and the dog park lot.

I didn't need his confirmation to continue my accusation. "You're the one who nearly crashed into Clara's SUV at the grocery store. Are you in on this with him?" No. That wasn't right. I switched questions. "Why?"

"Jayne was pissed at that other woman. The one who was on TV with him." He jerked his head toward Henderson, still gulping for air and still some distance behind us. "She posted stuff on her social media about what she'd said on TV and I could tell Jayne was really,

really pissed. I thought if I crashed into her, Jayne would be happy and then she'd see me, despite what she said at that party."

"But…" I heard the faint sound of another vehicle approaching. Surely fate wouldn't send a tailgating hearse *now*. If it was anybody except the hearse or Krystal—who would no doubt be completely efficient in dispatching me and covering up for Henderson—and if I could delay Henderson … But the only tool I had was Willie. "Jayne was already dead when you tried to crash into Clara's SUV, Willie. Because he—" I jerked my head back toward Henderson. "—murdered her. He strangled Jayne and then he dumped her body here in the early morning hours after the party."

"What the hell?"

"That's right. It was Henderson Nickell who killed Jayne. *Your* Jayne. Who was going to help you out, support you on the road until you made it big. He murdered her."

Willie let me loose.

"Don't let her go," Henderson ordered.

With fleeing-Bryan-Ferris speed, I had already cut the distance to the gate in half.

I looked back over my shoulder, hoping Willie would swing on Henderson, bring him down with one blow.

Nope.

But Willie did stand in front of him and shout, "You killed Jayne? What the hell? What the hell?"

"She's lying. She's—"

Willie pushed him.

Not exactly hero material, but it knocked Henderson back. He stumbled, couldn't catch his balance. And then his head cracked into the Vonner family monument and he crumpled to the ground.

"Sheriff's department! Stay where you are!"

That was Teague. He gave me a quick look at he charged past me, with Deputy Hensen off to his side. "Get out of here," he ordered.

"That's what I was doing," I muttered.

But he and Hensen were busy taking charge.

EPILOGUE

WHILE I WAS living with Aunt Kit in Manhattan, she insisted I re-read *The Legend of Sleepy Hollow*—though not aloud, thank heavens.

The commas, semicolons, and phrase-peppered paragraphs all remained. As well as the outline of the story and the indelible images of Ichabod Crane and the Headless Horseman.

What I hadn't remembered was the ambiguous ending, when the supposed teller of the tale says he doesn't believe half of it himself.

But even before that, there's disagreement about whether Ichabod was carried off by the Headless Horseman or decamped from Sleepy Hollow to teach elsewhere, while also studying law, which led to passing the bar, becoming a politician, writing for the newspapers, and presiding over a court.

Which to believe?

That's always a question, isn't it.

HERE'S A SHOCK. Henderson Nickell had not done a good job of covering his tracks, once people started to look. That involved the sheriff's department following his murder tracks and county investigators following his financial tracks. Henderson owned considerable property near ZigZag Cemetery. He hasn't admitted it, but everyone figures he planned to develop it and the cemetery was in the way.

Two other officials also fell into the investigative net. Adrian Jemson teetered on the edge for now.

The sheriff's department confirmed a black hoodie left at the party house belonged to Wellington Jemson—not through science. He'd left an ID in it with all his information, a photo, and a poorly doctored birthdate.

Willie Foglestedt left town as soon as the sheriff's department said he could. He said he had a record deal. Word filtered back that he was playing at a truck stop off I-75 for tips.

Krystal was definitely not singing *Stand by Your Man*. She is cooperating with authorities, while adamant that she had nothing to do with murder or financial crimes.

Clara and I pointed out she was the most likely person to have—at the very least—picked up Henderson from the cemetery. But the authorities' general theory is she was too smart to leave tracks herself, so they might as well cut a deal and get her testimony against Henderson and the others.

The Nickells' house was for sale in record time. She received permission to leave North Bend County, while staying in Kentucky. She moved to Louisville. I have no doubt she's landed on her feet.

Noah still worked at the Drain Commission office. Yakira, apparently, has taken him in hand and applied his nose firmly to the grindstone. Yakira was named Acting Drain Commissioner. Her colleagues were trying to persuade her to run for the position.

Doug Vonner appeared ten years younger. A man who saw a way forward to clear an obligation he'd carried all his life. However, he's not done with ZigZag Jane.

The county approved joining Doug in applying for funds to pursue the genealogical and DNA research on ZigZag Jane to confirm—or refute, but I think it will confirm—our conclusions about her identity.

Not a quick process. Doug also realized it might not produce the definitive answer. But he was more than satisfied with the progress. He was inclined to consider it a conclusion that needed only the cherry on top.

Even Urban leaned that way.

The day after my last trip to ZigZag Cemetery—I swear, never going back—Urban talked to state officials and reported back that license plates could be connected with a specific person—if the combination of letters and numbers wasn't ever used again. The ones on the Packard Twin Six had been used again.

Another dead-end.

But Urban wrote an article on behalf of the historical society extolling our research—along with his contributions, including ongoing research—and the Vonners' perseverance. He also included cautionary caveats that the solution to the mystery of ZigZag Jane's identity required further proof.

So did the mystery of ZigZag Jane's murder.

And that mystery would not be answered any more fully with DNA or genealogical evidence than it had been already.

We had our hypothesis, which fit all the facts known to us.

The facts not known to us ... Well, those awaited time travel, the afterlife, or a miraculous discovery of a handwritten journal. Preferably by Louis Kiel, in which he—going against type, as well as self-preservation—confessed to all.

Wasn't holding my breath.

"In fact," Urban said when we stopped by the historical society, "you did so well with adding to our store of knowledge about ZigZag Cemetery, which is furthering its preservation, I want to say there's another one you could take on in the southern part of the county where Union troops were sent to set up a camp. Problem for them was, Confederates had used the camp previously and the Union soldiers said the Confederates threw dead mules into the pond, contaminating it. They described green scum on it and wrigglers in it. One said it was as near to drinking mule soup as he ever wanted to be. Even boiling it, there were deaths from disease, likely from the water."

"Mule soup," Clara said in fascinated horror. "That's—"

"Thank you for the kind offer," I interrupted, "but we are off cemeteries. For good."

✧　✧　✧　✧

"HERE'S WHAT WE'VE pieced together. ZigZag Jane was actually Zelda Kiel or Kielwegen."

Clara, Ned, Teague, and I were around their dining room table with the dogs underneath, keeping our feet warm now that we'd hit a cold snap suited to November.

Talking about ZigZag Jane's story didn't rouse the ire of the men in our lives.

Teague, of course, knew all about Jayne Ulysee's murder. I'm guessing Ned did, too, from Clara. Though likely not the details of how Henderson Nickell was caught.

That was still a sensitive subject between Teague and me. Clara wasn't in any hurry to share it with Ned.

In a way, that's a shame, because he'd appreciate something Teague said.

I'd told him about Jayne using the same setup as she had with Henderson's parties for the Halloween party. When she let it get out of hand or deliberately pushed it there, it drew attention, which exposed what they'd been doing, which exposed him.

"He killed her to break the tie to what he was doing," I finished.

"Idiot," Teague said. "Murder's a tie that can't ever be broken."

He was right that Henderson Nickell will forever be tied to Jayne Ulysee. But I think the tie that can't ever be broken for Zelda Kiel was with John and her son, not with her killer.

As Clara and I were explaining to the guys now.

"Kielwegen? Related to the family around here?" Ned asked.

"Yes. Though not directly. She was married to Louis Kielwegen, who shortened his name to Kiel, and was known as Louis the K, short for Louis the Killer."

Ned whistled, stirring the dogs.

"Louis was part of the criminal underground selling alcohol during Prohibition. Bootlegging was a thriving business in Newport in the 1920s. After Prohibition's repeal, they shifted gears and kept going."

"I heard that about Newport, growing up," Ned said. "Mom couldn't believe the recent prices of housing there. She said it wasn't anyplace she'd ever consider living because of the criminals. They were cleaned out decades before, but she'd grown up with the stories and never shook the image."

"There've got to be descendants of those criminals still in the area. With DNA—"

I stop-signed Clara.

"Right. Sorry. Tell them about ZigZag Jane—Zelda."

"We found her in the census—"

"*You* found that, nobody else," Clara said. "You hit the galaxy far, far away that nobody had heard of yet."

The rest of us grinned at her.

"What? It's true."

Ned cupped her shoulder. "That's my Clara."

After a beat to let them smile at each other, I said, "She wasn't in that household in 1910, was there in 1920 as Louis's wife and with an eleven-month-old son named Ray, then wasn't there—or anywhere else we could find—in 1930 and beyond. Our theory is that, in the interim, she was murdered, found dead in the cemetery by Douglas Vonner on his way to school, and buried as ZigZag Jane.

"Over the same period, we tracked John Kielwegen. He's the son of another John, who was the younger brother of Louis. So John Junior is Louis's nephew. John Senior dies young. In 1910, when John Junior would be about fifteen, he doesn't show up as living with his mother and siblings. *But*, J.—just the initial, is listed in Louis Kiel's household in Newport. J.'s listed as Louis's nephew and he's the right age to be John.

"We also know John Kielwegen Jr. served in World War I and it was understood he came back a broken young man. Urban told me some people said he retreated to the woods around the Kielwegen cemetery because of a broken romance, some because he'd quit working for a gangster, some because of what he'd gone through in the war."

"We think it was all three," Clara said.

I nodded. "He became known as ZigZag John from his habit of

carving two Zs, one on top of the other on trees."

"Not zigzags?" Ned asked in surprise.

As I shook my head, I drew a Z on a napkin, then a second Z below it, leaving a gap. Right next to it, I did it a second time, but with the bottom of the top Z and the top of the bottom Z overlapping.

"Well, I'll be darned," Ned said.

"Isn't Sheila brilliant? All these years and nobody made the connection until her."

Now they all grinned at me.

I cleared my throat and continued. "After Jane's body was found, John shifted to markers in the cemetery, some citizens went after him. He killed one, and was hanged."

I drew in a deep breath. "That's the framework. It's interesting that there was a gap between John's return from the war and when he showed up in the woods. Might he have gone back to his uncle's in 1918 or 1919 when he returned? Jane—Zelda—was married to Louis by then. So she and John could have been in the household together."

I looked toward Teague. He was withholding judgment.

"What happened to Ray, the eleven-month-old in the census?" he asked.

I shrugged slowly. "No idea."

"Well, *some* ideas," Clara murmured.

Teague glanced toward her then returned to me.

I covered the least interesting scenarios first. "It's possible the child died—naturally or otherwise—before Zelda's death. Or that he remained in Louis's household, but died—naturally or otherwise—between the 1920 and 1930 census. Although he doesn't show up in death records."

"But you think..." Teague prodded.

I drew in a deep breath. "That it's possible Zelda tried to reach John, was caught and killed near or in ZigZag cemetery by Louis or his henchmen. What if she and John had a relationship after he came back from the war? John goes to or is driven to a life in the woods. Because of the war? Because his uncle suspected an affair? Because he didn't want to work for his uncle—Louis the Killer? A combination?

"For whatever reason, he leaves—before the 1920 census—while Zelda remains. But by November 1921 something drives her out, too. She's caught. And killed. Her son is never found or mentioned."

"Something drove her out—why do you think that?"

"If Louis decided to kill her, he had a lot of other places he could have had her disposed of. At his trial, the prosecutor said a benefit of his incarceration was there'd be fewer bodies clogging up the Ohio River. That was his MO.

"Why come here to kill her or to leave her body when the Ohio River was more convenient and familiar, whether he did the deed or had someone else do it. Though strangling *is* personal. Plus, as everybody's told me, these communities weren't considered close at that time." Teague didn't argue, so I went on. "John found her and—"

"Whoa. Explain that leap."

"The leaves covering her. That wasn't the style of Louis the K and his associates. More likely John found her first and did what he could to cover her. The first carving in the cemetery was a single Z on a headstone near where she died, next to the word *beloved*. John again. Then he returned to interconnected Z's resembling zigzags—for Zelda and Zacharaus, which was the full name of the eleven-month-old named Ray in the 1920 census."

I explained about the church records.

"That poor man," Clara said. "He must have loved Zelda. And Ray—Zacharaus—I bet he was John's son. He carved zigzags in the woods for his love and his son. One Z on the headstone after he found Zelda in the cemetery—he *must* have found her, arranged her so no one saw her face, then spread leaves over her like a blanket." Her eyes filled with tears. "And then, when he couldn't find Zacharaus, he returned to two Zs."

Teague frowned. "You're theorizing that after that first carving of the single Z he knew the boy was dead, too?"

"Or thought he was," I said. "If John still had connections in his uncle's household, he might know the boy disappeared at the same time as Zelda."

"The uncle killed the baby and that's what made Zelda run," Teague proposed.

It was logical. I hated it.

"Or, something pushed Zelda to leave. She'd try to get to John and they'd take their chances together, but the odds were against them. She wouldn't want to expose her son to that danger and she certainly couldn't leave him with Louis. So she left Ray somewhere safe. She never had a chance to tell John. Louis wasn't telling anyone the boy disappeared at the same time as his mother. In fact, he put out the word that Zelda went to Reno for a divorce ... like his first wife, never to be seen again."

I told Teague and Ned about the A.N. Observer item Urban shared.

"John assumed the boy was dead, too. Which drove him even deeper into whatever hell he was in ... and ended in his death."

Teague remained silent for a beat, before saying, "Okay, even if that's one possible way things happened, where does it get you?"

"Besides feeling better." Ned's mutter drew dark looks from Clara and me. "Sorry. But Teague's right. It's a nicer version of the story than some others, but we'll never know."

"Maybe you're right," I allowed, but only to make my next sentence more powerful, "Or maybe, with donations rolling in, Zelda's DNA will give us some answers. Eventually. First, to confirm it is Zelda. And then ... who knows? Maybe we'll find a descendant, a DNA tie that says Ray lived and had a family."

I thought about that later.

Some answers. Eventually.

Other answers could not come from DNA. Might never come.

Was that Douglas' handwriting that completed Louis Kiel's last name on the donor list? How did Douglas Vonner get the photograph with the Packard? Why did he keep it? Why keep it with the donor list—or was it kept with the witness accounts, including from the boy sure he'd seen a Packard the night of Zelda's death?

All those questions and more were part of a larger one. Did Douglas Vonner know—or suspect—Louis the K was connected to the woman known as ZigZag Jane?

If he did, I understood why he kept quiet at the time and immediately after, but why continue when Kiel went to prison? And even more in Douglas' later years, after Newport ridded itself of Louis the K's ilk?

Was it like Ned's mother, never able to shake the image once it took hold?

Only stronger and more visceral in Douglas' case. A teenager drawn to find answers about the young woman he found, yet recognizing answers might lead to Louis the Killer. And, later, maybe his head knowing that time had passed, but his heart unwilling to release the habit of protecting those he loved.

I remembered Doug repeating that his dad said he was sure Douglas kept secrets from him *like his dad didn't want to share all of ZigZag Jane with him.*

Douglas did better with his grandson—because the danger had receded? Yet when he passed the quest to Doug, had he still not been able to bring himself to share those once-deadly suspicions?

Like the ending of *The Legend of Sleepy Hollow.*

That's always a question, isn't it.

THAT NIGHT, TEAGUE took my hand in his.

It wasn't as romantic as it might sound. More like he was studying evidence.

"You cut your nails," he said.

"Yeah. It's hard to type fast with them too long. Besides, it changes the angle and my wrists hurt before my brain's empty."

"Interesting." Teague continued studying my hands like they'd committed a misdemeanor. Then he looked into my face and the charges rose to a felony.

"What?" I demanded.

He shook his head, with maddening finality.

He wasn't telling.

But I was.

At least one more thing … for now.

"I have some news, Teague."

"Do you? Something more you're going to tell me? What's that?"

"Not even Clara knows. She'll be excited, but I wanted to tell you first."

"I appreciate that," he said, dryness creeping in. "What is it?"

"Kit—my great-aunt Kit is coming to visit. For Christmas."

The End

For news about upcoming books, as well as other titles and news, join Patricia McLinn's ReadHeads and receive her twice-monthly free newsletter.

patriciamclinn.com/readers-list

You can buy this book and all my others, including print editions and audiobooks, from my online store. I've added direct-to-you buying options to better control how my books reach you, while having lots more elbow room to give you special bundles, early offers, and exclusive bonuses.

Patricia's Bookstore

shop.patriciamclinn.com

Author's Note:

Thank you for reading *Death on ZigZag Trail,* book 7 in the Secret Sleuth series. Hope you enjoyed it.

Kentucky counties do not have Drain Commissioners. I didn't want to assign Henderson Nickell to a true elected position in Kentucky, where he might have done damage. To my knowledge, only counties in the state of Michigan have Drain Commissioners. I borrowed the name for Henderson Nickell's nonexistent Kentucky position from Michigan, figuring that was far enough away that he couldn't mess up Michigan.

Bonus epilogue:

Get your free bonus epilogue to *Death on ZigZag Trail.* Just sign up to Patricia's ReadHeads and receive a free twice-monthly newsletter on Patricia's books, more exclusive offerings, behind-the-scenes, news, consumer tips, and a pet or two.

Link to bonus: https://dl.bookfunnel.com/5atnc2s56w

Thank you for reading Sheila, Clara and Teague's latest adventure! Santa Claus is coming to town, but guess who's coming first — Great Aunt Kit. And if Sheila and her fellow sleuth Clara want to give her author relative what she most wants, they'll wrap up a murder. The New Year just might ring in

Death on Puzzle Place

Sheila, Clara, Teague and friends ask if you'll help spread the word about them and the Secret Sleuth series. You have the power to do that in two quick ways:

Recommend the book and the series to your friends and/or the whole wide world on social media. Shouting from rooftops is particu-larly appreciated.

Review the book. Take a few minutes to write an honest review and it can make a huge difference. As you likely know, it's the single best way for your fellow readers to find books they'll enjoy, too.

To me — as an author and a reader — the goal is always to find a good author-reader match. By sharing your reading experience through recommendations and reviews, you become a vital matchmaker. ☺

More Secret Sleuth mysteries

DEATH ON THE DIVERSION

Final resting place? Deck chair.

DEATH ON TORRID AVENUE

A new love (canine), an ex-cop and a dog park discovery.

DEATH ON BEGUILING WAY

No zen in sight as Sheila untangles a yoga instructor's murder.

DEATH ON COVERT CIRCLE

A supermarket CEO meets his expiration date.

DEATH ON SHADY BRIDGE

A homicide cold case heats up.

DEATH ON CARRION LANE

More murder is brewing in Haines Tavern.

DEATH ON ZIGZAG TRAIL

A spooky legend twists grave matters.

DEATH ON PUZZLE PLACE

Season's greetings: Whodunit?

More mystery by Patricia McLinn

Caught Dead in Wyoming series

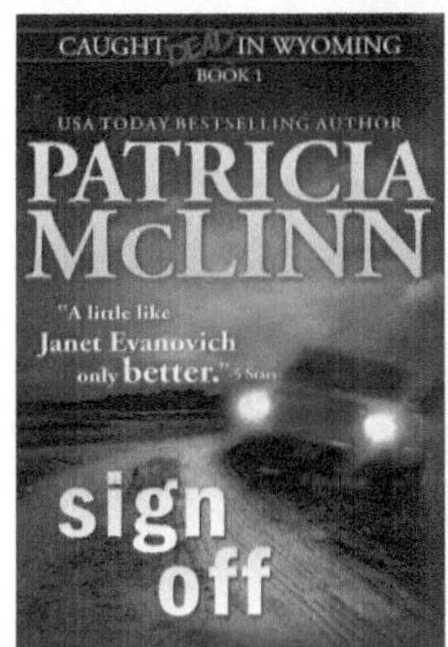

SIGN OFF

Divorce a husband, lose a career … grapple with a murder.

LEFT HANGING

Trampled by bulls — an accident? Elizabeth, Mike and friends dig into
the world of rodeo.

SHOOT FIRST

For Elizabeth, death hits close to home. She and friends delve into old
Wyoming treasures and secrets to save lives.

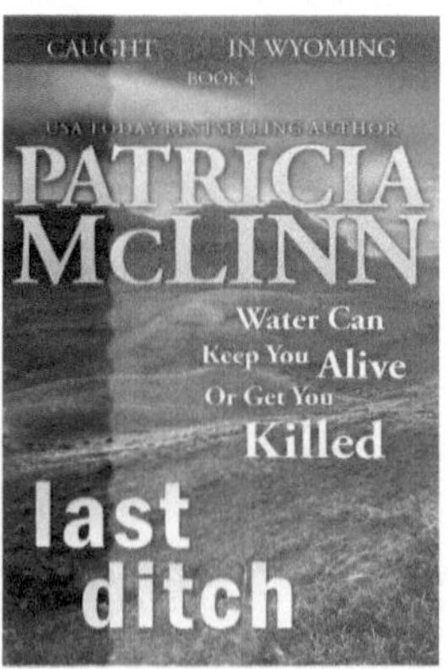

LAST DITCH

Elizabeth and Mike search after a man in a wheelchair goes missing in
dangerous, desolate country.

LOOK LIVE

Elizabeth and friends take on misleading murder with help — and hindrance — from intriguing out-of-towners.

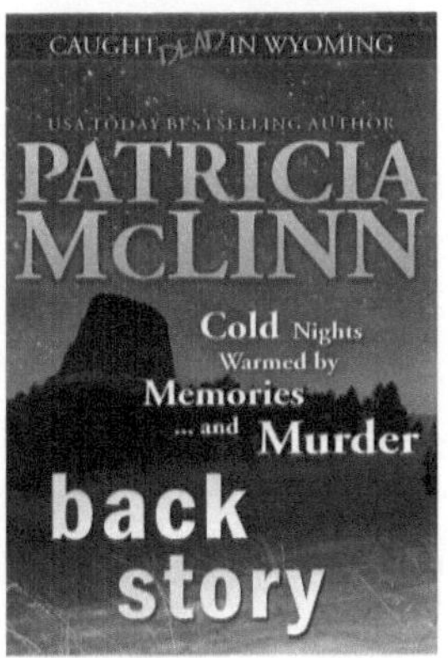

BACK STORY

Murder never dies, but comes back to threaten Elizabeth and team of investigators.

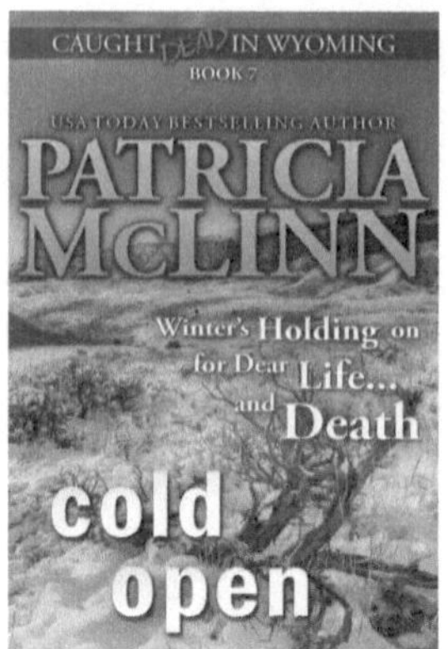

COLD OPEN

Elizabeth's search for a place of her own becomes an open house
for murder.

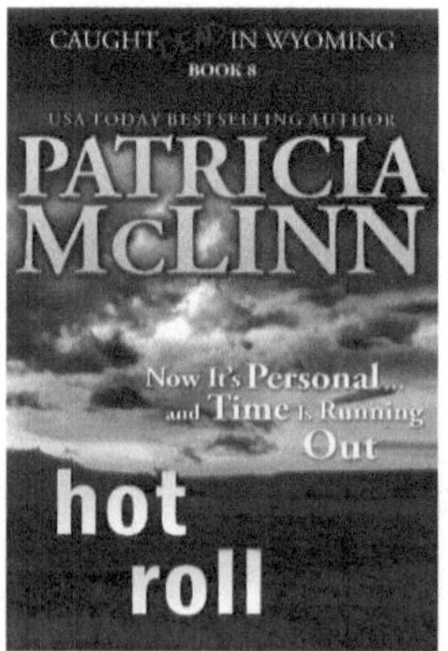

HOT ROLL

One of their own becomes a target — and time is running out.

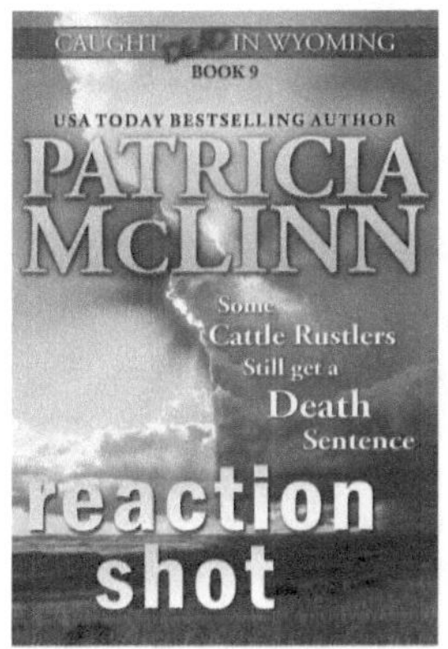

REACTION SHOT

Sometimes cattle rustlers still get a death sentence.

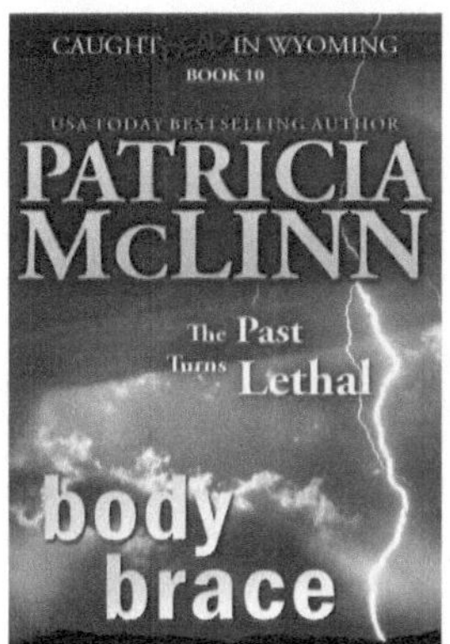

BODY BRACE

Everything can change, but murder still comes calling.

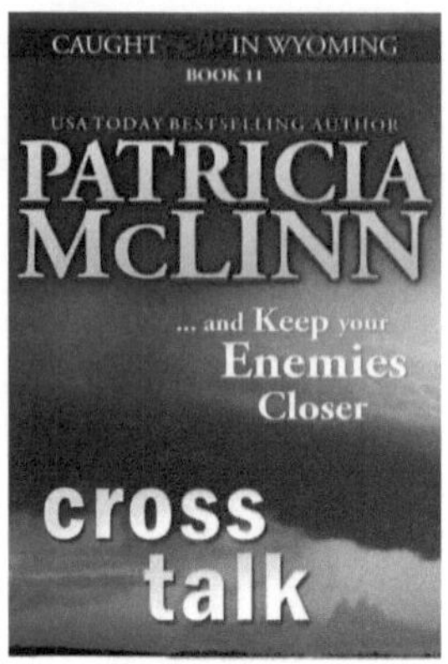

CROSS TALK

Prime suspect: The most annoying man in Sherman.

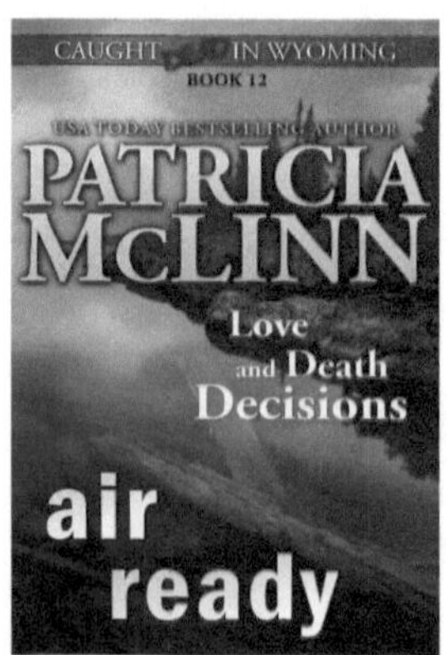

AIR READY

Love and death decisions.

HOLIDAY BULLETS

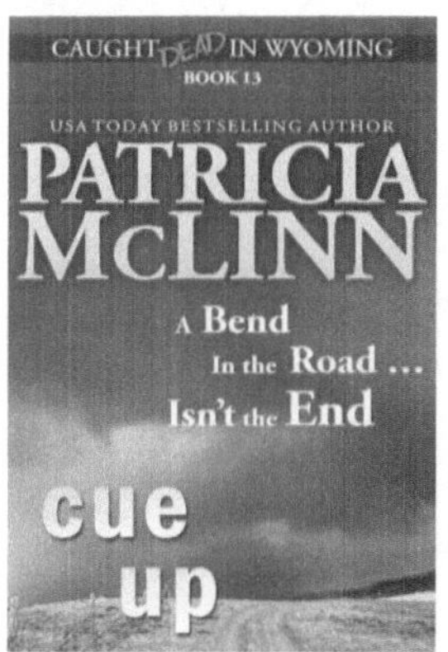

CUE UP

On the trail of murder.

"While the mystery itself is twisty-turny and thoroughly engaging, it's the smart and witty writing that I loved the best."

— *Diane Chamberlain, New York Times bestselling author*

"Colorful characters, intriguing, intelligent mystery, plus the state of Wyoming leaping off every page."

— *Emilie Richards, USA Today bestselling author*

PREMISE OF INNOCENCE

The last woman Detective Landis is prepared to see is the one he
must save.

"Evocative description, vivid characterization, and lots of twists and
turns."

— 5-star review

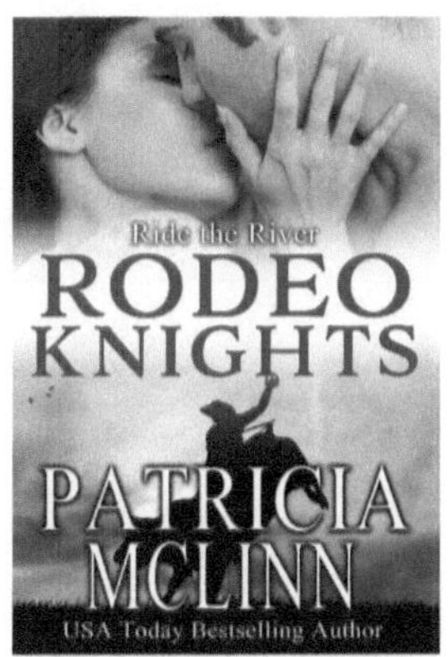

RIDE THE RIVER: RODEO KNIGHTS

Her rodeo cowboy ex is back … as her prime suspect.

Explore a complete list of all Patricia's books
patriciamclinn.com/patricias-books

Or get a printable booklist
patriciamclinn.com/patricias-books/printable-booklist

Patricia's Bookstore (buy online directly from Patricia)
shop.patriciamclinn.com

About the Author

Patricia McLinn is the USA Today bestselling author of more than 60 published novels cited by readers and reviewers for their wit and vivid characterization. Her books include mysteries, romantic suspense, contemporary romance, historical romance, and women's fiction. They have topped bestseller lists and won numerous awards.

She has spoken about writing from London to Melbourne, Australia, to Washington, D.C., including being a guest speaker at the Smithsonian Institution.

McLinn spent more than 20 years as an editor at The Washington Post after stints as a sports writer (Rockford, Ill.) and assistant sports editor (Charlotte, N.C.). She received BA and MSJ degrees from Northwestern University.

Now living in northern Kentucky, McLinn loves to hear from readers through her website and social media.

Visit with Patricia:

Website: patriciamclinn.com

Facebook: facebook.com/PatriciaMcLinn

Twitter: @PatriciaMcLinn

Pinterest: pinterest.com/patriciamclinn

Instagram: instagram.com/patriciamclinnauthor